LOVE

dhtreichler

Dedication:

To all those who have and continue to fight for equality and justice.

CHAPTER ONE:

gBeto Dahomey Brown, Attorney General, State of Texas

Although clouds fill the sky and a slight breeze musses with my hair, I am happy for the warm weather that has finally arrived after the cold damp days of a Fort Christian, Texas winter. We live close to the rocky and barren Permian Basin, that it doesn't get as cold as some places, but the aridness seems to chill me to the bone all winter long. I wait for the sun to show itself so I can feel it warm the skin on my face and chase the lingering cold away until fall.

I reach the mailbox at the end of our paved driveway, not a long walk in this development that serves both the upper reaches of the middle class like me and the lower reaches of the upper class like the Rutherfords across the street. The center line down our street might as well be a border between different nations. We live next to each other, but there is no way Nathaniel or I will ever live on that side of the street. Anne and John, her husband, aren't pretentious, but there are certain gatherings that take place there I will never be invited to join. The political meetings are another story.

As I open my mailbox and reach for the mail, I notice the For-Sale sign on the Williams house next door is gone. Cardboard boxes are stacked outside the garage. I would assume my new neighbors have moved in. *Wonder when I'll get a chance to meet them. The Williams family was there for what was it? Probably six months before I ever met them. And they didn't stay long before his oil company moved them to Nigeria. Never understand why companies don't move people who are ethnically the same to countries where they do business, rather than trying to fit a square peg into a round hole.*

Bills and more bills. At least the mail isn't all advertisements for one thing or another I don't need. We likely would not purchase the item or service based on a flyer even if I did. But then Nathaniel and I are at that point in life where we aren't acquiring things anymore. Experiences are more important to us than one more piece of furniture or a new painting to go somewhere. We'd rather travel someplace new and meet people who value different things than we do, to stretch our understanding of our fellow men, than go shopping in antique malls. Did that for how many years? More than I can count.

Nathaniel says we've lived here long enough. When a house needs repairs that means you've outlived your welcome. We disagree on that point. I tell him we need to update the house. *Replace the old appliances. Paint some walls. Rearrange the paintings and artwork. If all we did was move something from one place to another, it would seem all new, even though it isn't. We just need to look at the same things differently. To be able to enjoy them all over again. And clearly, we enjoyed looking at the things we have when we bought them. They have memories attached to them. Shared memories. But Nathaniel wants new memories. Maybe because in his current position, he deals with newly made bad memories nearly every day.*

I close the mailbox and look back towards our two-story solid reddish brick home, when I hear the front door of the Williams house open. I expect to see Joy coming out for her mail, but a petite young woman emerges. *Looks to be early twenties, fashionably dressed which tells me she's trying to look casual, but also wants others to know she's someone of substance, at least when it comes to bank accounts. Not a blonde, or bottle blonde, like so many these days. She walks with a grace like she's had years practicing dance. Light on her feet and the posture reflects a conscious control of her movement.*

In only a moment she sees me, smiles and approaches. "Hello, we're your new neighbors, the White's. I'm Sarah and my husband is Demetrius."

I nod as is the custom now where social distancing remains an expectation, even though no particular strain of virus is rampaging through our community at the moment. "gBeto Brown," I respond with a smile.

"I hope you won't take offense at this comment," Sarah White almost apologizes, "But the first time someone mentioned your name I thought they were talking about Geppetto. You know, the toy maker of the Pinocchio story."

"I get that a lot," I admit, knowing how unusual my name is. "And I assume you'd like to know what gBeto means. How did I ever get a name like that."

"When I learned we were going to be neighbors I did some research," she heads off my impulse to tell her the whole story. "gBeto means huntress in fon, the language of the Dahomey tribe. Means you were named after the Amazon women of Africa, who constituted a significant portion of the Dahomey army starting in the 1600's and lasting into the turn of the twentieth century."

"Then you know my maiden name is Dahomey," I seek to confirm how much homework she's done, now curious why she's taken the time.

Sarah White nods. "But what I've not been able to establish is why your parents decided to name you after the huntresses of the Dahomey tribe."

"I grew up in Edge Hill," I begin.

"The poorest neighborhood in Fort Christian at that time," Sarah responds.

I nod and continue, "My father was a day laborer, always working for minimum wage when he had any work at all. My mother took in neighborhood children, allowing their parents to work. We weren't dirt poor; dirt would have been a luxury."

"Your official bio says you were self-made but I had no idea..." Sarah admits.

"My father could barely read and write, but my mother... she read to the children all day long. She read for herself all night long. My mother is one of the smartest women I've ever met. But she was completely self-taught. She dropped out of school at fourteen when she had me. Never went back; but she read everything. She's the one who named me, because she wanted to remind me every day that people are hunting me. If I'm to survive in this world, I need to be able to take care of myself."

"Is that why you became a lawyer?" Sarah inquires, without any indication of anything other than curiosity.

"My mother impressed on me the importance of words. That they can have different meanings depending on how they are used. That words can lift people up or bring their worlds crashing down. I'm a huntress, but the law is my weapon. I train myself with the same intensity that the Dahomey warriors did two centuries ago. Did you know they could bring down an elephant? One of the hardest beasts to kill in the wild. Anything a man could do, they found a way to do it as well, if not better."

"You have a fascinating history around your name," Sarah notes. "Never thought about how a name can define someone in quite the way yours seems to."

"I'm sorry, Nathaniel tells me I can be a bit too intense some times," I hear her backing away. I didn't intend to do that. "Tell me about Sarah White." I smile at her.

"Not much to tell really. Just graduated, got a job and married all about the same time. We found this house and just loved it. So here we are."

"That won't do," I protest. "You know who I am. Even did the research. Either you could tell me about you and your husband or give me a link. Then I can explore your life the way you have mine."

Sarah seems to consider the options, but elects to fill me in a little more. "I grew up here. Graduated with a concentration in performance arts, but found in college that good in Texas isn't good in New York. I changed my major to media studies. Related, but I'm not the one in front of the camera now."

"What was your favorite part?"

4

LOVE

"You know there really aren't all that many great roles for women. But I really identified with Ophelia in Hamlet. That if you let yourself become dependent upon the affections of some guy, it is likely to drive you mad."

"Did that happen to you before you met your husband?" I wonder aloud to see what kind of reaction I get.

She smiles broadly. "You're making an assumption that I got over whatever happened when I was younger. Actually, I didn't. All through High School I was constantly with the son of the richest family in Southlake."

I nod, recognizing the richest area of the Fort Christian suburbs. That would indicate she likely went to the same private school. Wonder if that was on a scholarship or full tuition.

"Everyone thought we were the perfect couple. He was more athletic, but I was smarter. We looked good together. King and Queen of Homecoming senior year. Everyone wanted to be us. But he went to Harvard because that's where seven generations of his family attended undergraduate school. I went to Wesleyan. We were in the same city, but I never saw him again. It was as if I didn't exist anymore, now that he was with women of his class. Old money."

"Sounds like we came from different places," I note, trying not to sound unsympathetic.

Sarah White nods as if she had already come to that conclusion. "I don't want to sound…"

"You don't," I reassure her without the need for her to say more. "Tell me about your husband. How did you meet?"

"We both did an internship at the Boston Globe last year. When we met, it seemed we just knew we worked well together. It was almost as if we had one brain and the other could find something to complement what the other was working on without the need to ask."

"Must be nice," I offer.

"And the sex was incredible… in comparison. The first guy was a premature…"

"I get the picture…" I save her the need to be any more explicit.

Sarah glances over her shoulder as I look beyond her. A tall and thin greying man and petite dark-haired woman, both dressed country club casual, come out of her new home and approach us. As they get close Sarah introduces us, "gBeto Dahomey Brown, these are my parents, Thomas and Margaret Flannery."

Thomas' reddish complexion is freckled. Margaret looks more Mediterranean, *Italian maybe and her dark hair is nicely colored.* I wonder who she uses as a stylist. *Sarah clearly takes after her mother's side of the family.* I nod to each as is the custom. They reciprocate. "Your daughter was just telling me about how she met her husband," I respond.

"Her life has been a whirlwind," Margaret Flannery responds with a bright smile and loving glance at her daughter. "Graduating early, and now a new home." She touches the shoulder of her husband and glances at him wistfully. "Things weren't quite like this when we were first starting out."

"The next generation will find things even more different when their time comes," I offer some perspective to her reflection.

"These must be interesting times for you," Thomas Flannery observes, clearly looking for me to say something about my work.

"I prefer the word 'challenging' only because of the old Chinese curse about living in interesting times. Finding justice for all is never an easy or straightforward task."

"But as our state Attorney General you seem to do a better job of it than most," he responds which means he's at least a supporter.

"Thomas Flannery, why do I know you?"

"Nothing bad, I hope," he smiles at me with a relaxation that indicates he has not been subject to suit from my office.

"Sarah said she changed her major to media studies, are you the owner of Continuum Media?"

"My partner and I started that little firm a decade ago after working together for a number of years. I ran the operations and he sold the advertising. Now I have people who run the operations and he has people who sell subscriptions and advertising. I always say when you find something you're good at, keep on doing it."

"Sarah is following her father into the business?"

Sarah pipes up now, not to be overshadowed by her father, "It's not like that. I want to take the company into new areas, but he tells me I have to learn the fundamentals before I change the world. I'm writing blogs on the current events of the day."

"She's doing the news," Margaret Flannery gives me the short hand. "The core of our business is news. Whether sports or business or metro, it's all important for the American people to be informed."

"I absolutely agree."

"I promise not to ask you…" Sarah begins apologetically.

"Don't worry about it. I have an open door to the media and am transparent where the law permits me to be."

"And that's the issue, isn't it?" Sarah comes right after me. "The law. It protects the guilty from having to inform the larger public of the threat they pose."

I take a step back recalibrating my expectations of Sarah White, journalist. "In some instances, but the law is there to protect the innocent as well as prosecute the guilty. My job is to make sure the guilty suffer the consequences of their behavior."

I glance up to see Anne Rutherford, trim and blonde, approaching us from her drive. She's also apparently come for her mail. "Morning

Anne," I greet her. "Let me introduce Sarah White, our newest neighbor and her parents, Thomas and Margaret Flannery."

Anne joins our circle and nods to each with a big smile. "Welcome to our quiet neighborhood. We aim to keep it that way, but gBeto challenges us by showing up in the media all the time. You know how some people are," her smile reveals her genuine affection for me. I wink at her, acknowledging it.

"Full disclosure, Sarah works for her father's media company. I would have to expect there will be no peace in the future for either of us." I kid everyone hoping no one takes offense.

"Flannery…" Anne reflects. "The Flannery's in Southlake?"

Margaret rolls her eyes apparently knowing where this conversation is going. A deep sigh. "Guilty as charged."

"Then you are very welcome. You are known by your philanthropy. My husband and I are grateful you are generous, as it causes the many organizations looking for support to ask for less from us. Thank you." Anne sort of bows to them.

I touch Sarah on the shoulder, "You and your husband must come over some evening soon, so we can get to know you better." I retrieve a business card and hand it to her. "Give me some dates that work for you both and my husband Nathaniel will find an appropriate wine to share with you." I nod to Thomas and Margaret, "So nice to meet you both. We promise to look out for your daughter and her new husband."

I nod to Anne as my phone rings, "Yes?"

"Police involved shooting. White officer and Black victim," LaMance Freeman, my number two, uses short hand to tell me it's not going to be a good day. She's also telling me I need to come straight into the office to respond to the media that has started showing up.

I look at Sarah and her parents and wonder if I'm going to have more trouble creating separation from work and homelife. *That would not be a good thing.* "I'm on my way."

CHAPTER TWO:

gBeto Dahomey Brown, Attorney General, State of Texas

LaMance needs to either eat a little less or wear less tight-fitting clothes. I could tell her that, but it would probably cause her to eat more, worried about why I'm pointing it out. I know as Chief Prosecutor, that if this case goes to trial, she will be the lead attorney. That will add stress, and she'll balloon even more. Not a good thing, but how do I convince her not to binge eat? Nathaniel would say it's not my problem. But it is, because she's not just another attorney in my office, but also a friend going back to law school days.

She approaches my old wooden desk in the tiny office I use in the Waters Street State Office Building. The last attorney general used the larger office down the hall. I turned it into a conference room, which we needed more than for me to have a large space. I nod to her and look back down to the laptop on my desk where I've already watched the dash cam video of the incident nearly a half-dozen times. A better vantage point would make this case much cleaner.

"I don't think there's any doubt about what happened," LaMance informs me, and I assume she's watched it more times than I have.

"The outcome maybe, but I'm not comfortable about what happened during the five seconds when Bo Madison went out of frame. It was close to the actual shots being fired."

"You think the officers deliberately blocked the dashcam?" *LaMance apparently is wondering the same thing I am.*

"At first I didn't think so, but the more times I watch it…"

"I had the same impression," *LaMance confirms I'm not just*

9

seeing things. "You know this is going to end up in our lap."

I nod, still watching where the shots are actually fired. Bo Madison has just stepped back into frame, and I see the bullets striking his body. I haven't really even thought about how many times the officer fired his weapon. A judgment call, I already hear the defense attorney telling the jury. How many bullets does it take to kill a two-hundred-and-twenty-pound record setting running back? He may not have played after college, more than a decade ago, but that's still what the news people will zero in on.

When the video ends, I glance back up, shaking my head, still thinking the five seconds could tell me much about what happened. "We have to hope someone surfaces with a video from a different angle," I tell LaMance.

"The investigators didn't identify any witnesses. Everyone they talked with, who heard the shots, waited inside for a bit before coming out to see what was going on."

"Waiting to see if any more shots were going to be fired," I surmise.

LaMance half nods and half shrugs in response. I've seen her do that whenever she sort of agrees but is telling me we'll never know for sure.

"Who are you going to assign to work this up?" I ask wondering if she will pick the same team I would, given the high profile and sensitivity this is going to have.

"Scottie," she responds. "I'll let her decide who she needs based on the reports that are filed."

I nod agreement with the plan, although I think I know who would be the most thorough and also discreet. That's been a problem for us in the past. On the high-profile cases it seems there are leaks to the media. Usually not significant, but on more than one occasion, I'd have felt a lot better if certain facts hadn't gotten out before the trial. Don't know as they changed the outcomes, but they worried me then. A similar set of leaks could make this a very difficult prosecution, if it comes to that.

"Have you talked with Mayor Richards yet?" LaMance won't talk with her if she is going to prosecute the case herself, she's hopeful I can give her insights that won't be a conflict.

"Called her on the way in. At that point she hadn't seen the dashcam yet. She only had sketchy information. Too early to really have a discussion. We're supposed to chat before her four o'clock press conference."

LaMance decides to poke at me, "You chat with a lot of folks, but I don't ever hear of you discussing facts, or pushing boundaries. Why is that?"

My sheepish smile finds its way to my face, "I can chat with a bear that's pulling honey from a tree. But if all I do is poke the bear with a stick, warning him away from the tree may end up with a very different response."

"You can chat with the mayor today, but from what I see on the video, I don't think you're going to be able to keep from poking her. And when you do, you'll be poking your loving husband at the same time."

"I'm not there yet, but I'm distinctly aware of the probability that could happen."

"Will happen," LaMance pushes back. "Have you talked to Nathaniel since I called you?"

I shake my head, "He's got to be busier than I am, talking with everyone involved, the officers who responded to the scene immediately afterwards, and the medics… who came and ultimately took Bo Madison to the hospital, although the reports are he was already gone by then."

"And Nathaniel won't be able to talk with you about it, will he?"

"Probably very little. He'll be able to confirm things showing up in the media, but that's about it."

"You knew this might happen when you ran for the office," LaMance points out.

I nod again with a big exhale, which probably says what I think about the situation more than any words I might use. I catch LaMance's grimace, indicating she knows how hard it's going to be for Nathaniel and I, not to get the other into trouble. Knowing the defense attorneys will be looking for any indication of collusion against their officer.

"We can hope the internal affairs report exonerates the officer and then we won't have to deal with any fall out from your relationship," LaMance concludes.

"You've seen the video. Do you really expect that?" I'm surprised by her comment.

LaMance shakes her head as I knew she would. "The video leaves no doubt the officer involved used maximum force in this situation."

"While there are five seconds obscured, absent Bo Madison producing a deadly weapon of some sort, that's not seen when the shots were fired, it did not appear to be a situation threatening the officer," I complete the thought.

"What do you think happened in those five seconds?" LaMance asks.

"The only thing I can tell for sure is Bo Madison apparently turned away from the officers. When the camera became obscured, he was walking away. When the shots are fired, he's apparently moving towards them, but I can't tell if it's with intent."

"Thereby making it hard to know what we have here…" LaMance suggests.

"We have a dead civilian, that's what we have." I leave no doubt as to our focus.

"They didn't give him a chance," LaMance observes.

I nod. "You could always sit and stay a while..." I point my head towards the one chair in my office where she usually sits when we have some of our longer discussions. LaMance glances at it. She shrugs, apparently deciding we haven't concluded this discussion yet.

"This one won't be like the others," I point out. "The mood of the country has shifted. We will have to bring charges against the officers involved, even if only for use of excessive force. You might as well get a jump on it. Have Scottie start right away."

"I already talked to her," LaMance confirms she's thinking the same. "She has a little different take on the dashcam video."

"Oh?"

"She thinks the officer to the left of the shooter glanced back to see if they were obscuring the camera. It was fleeting, and almost looks like he was saying something to the shooter instead."

"Collusion?" I have to ask as that is all I can think of to explain what she describes. I start the video again and ask, "Where was that?"

"Just after they came up along-side him."

I fast forward to that point. LaMance gets up and comes around to look over my shoulder. She points as she says, "There."

I stop the video and look at the left side officer. I watched that scene over and over and just thought the officer was saying something to his partner in the heat of an encounter. Now I'm seeing it may have had an entirely different meaning. "Not conclusive," is all I can say.

"No, but clearly suggestive."

I nod as LaMance returns to the chair. "I'll look forward to hearing what else Scottie and her team come up with. What's the media saying?"

"That's the curious part," LaMance responds as if she's still mulling the question herself. "There hasn't been much of a reaction by anyone yet."

"It's early," I react without really thinking it through.

"Yes, but given all that's been going on around the country, I'd have thought there'd be a flood of accusations by now."

"What do you make of it... the silence from the usual suspects."

"Probably talking amongst themselves, you know? Let's coordinate our comments. Rather than the usual scattershot approach... maybe they're going to present a petition or something. Afterall, since the scattershot approach hasn't gotten the results they want, maybe it's time to try something different."

I nod, realizing she's probably right. "How many signatures you think they might get for a petition like you're suggesting?"

"You're worried about Nathaniel now, aren't you?"

I grimace without responding, clearly showing LaMance I am. "He'll be just fine, but I can see some of them suggesting he's part of the problem, because he's not been part of the solution."

"He's only been Commissioner for what?" LaMance asks searching her memory.

"Eighteen months," I fill in the blank.

"Hardly enough time to reverse two and a half centuries of racism," LaMance tries to reframe the situation.

"A number of people didn't want him in that role, since he'd been in the department for a long time."

"Nearly half the people who voted in your election didn't want you in this role either as I remember."

"That was the primary," I point out.

LOVE

"In Texas, that's the only election that counts, really."

I hear what she's saying although at the time it didn't seem that way. I had to work day and night to convince voters I wasn't going to do all the things my opponent was saying, to scare them away from me. And until now, I've kept my promises. Haven't done any voter approval poles since I haven't faced reelection yet, but that's coming up. I'll most likely be rated on how well I do with this… if it goes to trial, as we both believe it will.

"Did you catch Walter's speech yesterday, before all this happened?" Walter Rutherford is the Governor of Texas, my neighbor Anne Rutherford's brother-in-law, and my boss.

I usually see all his speeches, but in this case, I was in court observing a civil case one of our newest prosecutors is trying. I make an attempt to see how they do, when an attorney first joins the office, to make sure I've not made a mistake. In this case she performed quite well, winning the case with a well-constructed argument and strong closing statement. "No. Should I go take a look at it?"

"If the shooting hadn't occurred, I'm sure it's what we would have been talking about this morning."

"Increased consumer protections, more money for the special victims unit, or a request to revisit sentencing guidelines?" I zero in on the topics he's discussed recently.

"Better you watch it first. Then we can have this discussion."

"Fair enough," I concede. "What else do we need to discuss this morning?"

"You cancelling the staff meeting?"

I look at the clock and see I've not left myself the usual prep time to be ready to work through the active cases. I don't like to appear unprepared, which at the moment I clearly would. "Probably best. I'll send out the email to everyone when we finish."

I don't like to cancel it because we generally surface all kinds of issues we can work through as a team. I know the younger prosecutors learn a lot in those sessions. But there's no way I can be credible today.

"There's one more thing," LaMance sits back, which generally means she's bringing up something she knows I'm not going to be happy about. "The Prescott case…"

She's right, "I don't do custody cases."

"It's not a custody case, per se. Okay, that is part of it, but what do we do with the criminal portion, if you carve off the custody issue?"

A young Black mother accidently killed her abusive husband, who was trying to murder their six-month-old daughter by drowning it in the bath. Said its incessant crying was keeping him up at night. Said he couldn't work, because he was too tired. Said his boss was going to fire him if he nodded off at work again. Since he operated a sky crane, that was a major problem.

"Mrs. Prescott admits she killed him, although given the circumstances of trying to save her daughter's life, it would indicate a reduced sentence. But she's still guilty by her own admission."

"It's not black and white," LaMance pushes back.

"No, it's just black," I point out. "Black mother, Black father and black baby. And that's why nobody cares. If it was a white family, it would be a whole different discussion. It's almost like some people think the world would be better off if all Black people killed each other off. We can't get in the middle of this case from an advocacy perspective. We follow the sentencing guidelines and we let child protective services provide a temporary home for the child."

"But it's just a baby," LaMance protests. I understand why. "This is the most important time for the mother to bond with her baby. If she loses that contact now their relationship will never be the same. You increase the probability the child will have emotional issues for the rest of its life. You create barriers the mother will never overcome. Why don't you care about that?"

CHAPTER THREE:

gBeto Dahomey Brown, Attorney General, State of Texas

I'm watching the replay of Walter Rutherford's speech when he walks into my office, something he almost never does. The tall and thin former Exxon executive looks every day of his sixty-six years, although that wasn't the situation when he took office four years ago. Then he walked with the springy step of a professional tennis player, which he'd nearly become after attending both Texas A&M and the Colorado School of Mines. It's been a while since anyone can remember him losing a match, although the springy step has given way to a deliberate pace where his head is more likely down contemplating some issue and less engaging of the eyes of those he passes by.

He makes eye contact as soon as I look up from the screen. "Walter…"

"Does this mean you're studying my comments to formulate a response to my challenge to you, or are you seeing them for the first time, because someone reminded you I'd spoken to the media yesterday?"

"Kind of a combination of the two…" I admit.

Walter fluidly places himself in my only chair and glances at me with a question in his eyes. "Now I remember why I seldom come see you. This must be the most uncomfortable chair in all of Texas."

"Keeps meetings short," I point out.

"Then maybe you wouldn't mind if I borrow it for my office?"

"Not at all. Then I can have only stand-up meetings and they might be even shorter," I kid him knowing he's not serious and just setting the stage for what's really on his mind, although I think it's not necessarily what's on the speech video I've been watching.

"What are your impressions?"

Walter does this to me all the time. Puts out an open-ended question like that to see what's on my mind before he goes to what's on his. But in this case, I think we'll be talking about the same thing. "The video raises some troubling questions."

"Mine or the shooting?"

"Actually both, although I've not gotten to the end of yours yet. You'll have to forgive me."

"I assume you've been busy."

I nod in agreement and continue, "We have Scottie doing the work-up on the shooting."

"She the best you've got for a case like this? I don't remember her doing a police shooting before."

"She hasn't. That's why we wanted her to take a look at it. Virgin eyes. No preconceived thoughts. Just look to see what she sees, and determine what the evidence tells us."

"Has she ever lost a case?" Walter seems to be zeroing in on something that's bothering him.

"Just her first one. That taught her she wasn't preparing properly. She has just been a demon on the prep side ever since."

"Give her a chance, but if she's not cutting it, make a change earlier than later."

"What's your concern?" I have to ask as he never gets into this kind of detail on a case.

"Riots," Walter responds quietly. I almost ask him to repeat what he said, but decide that would not be wise.

"What are you hearing?"

"Nothing, no one's calling. No one is giving me advice about how to handle this one. That never happens."

"You're uneasy about the fact no one has called for the officer's dismissal, trial or execution?" I'm trying to put his worry into perspective.

"Usually it's in the other order, but yes," Walter acknowledges, "That's what I'm concerned about."

"Have you had this conversation with the mayor yet?"

Walter looks up at the wall clock to my right. "That's in an hour."

"What's going on? The dashcam hasn't gotten out, there weren't any witnesses. Why is this the one that's going to send people out into the streets?"

Walter raises an eyebrow, pulls out his cell phone, scrolls through and selects something before handing it over to me.

The image is of the shooting, but from a different angle, and quite far away. "Someone shot this from one of the surrounding stores?" I ask, although I'm orienting to figure out the answer myself.

"That would appear to be the case. Jamison, my legislative assistant lives near there. Said it looks to be from the Seven-Eleven on the corner. Probably someone who was filling their car and drove away before the investigators arrived."

I hand the phone back to him, "At least now we can see the five seconds before the shots were fired. The dashcam is obscured. Scottie thinks intentionally."

"Do you agree?" Walter is clearly considering this news.

"It's not a hanging video," is all I'll say.

"Ambiguity," Walter pronounces. "It will be the death of us all."

Walter thinks about something for a long moment before continuing. "What's your sense of where this is all going to end up?"

"I'd not thought of riots, although LaMance raised a concern earlier about how quiet things have been since the report. She thought a petition, which just didn't seem right to me. A riot? Now that's a whole different response. One the minority communities have resorted to in the past."

"Not just the minority communities," Walter reminds me. "Not the last time. And using law enforcement to contain the riots didn't work either. Just made it worse most places. If riots happen, I think it's you and me and every official in my government out in the streets talking to people and calming them down. Asking people to return to their homes and let the legal system provide the justice they are seeking."

"A tall order," I point out." What happens if the courts don't do anything?"

"That's where you come in," Walter has finally gotten to the point. "You'll need to weigh in on jury selection, you'll have to have your top prosecutor on it. We will have to ensure the case is complete and no shred of evidence escapes us. I'm not prejudging this incident, but I'm not going to let it tear our communities apart. The case has to be airtight, one way or the other. No one who reads the decision should have any question that justice was done."

"But what about all those who don't read the decision?" I push back.

"Can't force them to do their homework. But if the right people know we have done our jobs, it will be much better for all of us."

"I understand," he's talking about the media. I have a brief flash of Sarah White probably triggered by the implication of the role the media will play in what happens. *Where will a Sarah White come out on a White cop killing a Black man? With her privileged background, will she even care to report on it? Are the people reading her blogs just like her? I don't know. Never considered it before.*

"Next topic, the other video."

"Your speech," I respond to show I'm following him.

"You didn't get to the end," his eyes are twinkling now as the heavy stuff is over.

"No, sir," I admit embarrassed.

"Why do more corporations register in Delaware than any other state?"

"I would describe their corporate laws as business friendly," I respond as a way of saying corporations can get more favorable court decisions based on their laws than in other states such as Texas.

"We have lost a number of companies that have chosen to set up operations in states like North Dakota and even Iowa. I've set up a citizens task force, which is what you've not gotten to yet, to study what we can do to make our business climate even friendlier. I said at the end of that video you're watching I want my legacy as governor to be that we are the state that provides economic security to our residents through the private sector and not at taxpayer expense. Now that's a tall order, but something that should be manageable given our oil and gas revenues, and increasing corporate relocations."

"What is my role to be in regards to your new task force?"

"You and Ronald Amundsen are the co-chairs."

"The Chairman of AT&T?" I'm speechless. But then the question I have to have an answer to bursts through, "Why me?"

"Because a major part of it has to be overhauling parts of our corporation laws. You know them better than anyone else in our state. You have to enforce them. You have staff members who know where the bodies are buried. You and your team can feed the citizens task force with proposals that will make Texas the state that leads the nation in economic security.

"What's Ronald's role versus mine?"

"AT&T has stepped up to lend us resources for any studies we wish to undertake as part of the work of the task force. They will research what works in other states, what inhibits growth and what stimulates it in the fashion we want. They will pay for experts to come address the task force on any subject we believe could assist us in reaching the goal."

"Will he be weighing in on the solutions or just providing resources for the citizens to decide what is best for all of Texas?"

Walter shifts his position a bit uncomfortably. "I worked for Ronald on two different occasions before he left for AT&T. He will have opinions. He uses them as screening criteria for what is presented to him. He waits for you to build your case, which he then evaluates against his opinions. If you've built a strong case, he will change his opinion. If not… he will make it difficult for you to move forward until you come around to his opinion."

"You're not making this sound like fun," I point out.

"Fun?" Walter seems surprised I would select that word to describe the work he wants me to undertake. "Fun is what you have on your time. Our state is in a war with every other state for jobs and the people who will fill them. If we don't make Texas a more appealing place for companies, then the citizens of Texas will have no choice but to move where the jobs go. Staying here after they leave is a zero-sum game, because with fewer and fewer people living here, tax revenues decline. We have fewer and fewer dollars to invest in infrastructure and provide social benefits to them. Don't you see? I'm asking you to be the general of the economic war we are fighting."

"Along with Ronald who will clearly think I'm a private in this war."

"He will only think of you that way if you give him cause to. You played a major role in my campaign. You leveraged that experience into a successful campaign of your own. I know how you think. I see how effective you are. If I had any doubts about your ability to hold your own with Ronald Amundsen, I never would have asked you to take on this role. I fully expect you to drive this initiative. Ronald will be too busy managing AT&T. He just won't have time to study the issues you will. To evaluate the options the various members bring forward, to weave it all into a comprehensive strategy, to ensure the future of our state. To create my legacy."

"What's all this talk about legacy?"

Walter rises and begins to pace. "If I were to leave office today, what would the citizens of Texas remember about my administration?"

"People would remember you as honest, fair and forward thinking," I suggest.

Walter stops and looks at me, "Is that how you will want people to remember you?"

"I really haven't given it any thought, why?"

"To me, that's like kissing your sister. I want people to remember me as someone who made their lives better. Someone who wasn't here just for my own greater glorification. Someone who made Texas a truly great place to live, raise a family and work, contributing to the greater economy disproportionately to our size."

"Why the economy? All you read about is the culture wars."

"Exactly why we work on what truly matters to each and every person who lives here," Walter is going to the heart of the matter. "The ability to make a decent living, one where each person can afford to raise a family while giving them whatever lifestyle they want."

"I see that, but we already have one of the largest economies in the world and second only to California in this country."

"That's the beauty of what I want you to go look at. The pandemic changed everything. More people work at home now than ever before. We can attract jobs for those people to work from their homes without having to build giant industrial parks. We can lead the nation in smart jobs, if you will. Where people use their ingenuity, their intelligence, their insights to create value and sell it around the world."

His vision is starting to make more sense to me now. "You don't want to attract companies; you want to attract jobs that can be performed anywhere. Part of the new gig economy. But the gig economy doesn't create the kind of permanent jobs we're used to seeing. People work short term assignments and move on to the next. They may, or most likely, won't have benefits. I'm not sure that creates the kind of economic security you're looking for."

Walter nods but begins pacing again, "There will be some gig jobs, but the big companies provide the permanent jobs with full benefits. They've been letting their employees work where they want as long as they have broadband and reliable connections. That has to be a part of the solution. We have to deploy the fastest, most reliable and widest broadband anywhere. People need it to easily work anywhere in our state."

"This isn't just a change in a few laws," I realize. "You have a much bigger vision."

"Watch the rest of my speech. You'll see where I'm going."

"I'll do that. And as I have questions?"

"Every Monday morning at seven am, you, Ronald and I will be having breakfast to strategize. I want weekly press releases on what we are considering. I want to excite the people, give them hope and paint a future they will identify with."

"Against the drumbeat of another cop shooting a Black man," I remind him.

CHAPTER FOUR:

gBeto Dahomey Brown, Attorney General, State of Texas

Nathaniel won't look at me as he enters our kitchen from the garage. I instantly see the taught muscles in his jaw, the restrained power of his muscular body, seemingly wanting to burst from his slightly stooped stance. Almost like he wants to run through a line of football players, taking as many down as possible, as he eludes their grasping hands and arms on his way to the end zone. Just like he did when we were in college. If I didn't know better, I'd say it looks like he's become grayer in just the last twenty-four hours. His short black hair seems a shade lighter today. *Is that even possible?*

He flings his black suitcoat over the back of a chair on his way through. The colorful tie he chose this morning is nowhere to be seen. *Probably still in the car.* He seems to be on a mission. When he disappears into the wine closet, I know what kind of day it's been. We seldom drink alcohol during the week, saving it for parties and the weekend when we're not as concerned about responding to calls from the governor, or in his case, the mayor. The fact he's into the closet on a Tuesday speaks volumes about his day.

As he reappears, his first words to me are, "Rosso di Montalcino, five years old. How does that sound?" I know he's talking about whether it will go with whatever I've prepared for dinner. Not that I prepared it today, as during the week we almost always pull something from the freezer left over from a meal we prepared together over the weekend. I'm the chef. He's my sous chef and person in charge of cleaning up. It's one of the things we can do together, while we discuss things of interest, importance and necessity, usually in that order as we create a culinary classic to share. Tonight, the discussion will be of necessity.

"Fine," I respond to his query. "Chicken penne pasta with a red vodka sauce. It works."

"The sun-dried tomatoes and hint of mascarpone really made that special," he reflects for me and tells me at the same time he was hoping I'd pulled that one. I did, but only because I was feeling I needed something extra tonight given my day. But now I'm glad tending to my wants has addressed his as well.

"How did Tuesday get to be wine Wednesday?" I respond to the bottle in his hand. This is a joke as we have a friend who always drinks wine on Wednesdays. She tried to get us to join her. We did for a while; but we both were uncomfortable about being impaired during the week, even if it was in the off hours. The problem we both have is that during the week there really aren't any off hours. At least not any more. When we were first married, we often did things during the week with friends. A play, or dinner, or movie even. But as we rose higher in our respective organizations, that just didn't seem to work for us anymore. Too often we were called out of whatever event we were attending. When we realized that neither of us ever got to dessert when out for dinner, we simply gave in to the reality of our situations. We have uniformly declined dinners during the week that aren't business related.

"The mayor and I had a little heart to heart…" he looks at his watch, "about an hour ago."

I stop breathing afraid of the implication of his comment, realize what I've done, and quickly start again in such a way that it won't sound like a gasp, although it's hard to pull off. *I don't want Nathaniel to think I'm afraid of what he's going to tell me, but I am.*

"I'm suspended with pay until the internal investigation is complete," Nathaniel glances up at me sheepishly. "You know, when I put that policy in place last year, I never thought it would come back to bite me. And now that it has, I'm trying to decide if I regret putting it in place to begin with."

I remember the long debates we had over this very topic.

Nathaniel wanted to put pressure on the policemen he is commissioner over. By requiring that the commissioner is suspended with pay each and every time there is an officer involved fatal shooting, until the internal investigation is filed. It would ensure there is no undue pressure on the investigating officers. Great in theory, but we are about find out how it works in practice. The fact the Fort Christian police department has avoided a fatal officer involved shooting during his tenure was an early indicator that maybe the policy is working as intended. But now, we will see whether the flood gates have opened.

"It's the right thing," I come to him and put my arms around him for a hug as he lifts the wine bottle high over us and he gives me a kiss, although the usual smile is missing. "How long for the internal affairs investigation?"

"A couple weeks, hopefully," he responds before disengaging to find the corkscrew, and open the wine he desperately wants. Nothing more is said until he has accomplished his mission and poured a glass for each of us. "To better times, may they arrive sooner than later."

We clink glasses before the sip. I remember this wine. Distinctive taste we both enjoy. Probably why he chose it. "What did she say when she suspended you?" I dig knowing there has to be more to the situation given his behavior. If it was all procedural, I doubt we'd have an open bottle on a Tuesday.

Nathaniel looks away from me. *Not a good sign. He has to consider what to say to me, even though he's had the whole drive home to do that.* "She talked about the immense pressure she's under to ensure Black men aren't victims of the department."

"And you aren't?" I respond without thinking, but knowing how much he has been focused on just this topic ever since taking over the top job in the department eighteen months ago. The only viable internal candidate who overcame considerable community resistance to anyone from the department rising to the top job given the history here.

Nathaniel pours a little more wine into his glass even though it is still quite full. Tells me he is still wrestling with a part of the conversation with the mayor he hasn't shared yet. I wait until he looks up to me again. He catches my eye and sees what I'm doing. He apparently realizes he has to give me more than he has. I still wait as he takes another sip. "Okay. It wasn't quite that straight forward."

"What was it?"

"She said she regretted giving me the chance as my policies haven't avoided the current situation. If she'd hired someone outside, there may have been a more thorough shake up. Maybe gotten rid of the old dinosaurs."

"Was she referring to you since you've been working that very issue?"

"I knew you'd take it that way," Nathaniel takes another sip.

"What do you mean?"

"Let me just say it was clear to me she'd rather I just resign," he puts it out there apparently knowing he won't be able to avoid the subject much longer.

"Did you ask her?" I push back knowing he's too sensitive to things sometimes.

"No. And even if I had, she probably wouldn't have told me the truth."

"Has it really gotten that bad?" I ask surprised by this revelation. "I thought you had a good relationship with her."

"She's up for re-election," is all he has to say. Tells me that if they've had nothing but positive interactions for his whole term, if the mayor thinks this event has jeopardized her reelection chances, he's just a sacrifice to the election gods regardless of what she really thinks about him.

"Seems to me she doesn't have real competition, or are you hearing something I'm not?"

Nathaniel muses for a long moment before answering, "Every member of council thinks she or he could do a better job. Will one or more of them challenge her? If even one thinks this could be an opening to enable a change at the top, that member of council will jump in with both feet. And if one does, I won't be surprised if more join the fray."

"She's feeling the heat," I suggest to verify what I think I'm hearing.

"I think she's doing everything she can to head off a challenge behind the scenes. If I resign, that makes it easy for her. She can immediately start a search for my replacement while the investigation plays out."

"I know you looked at the tape..." I start down the path I know he won't follow very far, but I'm pushing to reassure him he's not at fault for what happened. *Hoping he'll realize he shouldn't resign, at least in my opinion.*

"And you know I can't discuss it with you since you will have to prosecute the case if it goes beyond the department."

"I'm only trying to get you to look at the political ramifications..."

"Can't go there either," Nathaniel is very clear he wants to change the subject even though we've not resolved anything. But maybe that's where he wants to leave it. Unresolved. Let me work what I have to and he'll work what he has to, even though we are both going to suffer the consequences of what happens next.

"I take it you haven't offered to resign .."

Nathaniel shakes his head as a way of confirming my question without saying anything. "Look. I'll be talking with the mayor every day. Even though I'm on suspension. I'm still her primary advisor for police matters. While I can't talk with anyone in the department, I still review everything and offer my professional insights for her consideration. She can ask me questions based on the reports. I intend to fulfill that role and see where this goes. We have made giant strides in a very short time, although she asked me straight out if I had any idea this could happen."

"And what did you say?"

"That in the moment anything is possible. It all depends on human dynamics, perceptions, relationships, prior experiences and sometimes it just comes down to someone having a bad day for some reason, totally unrelated to the incident that pushes events in one direction or another."

"Sounds like an excuse…" I confirm.

"That's apparently how she took it."

"She wanted to know why this happened. What you are going to do to make sure it can't happen again."

"That's all clear…" he looks at his watch, "two hours later, but at the time…"

I hug him again, holding him as reassuringly as I know how. I feel a wee bit of his tension release. Don't know if it was the hug or the first effects of the wine. Whatever, I'll take it. He needs to step back. "No matter. We will get through this together, just as we have all the other challenges we've faced to get here."

Nathaniel kisses me again and releases me. The tension is still as prevalent in his jaw. Whatever release he felt was likely minor. I'll have to do a better job in bed later, although he sometimes struggles in that situation when he's really tense over something at work. I better not get my hopes up too much.

"You know I don't know what to do since I've never been suspended before. Do I spend the whole day baking bread, or cooking us a great meal? Do I watch television or spend the whole day scrolling through the various media?"

"Think of it as a long Saturday," I suggest. "What would you do on any given Saturday? Do that and then the next day think of it as Saturday and what would you do the next Saturday."

Nathaniel sort of half shakes his head and half nods, ending with a shrug. "Guess I'll read some of those articles I've been sitting on for the last several months. I keep saying I'll read them when I have time but I've not found the time, until now."

I kiss him again, "Good idea. You've had some of your best ideas after reading about something another department tried and had good success with."

"Yes, but I generally call up the chief or commissioner and discuss it with him or her. Get the inside view of what worked, what didn't and what might have worked better if only they had done something a little differently. Generally, we have to change what they have done to make it work here."

"That's what you've been good at… adapting something someone else tried. You see opportunities to make it better, make it effective, bring everyone together to solve a problem that just seemed insolvable until you worked it through with all the stakeholders. Convinced the early adopters there can be real gains for them."

Nathaniel seems more upbeat for a moment, but then the brightness disappears and his head drops. "Don't think I've seen anything that would address what happened here, in this instance."

"You're making an assumption," I push back. "You have what? A couple weeks to really dig in. Talk to your peers around the country. See what they suggest. Who do you talk with most often?"

"Chief Walsh in Raleigh. She seems to have a lot of similar issues," he instantly seems brighter again, apparently remembering one or more conversations.

"Since you're wondering what to do with yourself, why don't you help me with dinner? You need to get something in your stomach other than just wine." I kiss him again and head for the kitchen.

In only a moment he has followed me in and begins to re-engage with our immediate problem. "Chicken penne pasta, red vodka sauce with mascarpone and sun-dried tomatoes."

"You can make the salad. Anything special you want to add?" I ask but get an unexpected answer.

"Yes, the mayor wanted to know how I was going to ensure we don't talk about the events in case it ends up in court."

I stop and look at him, not sure what he told her, given the way he held this back until now.

"I told her I could move to a hotel if she would prefer... just until the internal affairs report is filed and she reinstates me."

"That's not going to happen... not from what I saw on the dashcam," I push back to let him know I think this is a bad idea.

Nathaniel waves his hand to remind me we can't discuss what we seem to be heading to discuss and that's what this whole issue is all about. "You're jumping ahead. At this point we assume..."

"You can assume anything you'd like, but this isn't going to end with the IA report and you know it," I'm mad he has held this back. "This is going to trial and that means you could be suspended for months and living in a hotel for months... and I assume we're paying for your little vacation accommodations. If you think you're going to have trouble figuring out what to do here, if you're in a hotel you'll be going up the walls... literally."

He waves me down and that only spins me up more.

"Moving out is an admission we can't separate our lives, that we can't act professionally and respect the law we are both sworn to uphold. I'd tell the mayor there is no need for you to move out for two weeks or two years, because we both know it could take that long with appeals and all that could intervene in a resolution of the case, when it becomes one. If you move out you better be prepared to not move back in... ever."

"Whoa," Nathaniel didn't anticipate my reaction. "Where is that coming from?'

"I'm prepared to document every source for every fact we collect in building our case, when that time comes. I am not going to introduce any evidence of any kind that would affect the validity of the case. I don't intend to permit the plaintiff to get off on a procedural. You stay, or you go and don't come back. Am I making myself clear?"

CHAPTER FIVE:

gBeto Dahomey Brown, Attorney General, State of Texas

Estella Velasquez has an outsized presence in any room or conversation. At just five feet tall, and well under a hundred pounds, one would expect she would not be the first person looked to in any debate. However, she has established her expertise and sage advice in many political discussions over the years, all without ever holding office herself. She chose to be a campaign manager and policy advisor.

I was lucky enough to convince her to be mine on both counts. The other thing about Estella is she always dresses in bright hues with colonial blue being her favorite color in the winter and red or white in the summer. They just happen to be the dominant colors of the Texas state flag. She has a cape made of a flag she wears at the year-end holiday events, which I am jealous of, but would never dare wear for fear of the comments I would get. I'm sure she has received many comments over the years, but she still wears it every holiday season to more than one event.

"It's not too early to begin preparing for the next election," she begins in her very direct style, and enunciation, which is influenced by Spanish being her native language. I often thought she didn't run for office herself since she was born in Ecuador, a country that would not have provided the same economic opportunities. Was that why she left her home at sixteen to come to the US, or was it another reason? She's never answered that question.

"Are you talking about fundraisers or organizing the get out the vote team?" I respond as we sit in my living room. She's drinking her favorite white wine, an Argentinian Torrontes, which I keep in the refrigerator just for her visits. Actually, bought a case in preparation for the upcoming election, since I know she will be over a lot.

"Have you decided? You're running for re-election?" she seeks confirmation since we've not had this conversation to date.

"Yes, although I've had some thoughts of not making the race. Last time I had more flexibility with my schedule. But frankly I'm not sure where I'm going to find the necessary time. That's not to say I don't want to return as attorney general. I just don't like the idea of having to take time from the job to convince voters to keep me."

"That's what you're supposed to say when you're up for re-election the fifth or sixth time. You have many fewer voters to convince than most people running for state-wide office and a significant registration majority for our party. While this isn't a cake walk, it's certainly not what you'd experience in many states."

I nod in agreement. Texas would not be considered a battleground state by any stretch of the imagination. Having the nomination as an incumbent makes the task a lot shorter and a lot more straight forward. Those facts certainly influenced my decision to run in the first place. "Yes, I'm in."

Estella consults her notes, "Your treasurer gave me a report on your campaign finances. Seems you still have a little less than a million dollars left over. The note he gave me is you received most of that after the polls showed there was little doubt you were going to win. People piling in on the sure thing. You'd already made all your media buys, paid your campaign staff and the decision was made you didn't need to up your spending at the end. You're actually in a very good place finance-wise."

"I had no idea it was that much," I just blurt out. "Are we really going to need to focus on fundraising?"

"You always focus on fundraising. If you don't need all the money you raise, you contribute to campaigns of those who need it more," she dashes my hopes that I won't have to spend much time asking for contributions. I've never been comfortable asking people to invest in me, knowing the only return is a fair and honest attorney general.

I nod, but I see her look, which is apparently reacting to my look of unhappiness.

"This year Walter's going to need some help," she reveals to me. I've heard nothing of the governor having a primary or even a strong candidate from the other party. *What's she talking about?*

"Walter?"

"Robertson's not returning to the ticket, but you knew that," she is planting seeds, what seeds?

"Are you saying the lieutenant governor, who has already announced he's retiring, somehow carried that ticket?"

"Financially he did," she confides. I've never heard anything about this.

"I knew he ran the senate finance team when he was a senator, but hell, Walter was at Exxon for decades, in senior levels, he's got to have a whole network of wealthy donors from his time there."

"He does, but that's not the point. The only person who can replace Robertson's contribution to the campaign is Smithson, who replaced him as senate campaign finance chairman. He can tap those same donors in the same way. But if we want to change the dynamic of who benefits from government largesse, we have to tap different donors. If the party is only beholding to the same corporate donations, the policies we see coming out of the state house will be the same as we saw last session. If we want to change those policies, we have to have others providing the funds to elect new voices, new visions and new directions."

"As attorney general why do I care about any of that?" I challenge her thesis as it relates to my campaign treasury and fund-raising efforts.

"Why do you have trouble seeing the dotted lines?" Estella

challenges me in return.

"Dotted lines? What are you talking about?" I have no idea.

"There is an opening on the ticket..."

"Walter will choose Smithson," I push back. "You said so
yourself. He brings the money and the connections and the experience
in the state senate. He knows the policies, the players and where the
bodies are buried. Smithson's been working for this ever since
Robertson moved up and gave him an opportunity to build his base."

"Are you White?"

This comment takes me back like a slap in the face. "What?"

"You sound like all those White people who sit back and assume
others are going to fight for what they want," she castigates me. "Or
maybe they just don't care about any of it because they have what they
want. A big house, cars in the garage, good schools for their kids and
enough money to do what they want. But that's not what we want. We,
as the minority community, don't have those things..."

"You're talking the larger we... aren't you? Because you and I do
have those things. We didn't, but things have changed enough that
some of us have achieved that level of social comfort."

"You don't have kids... if you did you wouldn't think that way. If
you were afraid your son was going to be shot by a White cop because
he was in the wrong place at the wrong time, you wouldn't talk about
others leading. If your daughter was constantly being harassed for
being Latino, like mine, or Black if you'd had one... you wouldn't be
quietly waiting for Smithson."

"Hold on," I raise my hand now to calm her down. "I know
exactly what you're saying and I'm fighting for those kids to have
justice every day I show up to work. I'm just saying, you want to fight
a culture war and I'm not into that. I want to eliminate the fear Black
and Latino kids experience in going out at night. But I want to do it by
ensuring the consequences of those who would harass or endanger

them are so high, that it disappears as a viable choice. And that's exactly what I'm doing in this job. Do I think we will ever win at the ballot box? There are six White people for every Black person and two White people for every Hispanic or Latino in Texas. That's just not a winning proposition. We have to take a different approach. And that's what I'm doing every day."

"I'm glad there's no media in here," Estella responds to my comments. "Your attitude isn't going to get you votes from either constituency. That's not what you ran on last time. You're Ms. Law and Order. Enforce the laws the legislature passes. There was no advocacy in that pitch last time and it worked. You were elected. And your reputation now that you're in office is you do exactly what you promised to do. Laws are enforced fairly and equitably. But you've also not had a high-profile case that galvanized the public's attention. And that's a good thing. But I'm afraid that may be about to change."

"Is that why you came to see me today?" I now understand the lecture I'm getting.

"I watched the dashcam tape. I saw the cellphone video. I don't know how that case doesn't go to court, your court. And it's going to be a no-win situation for you. If the cop walks, the minority community won't back your re-election. If he is found guilty the White community won't. The current power structures will favor acquittal. If you buck them, you'll not get a dime from the people you need or votes from the largest block of voters. Either way you either lose your job, your naivete, or any following in the minority communities. You become an Uncle Tom. And while you might be able to get re-elected by the White voters, you won't be able to do your job if the minority community doesn't trust you or support what you're doing."

"Maybe this case will make my choice for me," I suggest although I don't really believe that to be the case.

"Only if you let it," Estella responds with a challenge evident in her tone of voice.

"You've obviously given this thought," I observe. "What would you have me do?"

"That's the interesting part of this whole discussion…"

"I don't know what you're saying," I respond curious but not sure what she wants me to know or do.

"You're wrong about Smithson," she looks me straight in the eye.

"I don't agree," I dismiss her statement.

"Smithson is going to ensure Walter gets his donations, but he's already cut a deal to be the next Chief Justice of the Texas Supreme Court. Smithson's a lawyer and he loves the law. He does the political work because his father told him a long time ago that was the only path to becoming a supreme court justice. Smithson's not your competition."

"Competition? For lieutenant governor? I'm not a candidate… Walter's given me no indications he would even consider me."

"You haven't been listening." Estella doesn't say more but just looks at me as I process what she's been saying.

"Hold on. You've just been making the case I should step down as attorney general because I won't be electable after this current case. Now you're saying Walter is going to put me on the ticket with him? This just doesn't make any sense. What's in that wine you're drinking anyway?"

"Your wine, you tell me," Estella holds up the glass for me to see better. "Stop and think about it."

"I am, but I'm not coming to the same conclusion you are."

"You are about to be on two of the highest profile events in our state going into the convention this fall."

"How did you know about the commission?" I wonder aloud.

"Do you think I'm not talking to Walter's campaign team? Of

course, I am. I work for them as well."

I knew that, but hadn't considered it. I shrug.

"I'm not saying you're the nominee, you've got a few hoops to get through to get to that point, but Walter's actions would say the nomination is yours to lose. And you're in the perfect place to do just that, if you're not smart about everything you say or do between now and the election."

"What are you saying? That I need to run everything I want to say publicly through an election filter?"

"No, I'm suggesting you need to run everything you're going to say past me before you say it. I need to see everything you write that will ever see the light of day. And that means everything you write."

"I'm not going to run legal decisions past you."

She doesn't say anything, just looks at me like she did before, saying with her eyes what she's not about to say in words, which is *do I want to be on the ticket or not?*

"You're going to have to give me some time to think about this conversation. I haven't given it any consideration because I thought Robertson was going to stick around for a second term. Everyone did, didn't they?"

Estella shakes her head, "Walter knew when he put him on the ticket last time. Walter needed someone from the legislature since he came from the private sector. He also wanted someone who could be seen as guiding him, without being a threat to replace him after just a term. Robertson was perfect for that role, but now Walter is more concerned about a legacy…"

Walter used that term in our talk…

"He wants to lay a foundation for good governance that will continue after his time in office is up. He wants to transition to a younger generation that comes at governance from a rule of law perspective. Someone who understands that how laws are interpreted is just as important as the intent of the law in the first place. Does this sound like Smithson?"

"You think safety and jobs are the winning pitch..." I point out.

"That's high on Walter's list, but he knows he only has a limited ability to affect it given the current make-up of the legislature. I think, and I could be wrong about this, that Walter hopes if you are his running mate, you will encourage more minorities to contest for seats in the legislature. If not this year, in two and four years from now."

This is why Estella, all of five feet tall, carries such an impact in legislative and political discussions. She sees all aspects of the situation and is able to project how things could play out. She formulates strategies of how to respond and how to shape what will happen. Since taking office, I've spent exactly zero time on either until today. And I'm sure that's why she's here. Because I've not been playing the political game, even though Walter and maybe others have been setting me up behind the scenes. I wonder if that's because I haven't been overtly political or ambitious. I've done my job to the best of my ability, and been good to my campaign promises. Does that make me different from other politicians? I don't know, but I suspect if I'd been openly ambitious, I'd not be on Walter's list.

"You clearly know more about what's going on than I do," I respond finally. "But don't you think Walter's likely to back off if things don't go well on the recent shooting? I don't know how you win political points from a proceeding on that topic. A large number of folks aren't going to be happy no matter how it turns out."

"That's where you have to work your magic," Estella leans forward as if conspiratorially. "You have to communicate the case in such a manner that no one can question how it is conducted or how it is resolved. Communications. Isn't that the keystone of any good politician? However it turns out, you have to communicate that the result is justice for everyone, and a precedent that will ensure the next person who finds her or himself in that position will get similar equal treatment under the law. That's what you do, now you just have to communicate it."

"Much easier said than done," I respond now deep in thought about this news. Another layer of complexity in an already difficult minefield to traverse.

"Now we all get to see what you're really made of," Estella nods to me, takes a final sip of her wine and rises to excuse herself as I barely notice.

CHAPTER SIX:

Mayor Jenny Richards, City of Fort Christian, Texas

Bethany, my slender and long dark-haired media relations manager pokes her head into my Spartan office, "The media is gathered in the conference room, Mayor Richards."

I've just been on the call with Nathaniel. I'm surprised how hard he seems to be taking his suspension. And even more surprised he doesn't seem willing to just resign and give me a free hand in this matter. I should have known it would come down to deciding his fate, rather than leave it in his hands. He's a product of the department. I can see where walking away would seem like quitting a team you've played on your whole life. "Be right with you."

A quick review of my notes, just to ensure I have the basic facts in my head. Then, and only then, I rise and follow Bethany down the hall.

"Morning," Peterson, the lanky and balding city treasurer nods to me as we pass in the hallway. In only a moment I'm in the conference room and see every seat is filled around the room. A few more are standing in the back. *Everyone has a recording device. I expect to hear myself all day long if I care to check what anyone is saying. But that's Bethany's job. She'll give me a summary as needed.*

"Good morning, everyone," I offer as I take a seat at the head of the faux wood conference table. Would have been nice to have a real wood table, but my predecessor was an infamous scrooge and only bought the cheapest of whatever was needed. I'm not a spendthrift, but look at the useful life more than just the initial price.

"Mayor Richards," the young woman from Continuum Media starts things off, *what's her name?* "In regards to the police involved shooting yesterday."

I nod having expected it to be nearly the sole subject we will discuss today.

"What actions have you taken as mayor to address the situation?" she continues.

"Sarah, is it?" I ask as her name pops into my head. I like to make these meetings as personal as possible to keep on friendly terms with the media.

"Sarah White," she responds with a nod.

"Sarah, that's an excellent question and probably appropriate to be the first one. The tragic events of yesterday are regretted by every member of my administration. We all extend our condolences to the family of Bo Madison. Whenever a life is lost, we all take it very personally, and vow to follow the evidence wherever it leads as we investigate. Our paramount interest is in seeing justice done for all parties concerned, and indeed for all residents of our city."

"You have referenced an investigation," Sarah asks. "Could you provide us detail on that?"

"Yes, as you know, it's standard procedure for the internal affairs department within our police to conduct an independent investigation of any and all incidents where an officer discharges his or her weapon, regardless of whether anyone is injured or not. In the event of loss of life, either police officer or civilian, the investigation team consists of at least one officer from a police organization in another city."

"Who is that officer?" Daniel Holt, the ex-Marine from the Fox News affiliate in town asks. Someone said he never fought when on active duty as he was assigned to media relations for his entire tour. Must be connected somewhere.

"Sergeant Tim Scott of the Houston department. He heads up their internal affairs team," I respond.

"Tim Scott? Is he White?" a young Black man in the back who I don't know asks.

"Who are you?" I respond, trying to sound neutral, but wanting to know who is asking what questions.

"Tic Rogers, I have an independent blog site a lot of folks have been making attributions to."

This could be dangerous as I have no idea who is following his stories or what slant he's likely to take. "You here in Fort Christian?"

"No, Ma'am. I'm from Tulsa. Drove down just for this story."

"Not much else going on in Fort Christian that would be of interest to your audiences," I respond.

"Actually, you have a number of things I'm looking into while I'm here. You're likely to see a series of blogs on Fort Christian over the next several weeks."

"What kinds of things?" I pursue since I still have no idea who or what I'm dealing with here.

"I thought we were supposed to be asking the questions," draws a laugh.

"We'll get back to that, but I'm just interested in who is following this story and why. Could you provide a little more insight?"

"My stories have been picked up by Bloomberg, Axios, Politico, Sierra Club, Environmental Defense Fund, and a series of organizations. I'm not one dimensional. I follow a good story regardless of who is likely to link in."

"You're looking at our initiatives to improve our air quality, our economy and our political transparency?" I suggest.

"Among others," he responds indicating it's more likely the social justice angle on the shooting. This story isn't going to remain local long.

"Thank you. For the record, Sergeant Tim Scott is a Black officer on the Houston force. He is a former Marine infantryman, has been with the Houston department for twenty-seven-years and has a distinguished record as an officer."

"Distinguished in what way?" Tic Rogers follows on.

"If you're asking has he ever killed anyone in the line of duty, the answer is no. He has been wounded on three separate occasions while making arrests and has wounded civilians on two occasions, both of which occurred when he himself was already wounded. He has been able to avoid lethal use of force in his career, while compiling an impressive record of arrests and maintaining the peace in his city."

"Is he the lead investigator?" Sarah White again.

"No. Lieutenant Childers is the lead investigator, as he is for all internal affairs cases in our department."

"He is white." Tic Rogers again.

"Lieutenant Childers is white," I acknowledge. "Has been with the department thirty-two years and often serves on investigations for other departments because of his reputation for objectivity and thoroughness."

"Has he ever killed anyone in the line of duty?" Tic Rogers again.

"Yes. As a highly decorated officer, he has been involved in some of the most dangerous situations faced by our police. He spent most of his early years on the drug watch, which as you likely know resulted in a significant number of large-scale raids with unfortunate loss of life amongst our officers, the drug dealers and innocent civilians. These operations were necessary to reassert control over certain areas of our city where the drug dealers established themselves as the local authorities, a situation we could not allow to persist."

Tic Rogers, looks up from his cell phone, "I'm reading an article from about ten years ago where your Lieutenant Childers was cited for using unnecessary force to obtain a confession. Is he really the best person to lead the investigation into charges of unnecessary force that led to an unnecessary death?"

I have to think back since that was before my time on council, "I don't have first-hand knowledge of the events you have referenced. All I can say is that in the eight years I've been an official of the City of Fort Christian, Lieutenant Childers has only been cited for bravery and the tactful handling of tense and explosive situations, that could easily have gone in the other direction."

"Is the problem that you are blind to the fact your police department is steeped in racism, profiling and taking the easy way to maintain control, which is to intimidate anyone who is of color or not from the right neighborhoods?"

"Would you say you have an agenda, rather than a desire to be objective in gathering facts and obtaining ground truth as to what happened?" I push right back as I can't allow those charges to stand.

"Agenda?" Tic Rogers seems unprepared to answer the question. But then his response is swift, "Your agenda is to keep the city safe for the White folks who pay your taxes. Keep their streets paved and garbage picked up twice a week. Your agenda is to keep the status quo while the people of color in your city suffer daily humiliations, indignities and harassments from your White policemen and their striver token Blacks who only want to keep their jobs at the expense of their dignity."

"This isn't a debate, Mr. Rogers," I stay on the offensive to counter his. "This is a media relations update by the city. You infer political motivations without facts. You wish to label where there is no proof. You wish to denigrate the many men and women who serve this city to make headlines, to entice Mrs. White's media company to pick up your story, all to help you create a reputation, and therefore, make a living by tearing down the hard work of many in service to their fellow citizens. This is an open meeting, otherwise I would ask you to leave."

Sarah White jumps back in, "Mayor Richards, what actions have you taken in relation to the officer? Your procedures call for you to suspend him with pay until after the internal affairs review is complete. Have you?"

"Yes, the officer involved and his partner have been suspended with pay pending the release of the report. At the same time, we have suspended Commissioner Brown per the protocol he was instrumental in putting in place last year."

"Commissioner Brown?" Sarah seems surprised.

"Yes. The commissioner put into place a protocol last year that whenever there is a loss of life resulting from an officer involved shooting, the commissioner is put on suspension with pay. The thought is to ensure she or he will not be able to influence the course or nature of the internal affairs investigations."

"The commissioner recommended this policy?" Sarah White wants to confirm.

"Yes."

"But why would the commissioner want to do that? Seems he would want to be driving the investigation to get to the bottom of things as quickly as possible." Sarah seems to be still puzzling on this revelation.

"Believe me he does," I shake my head thinking about the last conversation with him. "But Commissioner Brown wants to make sure the internal affairs team feels free to go wherever needed to obtain all the facts, regardless of how negatively they may cast the department, without fear of embarrassing the commissioner. If at the end of the day it becomes clear the commissioner has not managed the department in a prudent manner, it is easier to remove that individual if they are already on suspension."

"I take it this is the first time this protocol has been invoked?" Daniel Holt jumps back in. *Nice to know he hasn't gone to sleep on me.*

"Yes."

"And it's been on the books for over a year?" he follows up.

"Yes."

"That would mean you haven't had an officer involved shooting death in over a year."

"That's correct." I wonder where he's going with this line of questioning.

"Is that a record or something?"

"Mr. Holt, there are approximately a thousand deaths of civilians each year at the hands of police officers. There are nearly 18,000 police departments. That would indicate the vast majority of them do not have a civilian death at the hands of a police officer for many years running. I am clearly not proud of the fact we had one this year. It is only the second to occur in Fort Christian during my years of service to the city. No, it is not a record. If anything, it is something we should all stop and consider for a long time. Why did this happen? Why did it happen now, and what can we do to make sure it never happens again in our city?"

"Isn't that a bit unrealistic?" Tic Rogers seems to think we should be killing people on our streets daily or something.

"I don't think so," I respond. "If anything, it's not ambitious enough. No one should die in our city other than from old age. That may be unrealistic, but that is what I personally strive to achieve."

"What will it take for Commissioner Brown to be reinstated?" Sarah White again.

"An internal affairs report that does not point the finger towards things he could have done or should have done to prevent what has occurred."

"How likely is that?" Tic Rogers chimes in.

"I am hopeful that will be the conclusion of the report. I have personally known Commissioner Brown for all my years of service to the city. In fact, I was acquainted with his wife even before that. I have to say he is someone of the utmost integrity, honesty and passion to make the City of Fort Christian a safe and orderly place for families to raise their kids, and for every one of every background to feel they are receiving equal treatment under the law."

"Given your glowing testimonial, how likely is it you will release the commissioner if the report is not as glowing as your description?" Tic Rogers trying to have something to talk about tonight.

"I will read the report with an open mind, will assess the evidence collected, the recommendations forwarded, and make a decision that will be in the best interests of the city and its residents, after consultation with council members and our city legal team, not out of personal loyalty to any one person."

"What about the officers involved in the incident?" Sarah White shifts the focus back to the officers directly involved.

"The same procedure will be followed," I try to keep it simple, although I know it won't be. "After reading the report I'll talk with the other council members and our legal team to determine the best course of action for the city."

"If criminal charges are involved, who would bring them?" Tic Rogers seems to have taken over the meeting now.

"The State Attorney General's Office," I say as simply as I can hoping to avoid discussion on that subject. "They will be given a copy of the internal investigation report and will conduct their own investigation before determining whether charges will be brought."

"We won't know right away," Sarah White seeks to confirm.

"Depends on whether they believe they have enough to warrant an investigation based on public information or not," I respond hoping we are getting close to the end. *They seem to be going further afield. I don't have much more I can offer.* "They may not wait. That would certainly be their prerogative. Formal charges won't be made prior to release of the internal affairs report, if precedent holds."

"Where is the Black community in all this?" Tic Rogers asks, looking around the room where he is only one of two persons of color. "Why aren't they storming the barricades?"

CHAPTER SEVEN:

Sarah White, Director, Content - Continuum Media

I'm writing my blog in my tiny cubicle when Dad comes by and plunks himself in the chair. I'm the only one without an office who has a chair, even though I really don't have the room for it. I think I got one because Dad likes to come by. While I love seeing him, and value his advice, I get the impression some of the others here aren't as thrilled by seeing him talking with me and not them. But what can they expect? He is my father. The fact he owns the company, well…

"Anything interesting come out at city hall?" he asks as if he's only semi interested.

"Tic Rogers was there," I offer as I know he'll be more interested in who else may be running a story than the actual content.

"Is he that freelance guy…"

"Who sells his stories to most of our competitors, but you would never use, because he always comes at the story with a singular focus."

"You know what he's going to say before you read him, so why bother?"

"A lot of people are reading anything with his by-line," I remind him gently that he needs to keep an open mind. "Apparently there for the ACLU, if I read his questions right."

"You think this story is going to blow up and go national?" Dad seems to gain a little more interest now.

"Will if he or I write it that way," I suggest to see what he does with my implication.

"Is it a national story?" *He's not sure. I can tell from the tone of his voice.* "Or is it simply the cop had a hangover and got sloppy?"

"Where did you get that from?" I've not heard anything about this allegation.

"You forget I've been at this a while," he smiles at me with that fatherly smile he reserves for key lessons he wants me to remember.

"… and have friends in high and strategic places," I paraphrase his answer the last time we had this discussion. "But really, who told you that?"

"My inside source in the department. She usually has the scoop on all kinds of things that aren't generally known."

"Will that come out in the internal investigation?"

Dad considers my question. I can always tell when he's not sure about something, because he scrunches up his face almost like he's feeling some pain or something. "If it's a typical investigation, and they let the union read the report before it goes public, probably not."

"The union?" I didn't know the union would have anything to do with the report until after it is released.

"The union backed the mayor in the last election," he informs me. "There was a reason why they did. And it wasn't because she was going to hold them accountable."

"You're saying the report is not going to be more than a slap on the wrist?" I'm surprised he would predict this outcome. I'll admit this is the first major incident like this since I graduated and started work actually publishing articles. But I thought the system wouldn't be as rigged, as that is certainly what it sounds like to me.

"We'll know next week," he brightens and glances around the office, probably to see who is listening in on our conversation. "Won't we. How are you writing your story?"

I'm not sure I'm ready to share what I've written. It seems I need to reconsider it after this conversation. "That the mayor seems to be following protocol at the moment, while the investigation takes its course. But I think the bigger story at the moment is the suspension of the commissioner."

Dad seems puzzled, "She suspended Nathaniel?"

"It's a protocol he recommended," I want him to consider that angle and see what he comes up with.

He looks away and rocks gently in place apparently trying to understand the implications. "Hit that hard," he looks back at me with a serious look I seldom see from him. "That could be the real story. Does taking the commissioner out of the equation lead to a different outcome? Is it something we should try to convince other cities to adopt? Is the commissioner the root cause of the department's lack of discipline, or is that all smoke screen for a cop with a hangover who failed to use judgment?"

"You keep coming back to the cop having a bad day, is that the real story?"

"In the end it may come out, but don't count on it. At the moment it's gossip. Nothing more. You can't say it, you can't allude to it, but you always have to consider the developing story in light of the possibility."

"Is this how news works? We know the real story but can only report on those things we can establish as fact from sources who will stand up and repeat their allegations before a jury and provide whatever proof they have to back them up?"

"How many journalists have been burned when a source turns out to be full of shit, or to have set up the reporter for one of a hundred different reasons we never know about until after the charges have been put into print? The worst are the sources that seem credible, have some kind of proof to back themselves up, only to find the proof is fake in some way. This job isn't easy. If it were, we wouldn't be doing it because no one would value it. We get it right because we don't have a political view, aren't trying to do anything other than report facts and inform our readers. Your friend Tic Rogers? He wants everyone to see the world through his rose-tinged glasses. He writes that way. I don't want you to be like him. I want you to ask questions our readers have to answer for themselves. When you do that, you get more readers, you don't get punished by your advertisers, and you become credible in a way other media players aren't."

"I'll be successful as long as I follow those principles, just as you have been?"

"You need to follow them until you come up with your own based on the choices you make and the experiences you have," Dad is lecturing me again. "The world is changing way too fast for any set of principles to endure. If we aren't continually asking ourselves if we're doing the right thing, we will find someone else has replaced us. We're not in the business of winning hearts and minds, but we are in the business of lifting up rocks and pointing out what's under them. Our readers will make their own choices about whether they want to do something about it or keep on walking. Does that make sense?"

"For today we're asking our readers if suspending Commissioner Brown was a good thing or not, and if it is a good thing, should other cities consider doing the same?"

"That's what I'd write, but as I remember, I've turned the pen over to you." Dad's fatherly advice smile returns. "You coming home for dinner tonight or staying in the city to hang with your new husband and friends until all hours?"

"I think we're going to just do a quiet dinner at our house tonight. Demetrius has been after me to actually cook something, since we went out and bought a credit card full of appliances and cookware. I didn't know it was going to be expensive just to set up a kitchen."

"When it comes to a house, no matter what you think it can't possibly cost more than, double it and you're probably in the ballpark."

"Voice of experience," I nod.

"Your mother has redone every room in the house since you left for college, so yeah, the voice of experience here." He rises and I notice it seems to be more slowly than usual, but he continues, "Shoot me your draft before you send it on. I'd like to see how you're approaching the issue of the suspension," he then apparently thinks of something, "Was that with or without pay?"

"With," I see him seemingly agreeing with that approach. Apparently for some reason he would not have been as happy if it were without, as he nods and concludes, "Right." And he leaves me to my writing task. The governor's newscast pops up in a window on my computer screen.

"Good afternoon," he begins, glancing down at his notes and then at the audience which I can't see from my monitor. "As you can imagine, I've had a few calls regarding the recent shooting. Let me begin by saying I believe those who are handling the investigation are approaching it from the right perspective. They are seeking all relevant facts in the matter. The police investigators have spoken with all witnesses and gathered complete details of what was observed. The crime scene investigators have collected and analyzed all details of what was found where the events occurred. They have reconstructed timelines of the events and as much as possible transcribed the conversations that took place prior to and after the shooting. I feel confident we will have a complete report when the investigation is filed with the city."

Apparently one of the journalists present wants to ask a question as the governor shakes his head before continuing, "I'm going to ask you to hold your questions until I complete my remarks, otherwise important points may get lost. I have spoken with Mayor Richards and Attorney General Doheny-Brown. Both are personally involved and are working diligently to bring clarity to the situation, so justice can be the result. Now I know that may seem a strange comment when we are talking about a civilian death, but we are all looking at this as ensuring justice for everyone involved, whatever that takes. We are not making any assumptions, nor are we excusing any behavior. We are looking at everything, and have the best people available working it. I'll take your questions now."

I can't see who is asking the question. I just listen. "What do you think about the suspension of a Black police commissioner when you are investigating the death of a Black man at the hands of a White police officer? Don't you think it could be perceived the city took away an advocate for justice for a murdered Black man within the department?"

"Thanks for that question. I know Commissioner Brown personally. He is a fine public servant. What we have to look at is cause and effect. Why was the commissioner suspended? It was because he recommended a policy to do just that and the Fort Christian City Council agreed with him. That was the cause. Now the effect may be as you say, that an advocate for Bo Madison may be on the sidelines throughout this investigation. But at the moment you and I don't know if the commissioner would have been an advocate for him or not. You're making an assumption, which may have been correct, but we'll never know. Next question?"

"The deputy and now acting commissioner is white. Doesn't that say something?"

The governor seems perturbed. "If the mayor decided to suspend a Black commissioner on her own, I believe such a question may be appropriate to ask, but this was procedural. The mayor would have had to override a department procedure in order to not suspend him. Apart from those two sets of circumstances I don't think your question has any relevance to the current situation. Next question please."

"Was the city council vote an indication it didn't trust the impartiality of the commissioner? Wasn't it really an indication there were perceived problems in the department he wasn't addressing and the death of Bo Madison is the direct result of those failings?"

"I would have to redirect your question to the members of the Fort Christian City Council and the mayor as only they could answer your question. Next?"

"How could a commissioner, who has been a part of the department he oversees for twenty-three years, be impartial?"

"You obviously don't know Nathaniel Brown and that's all I'll say about that. Next."

"Does the attorney general have a conflict since her husband is the commissioner of police who has been suspended?"

"I actually thought this was going to be the first question you asked. Thank you for letting me get a few other points across first. In answer to your question, the husband of the attorney general is not being investigated in this case. He did not fire a weapon in the course of performing his duties. He has not taken any action that would result in an investigation of his performance. So, no. I do not see a conflict. If the recommendation of the report is for prosecutorial action, it will be against the officer or officers involved, not the commissioner."

Before the governor can recognize the next journalist, the same questioner continues: "But what if the report reveals something the commissioner did or failed to do that led to the death of Bo Madison?"

"That would normally be a disciplinary action by the mayor and Fort Christian City Council, not the attorney general's office."

"There have been calls for you to place her on administrative leave until after this case is resolved."

"Now why would I place the best attorney general we have ever had in this state on administrative leave when we have an important investigation going on? That makes no sense to me at all."

"To ensure she can't influence the outcome." The same reporter, I suspect it's Tic Rogers who is looking to stir any controversy to sell his blog.

"Isn't that the point? Shouldn't I want her to influence the outcome to ensure that justice for all is done? That's why you elected her to be the attorney general. Because we all felt she would do an excellent job of ensuring justice is the outcome of every legal dispute in our state. I'm not going to sideline her when she's needed more than ever."

The governor is certainly boosting gBeto. I wonder why?

"There are reports of a petition circulating. The petition is to establish an independent citizen's investigatory panel. To take this whole thing out of the government, out of the police department, away from the state elected officials and let the citizens decide what should be done. What do you think about that?" different voice, probably Daniel Holt looking for a prime-time filler.

"Such a petition would go to the Fort Christian City Council. You would need to discuss what action they may take with them."

"What would have to happen for you to suspend or place the attorney general on administrative leave?"

"I cannot foresee any circumstances under which I would take such an action. Why are you pushing this line of questioning? It almost seems to me you're looking to make the case more than it is. At the moment there are no charges pending. An investigation is underway to determine if charges are warranted, both within the department and by the state attorney general's investigatory arm. Both are normal procedures when there has been an officer involved shooting, whether lethal or not. You need to be patient, let the process take its course. Review the reports when they are released, and then push for a course of action if you are so inclined. But until then all these questions are premature and speculative at best."

"Governor, since your lieutenant governor has already announced his intention not to seek re-election are you considering not seeking a second term?" That's definitely Tic Rogers.

"The lieutenant governor has provided distinguished service to our state over the many years he has held office. It has been my privilege to have him as my partner in formulating public policy these past several years. But his decision is independent of mine. I intend to announce a new initiative that will ensure the continuation of Texas as one of the leading states in our nation. I intend to transform opportunity for every person who chooses to live here. You will be hearing more about this in coming days, but I really didn't want to take away from the discussion of the actions we are taking to ensure justice is done, which has been the focus of this meeting. Just for the record, I will be seeking a second term."

CHAPTER EIGHT:

LaMance Freeman, Deputy Attorney General, State of Delaware

Scottie outdid herself. I'm carrying the file she assembled on the officer involved shooting in record time. *Almost seems like she had an inside source or someone telling her where to go look.* I see gBeto's office door is open. I go right in. She is watching something on her computer screen; I hear the shots and instantly know she's watching the dashcam or phone video of the investigation I'm bringing to her. *Good. That means she's still focused on it, and not some other 'go do' from the Governor.* "You'll never guess what present Scottie has for you."

gBeto glances up and her expression changes from puzzlement to curiosity. As it does, she reaches out for the folder, which I transfer to her, and take a seat opposite as I always do. "I see something new every time I look at those videos. I don't ever remember that before."

"What is it this time?" I ask to see if it's something I'd noticed or not.

"Bo Madison didn't step out of the camera frame, someone turned the dashcam."

"Who? I thought all the officers were accounted for in the dashcam video."

"They were, that's what I don't understand."

"Was there someone else there that wasn't reported?" I find this hard to believe. Were the officers deliberately with holding important information?

"Definitely something we need to ask about," gBeto notes. "Make a note of it."

As I do, I have to ask, "What else have you noticed we may not have caught?"

"When the officers drove up, Bo Madison was sitting on the curb with his head down. He wasn't doing anything that would have drawn attention to him. Do we have any idea why the officers were there?"

"It's in the report," I point to the file in her hand. "Shop keeper reported him. Said he came in apparently under the influence of something and wanted to buy beer. Shop keeper refused, based on Bo Madison's behavior, and he became belligerent. Shop keeper asked him to leave but Bo accused the shop keeper of racism, pushed him from across the counter and left pushing merchandise off shelves, but only got as far as the curb where he sat down. Shop keeper called it in; afraid Bo Madison might come back in and try to steal the beer he wanted."

"What ethnicity was the shop keeper?"

"Indian or Pakistani, I'm not sure which," I recall from the file.

"Small man where Bo Madison was a football player?"

I nod. "Clearly intimidated. But what I don't get is why Bo decided he was racist. Most people from that part of the world don't get into that."

"Toxicity report on Bo Madison?" gBeto wonders aloud. "Was he on something other than alcohol?"

"That's another thing. Autopsy says he was sober and no drugs other than Naproxen, an anti-inflammatory. Indicates Bo was maybe dealing with some pain or stiffness due to inflammation, but the report is he should have been lucid and non-threatening."

"Was the shop keeper the one who was on something?" gBeto asks clearly taking the other side of the question.

"No way of knowing," I shake my head, but then remember what I read about the interview with the shop keeper. "The officer who took his statement said he was a little hard to understand. His English wasn't what you'd hope. Rambled a bit and mixed in a bunch of Pashto phrases."

"How did the officer know they were Pashto?" she asks going somewhere I'm not yet.

"Where do they speak Pashto?" I have to ask.

"Pakistan is one place, but also Iran. Are you sure the shop keeper wasn't Iranian? Would make a difference in how we proceed here."

"Why?" I don't see any difference. "This doesn't have anything to do with our country's relationship with Iran, or Pakistan for that matter."

"Bo Madison was a Marine in Afghanistan. Did two tours if what I'm remembering is correct."

"Where did you get this information?" I'm surprised she already has basic information. "We're just giving you the file."

"I talked to his parents," gBeto admits.

I didn't know anything about her making contact independently. That's not usual for us. "Why would you do that?"

"To reassure them we will follow this to the logical end, regardless of what we find."

"Trying to defuse?" I have to ask, although I'm not sure she will admit what she was up to.

"We have a higher standard we have to live up to than my predecessors."

"None of whom have ever been Black," I point out. "You need to get out of this 'I'm gonna change the world' mindset. Procedure is you wait for Scottie to get you the file and once you've reviewed what we have you still keep your distance, so we can operate without being compromised. Your role is the 'higher' authority. Someone they can appeal to if they don't like something. But when you go out like that, they go right to you in the first place and there's no appeal. You got to make the decision and then we're fucked, pardon my French, because the only appeal then is the governor. Not a place you want us to be."

"I hear you," gBeto glances at me. "But if we don't start being more responsive to the victims and their families, who is?" gBeto looks at the file in her hand for a moment before continuing. "It's up to us to do what's right. Talking with the families up front is right. Would you want me hanging back and not talking to you if it was your son who had been killed that night? Hell no. You'd be in talking to me the very next morning, demanding justice. Why should you be able to do that but not Mr. and Mrs. Madison, or any other family for that matter?"

She has me back on my heels because I know exactly what she's saying. If something happened to my son Kwame, I don't know what I'd do. Probably go shoot the son-of-a-bitch myself if I could keep my husband Tyler from killing him first. I know if that happened to me, she would be at my house that night. Nothing could keep her away. And it's not just because she's my boss and friend, or she's the attorney general, but because that's who she is. "You're right. We need to examine what we are expected to do, because that's what everyone else did before, and decide for ourselves if it makes sense. The times are different, the events are different and we are different."

gBeto apparently didn't expect me to cave in so easily because she pulls back just a bit and looks at me closer. *She wants to know why. I'm not going to tell her. She will just have to make up her own mind about my behavior.*

"Do you understand why the Pashto thing is important?" gBeto asks me.

"It makes sense. Scottie didn't have anything about that in the file. I'll ask her to run it down. Try to understand if..."

"Have her look at whether Bo Madison was suffering from

PTSD."

"His erratic behavior?" I guess.

gBeto nods. "Could also explain why he couldn't get off the curb if he was in the midst of flashbacks when the officers showed up."

"How could Scottie of missed all that?" I wonder aloud.

"She was doing her job, which is to collect the facts from the investigating officers and public sources. No one expected her to call up the parents and ask about their son."

"She apparently didn't do a search on Bo Madison," I point out.

"What would the public records have on him?" gBeto isn't going to take my criticism of Scottie's work. "Go look him up. I'll bet you won't even find him. Why would you? He's only served his country, among thousands of others, and worked menial jobs since his discharge. He's never set up a website or been elected to office or given millions to charity."

"Scottie usually has it all wrapped up in a bow for us."

"She does and I suspect she's done her usual fine research. But in this case, I suspect she's going to have to dig deeper when this comes back to us from the Grand Jury."

"That's a question I have for you," *I begin what I really wanted to ask.* "Do you want me to seat a grand jury to review this evidence or wait for the internal affairs report?"

"I'll tell you after I've read the file," she responds as she finally sets the file down on her desk as if preparing to read it, but I can tell *she's not quite ready to do that yet. Something else is on her mind.* "Have we heard anything more about potential protests?"

"Yes and no," I affirm to her disappointment. "Yes, there is something in the works. But no, no detail about what's being planned. A guess on my part? Likely they are organizing. When the internal affairs report is released, they can come out of the gates full throttle. That's what I'd do if I was sitting over there."

"A week or more of quiet before the storm," gBeto responds as if puzzling something. While she considers whatever it is. She opens the file and glances down. I see her head jerk back as if startled. "Michael St. James?"

"The officer in question. What about him?" I'm still trying to figure out her reaction to the responsible officer's name.

"What do we know about him?" she doesn't look up at me.

"The city hasn't released his records yet," I remember being frustrated about that reluctance to share. "Why?"

"I grew up with a Mick St. James," gBeto reveals.

"That was in Edge Hill?" I ask as I'll need to know that in order to confirm her question.

"Mick was the older brother of a guy in my class, who I knew a lot better. Just curious if it was him."

"Some reason you think it might be?" I'm curious as to whether there's something specific behind her curiosity.

"I didn't know him very well, he was what? Two or three years ahead of me. When you're a teenager, a year is an eternity. He wasn't interested in me and there was no way I was going to talk with him."

"Was he trouble?" I ask wondering if he was someone who harassed Black people then.

"You know I haven't thought about him in decades." Again, she doesn't look up.

I listen more closely to gBeto silently reflecting on Michael St. James. "I'm sitting here trying to remember what people said about him and frankly I just don't remember anything."

"Would he remember you?" I wonder about her description.

She seems to consider that question, "Probably, because I was friends with his younger brother and you know how it is. When someone from your High School does well, you want to associate with their success."

"Would that be an issue if you're prosecuting him?" I wonder aloud.

"I won't be prosecuting him even if it gets there. And there's no guarantee it will. I doubt it will be an issue."

"There something you're not telling me? Seems you're minimizing all these connections. But if there's one thing I've learned while in this office, nothing is ever what it seems. A casual connection ends up being a lot more than you would ever expect. If there's any way this could come back, now's the time to talk it through. We need to be prepared. You hear what I'm saying?"

"I do," gBeto finally looks at me directly. "No worries. As I said, not likely an issue. As I think back, I'm not sure I had more than three or four conversations with the guy ever. And besides, we're not even sure if our cop friend is the same guy I knew when I was growing up."

"I'm going to flag it any way. We can evaluate if there's going to be an issue. You okay with that?"

"I guess, why?"

"You're aware there's a group that wants you put on administrative leave. They don't want you to have anything to do with this case." I have to believe she saw the governor's media relations discussion.

"It's not going to happen. Why are you worried about it?" She did see the governor's meet with the media.

"You and I both know how this town works. You've got to give the governor cover so he can keep you out of the glare of the media lights. They're coming after you now and that's before they really dig in on Nathaniel."

She seems pained by my mention of her husband's situation. Apparently, it's not as simple as everyone seems to be painting it. I'll have to keep that in mind.

"I do indeed understand the need for fresh meat daily and until now it seems I've done a reasonable job of keeping out of the limelight…"

"But we can both see there are people out there that want to drag you in, and the governor. He didn't do you any favors with his glowing endorsement," I inform her of my opinion of the world. "I'll bet a whole bunch of prognosticators are thinking he's got bigger plans for you."

"The governor and I haven't had a conversation about anything not related to this office. I really can't comment on what may or may not happen down the road."

"Now that sounds like you've been practicing your political speak," *I react without thinking it through, but if I have to have filters on to talk to gBeto I'm in big trouble.* "Denying something in such a way that it leaves the door open to doing exactly what you're denying today."

"Did it sound credible?" she asks and now I know there's more than smoke about higher office.

"The words are the same, but you're less convincing and I have to interpret that as you're still not committed to whatever it is you think might happen."

"Or events will change the world one or more times between now and the next election."

Maybe she's just trying to be cautious if events spin her off in another direction. Maybe because she once knew a cop who many years later killed a Black man. Particularly if the victim's only offense was having PTSD and experiencing a flashback at the wrong time. "What's going on? You're acting coy and you're never coy."

"Governor wants me helping out on a special project to see if we need to change laws to create a more favorable business climate. But I'm just not sure it's a good time for that when we may be resolving the guilt or innocence of a cop who took a life."

I shake my head, "You need to be looking for the landmines that can blow up in your face, and come up with a strategy for dealing with each of them, starting with Michael St. James."

CHAPTER NINE:

Nathaniel Brown, Commissioner of Police
City of Fort Christian, Texas

The doorbell. What time is it? I glance at the clock on my desk. The one my union brothers gave me when I was named commissioner. They gave it to me because I could no longer remain a member. It's hard negotiating with Rick and John. They used to represent me when I was on their side. I don't like to think of it in those terms – sides. We're all on the same team. How can we be on different sides? But we are because the expectation is I'll be able to get the city to make concessions my predecessor couldn't. So far it hasn't worked out that way.

Seven o'clock – the doorbell. Oh yes, the new neighbors… gBeto invited them over for drinks. What are their names? I go to the door and as I do I realize I'm still in shorts and a t-shirt. gBeto's not going to be happy about that.

Young couple. What did gBeto say about them? Both just graduated or something. "Hi. I'm Nathaniel." I nod at them as is the custom and gesture for them to come in.

"I'm Sarah and this is my husband Demetrius," they nod back and come in, "I hope we're not inconveniencing you."

She's looking at my casual clothes. They are preppy in their attire. Could easily be on their way to dinner at the Country Club, or more likely have just come from there. She's short, dark hair and large eyes that seem to take in everything. He's taller, about six feet. Athletic, but more like a band majorette than linebacker. Funny how you get images of people you just meet. It will be interesting to see if I'm right. "Not at all, we've been expecting you," I close the door behind them and nod to the family room. "You just moved in to the Williams house. Very nice home, you should enjoy it."

"We love the big back yard. The former owners put in a marvelous garden and the landscaping is just perfect," she offers in response.

gBeto joins us, gives me the questioning look like why are you not dressed better? But she instantly engages them with the welcoming head nod. "Nice to see you again, Sarah. This is your husband?"

"Demetrius White, it's nice to meet you," he nods in return.

"Come in, would you like something to drink?" *gBeto is probably wondering where are my manners.* "We can accommodate most adult beverages."

As we walk into the other room she responds, "If you have a red wine, that would be terrific."

"I prefer white," Demetrius responds.

"I'm trying to avoid the stereotypes that women only like white wine and men only drink red," Sarah informs us as they sit. "But Demetrius really decided with White as our last name that he should drink white wines."

"And wear white clothes?" gBeto notes his attire, while she's wearing a yellow sundress.

Demetrius glances down and apparently realizes his earlier choice.

I pour the wine and hand them the glasses as they requested, "You know, I've not had a white wine in a while. I'm going to join Demetrius," I inform them as I pour my glass and catch gBeto's look that I should pour one for her first. I set my glass down and pour a glass of red for her, since I know she prefers it.

LOVE

As I sit down next to gBeto and hand her the glass, I hear her clear her throat. *What did I forget? Something.*

Anyway, "To new friends." We all raise our glasses, "May you not be strangers." *We all take a sip as I finally figure out there's no food out.* "Excuse me for a moment."

Now I'm beginning to panic as I completely forgot to make the snacks gBeto had asked of me. She's been busy all day and I'm the one with time, but I got caught up in reading reports filed on the Madison shooting. As I enter the kitchen, I find snack trays all prepared. Apparently, that's why she didn't answer the door. I pick up the trays and return to the family room.

Demetrius is talking, "... University of Texas Law School. It's only about an hour each way."

"You're second year?" gBeto asks.

"Yes. Thinking about specializing in contracts."

"He wants to represent professional athletes," Sarah finishes his explanation.

"Do you have any contacts? Firms already representing sports figures?" gBeto asks.

"One of my classmates is Randy Jackson's son," Demetrius enthuses. "His father represents like half of the Yankee ballplayers. We've talked about my interest. Randall, the son, has agreed to introduce me to his father when the time is right. Randall says his father's a tough sell, but if I can impress him, I might have a chance to join their firm after I pass the bar exam."

"Were you always interested in being an agent?" I seek to satisfy my own curiosity.

"Not until I met Sarah," he admits. "The fact she's going to inherit a media company someday, well... I just thought if we want our relationship to last, I've got to be able to contribute reasonably to the marriage. Wouldn't work for me to just live off the family business."

"I've met Randy Jackson," I admit. "He represents my old college roommate, Mitch Daniels."

"The former Jet's quarterback?" Demetrius is amazed. "He was your college roommate?"

"I was first string full back on the University of Texas team the years he was our quarterback. We became friends as freshmen and decided we got along well enough rooming made sense."

"Do you keep in touch?" still Demetrius *who almost seems star struck.*

I nod, "Usually get together when he comes to town to see his parents.

"What's he doing now?" Demetrius is trying to remember something.

"He owns a film production company. Makes most of the documentaries on sports events and sports figures. You see them all over the place now."

"I bet he knows everybody," *Demetrius seems to realize.*

"Pretty much. Be happy to introduce you to him sometime when he's here. You just never know. You might hit it off or you might not. Either way he's a good guy to know."

"What about you? Why didn't you go pro?" Demetrius asks.

I glance at gBeto to see how she's reacting to this hijack of her getting to know the new neighbors. *She seems fine. Almost like she's really interested in hearing this story one more time.* "As a running back, you take a real beating. I'd been playing that position since I was ten. While they don't hit as hard in Pop Warner games, I wasn't as good at protecting myself. By the time I graduated I was taped and held together by all kinds of braces."

"To say nothing of the pain killers," gBeto interjects.

"There was that too," I admit. "Randy was willing to shop me as a walk-on, but I would have had to convert to a linebacker which meant learning a whole new position."

I look at gBeto who isn't listening anymore. "And my heart just wasn't in it, even though I had the school record for yards gained from the line of scrimmage for like ten years."

"That was when what's-his-name... Bo Madison. He still has the record, doesn't he?"

I nod, knowing the athlete who broke my record was killed by one of my officers. Someone I've known since he joined the department. I see gBeto react to my silence.

"What about you, Sarah?" gBeto decides to change the conversation. "What are you aspiring to be other than CEO of your father's company?"

Sarah has put two and two together since her husband clearly hasn't. "I have this title, Director of Content. But Dad wants me to learn the business from the bottom up. He has me writing stories about major topical events. Everything from weddings to national and international affairs. There's a market for almost every kind of story. He wants me to develop a nose for what people want to know about. Wants to be sure I can really do the content job."

"Does he have you working with someone who has the nose?" I ask since that was the term she used.

Sarah nods, "Him. My father. He comes by every day to talk to me about what I'm writing about and what I'm learning as a result. There's no one better. That's how he was able to set up his own shop after stints with most of the majors. He kept getting promoted until one day he realized he didn't need someone else looking over his shoulder and learning from him. He left and took the top sales guy with him as his partner. That way he was sure he would be able to pay the bills."

"The strategy clearly worked," I note.

"Is this your dream job, or is there something you'd rather be doing?" gBeto asks. I think it a strange question given the family business angle, but she has something on her mind.

"You've met my dad," Sarah looks at gBeto. "I've never had a conversation with him that didn't somehow get back to the expectation I will run the company someday. I better prepare and really learn the business. Explains why he started me out in content. That's the basis for the business. Content is what we sell. I need to thoroughly understand it."

"Never wanted to be a doctor or astronaut?" gBeto pursues.

"Maybe for an instant, after a doctor saves someone's life or a woman astronaut completes a spacewalk at the International Space Station. But not really. It just wasn't an option for me."

"How did you meet?" gBeto wants to steer this away from the shooting.

"We met my Junior year at Wellsley," Sarah continues. "We were at a dance and I just kind of picked him up. He was talking with some of his friends. I went over and asked if he was going to stand there talking all night or ask me to dance."

"We'd just won a game no one thought we could," Demetrius defends himself. "We were just happy. I wasn't really even looking around, although I did notice her when we came in, but she was dancing with some other guy so…"

Sarah pokes Demetrius, "You said you were just waiting for him to go dance with someone else and then you were going to make your move."

"That's true, but he just kept dancing with her…" Demetrius looks to us, clearly having had this conversation with her more than once.

LOVE

"Because you weren't coming to my rescue…"

"But I was going to," his excuse is sounding more like one.

"You were all into your guy thing. Showing them you were Mister Macho. Waiting for me to make you look irresistible."

"You did… by coming over and making it look like I was…"

"Cute," Sarah cuts him down a peg from where it sounded like he was going.

"I was cute? Not ruggedly handsome? Not the star pitcher who won the ballgame?" Guess I got that wrong. Band Majorette, pitcher… from the perspective of a running back, pretty close.

"You struck out the other team's homerun hitter in the bottom of the ninth?" I guess.

Demetrius shakes his head, "No. I gave up a run in the top of the nineth that put them ahead by one, but I came back in the bottom of the ninth and drove in two runs. The other team thought I was an easy out, as I often was, but their pitcher was up on his pitch count and tossed a breaking ball that didn't."

"A pitcher who saved a game with his bat," I note. "Commendable and I'm sure it will be part of the family lore that will be told year after year at family get togethers."

"I hope so," Demetrius grins.

"Anyway," Sarah continues. "Since I was at Wellesley and he was at Boston College, we kind of went our different ways as the year progressed, but we both got summer internships at the Globe. Not planned that way. Just kind of worked out. Anyway, by the end of the summer we just knew we worked together."

"How did you decide on your new house?" gBeto changes the topic once more.

"I wanted to be in the neighborhood with the best schools in the city. I went to Catholic schools and don't want that for my children."

"Why not?" I ask without considering if this would be too personal.

"The abuse issues in the Church just really bother me. My mother agrees."

"But not your father…" I guess from the way she phrased her response.

"Dad says Catholic schools provide a great foundation and can better attend to the learning needs of bright kids. And that's followed by, 'they were good enough for him and mom and me. They should be good enough for any grandkids."

"And you are split down the middle between your mom and your dad." gBeto surmises.

Sarah nods reluctantly. "I never want to have to take sides, but they do that to me all the time."

"What about you Demetrius? What's your opinion?" I pursue the other side of this discussion.

"I went to public schools throughout," Demetrius looks at his wife, again confirming this has been a source of more than one discussion before buying the house. "I certainly think the public schools out here are more than good enough for my kids."

"Good schools. You could find that lots of places besides here," gBeto wants a fuller answer. Must be the prosecutor in her coming out.

"My Dad's partner suggested looking in this neighborhood. Not this specific house but he said the schools are good, property values are going up and it's convenient."

"To say nothing of nice neighbors," Demetrius tosses in.

I raise my glass, "To nice neighbors."

"Does he live here?" gBeto follows up apparently wondering why someone would recommend this area if they didn't.

"No," Sarah responds. "I think he lives in a condo downtown. He's always been married to his work, so he likes being within walking distance of the offices."

"Well. We're just happy he made the suggestion and you found a nice place to call home." I decide to move gBeto on from that topic.

"Why did you choose to live here?" Demetrius asks although I can't ferret out why.

I look to gBeto, letting her answer.

"Anne Rutherford suggested we look at this house. She'd known the family that built it and had lived here all their lives. Anne knew it had been kept in great shape. She insisted we come look. We did and knew it was the right place for us."

"She lives in the big house across the street?" Demetrius is trying to piece things together.

I nod.

"And her husband owns Oil Field Services that supplies Exxon, where his brother Walter, the governor, used to be a top official…" Demetrius is putting the pieces together nicely. He'll be a good lawyer.

CHAPTER TEN:

Daniel Porter, Editor, Fort Christian Morning News

I expected this call hours ago. Mayor Richards must have called in her damage control team to discuss what to say before she called me. I can expect this to be nearly scripted.

"Mayor Richards, good morning to you."

"Daniel. Why?"

"Why what? Why did I write the editorial? Why did I ask you to do your job? Why did I take the side of the Black and minority communities in this city that's overwhelmingly White? Why did it take you so long to call me?"

"Daniel. I thought we'd developed a good working relationship. I've always been transparent. If you had a question, when have I not given you a straightforward and honest answer?"

"Yesterday," I respond without hesitation that based on the silence tells me she did not expect this response. "Yesterday I asked you when you were going to release the internal affairs report."

"And I told you. When council has had sufficient time to consider it."

"You know every thinking person in this city sees that as a cover-up. What can you sweep under the rug? What words can you change to defuse the furor that will descend on council the moment anyone reads what really happened, if the report dares to describe it."

"Are you saying you think council will try to re-write the report?"

"Influence word choices?" I clarify what I'm thinking, "Absolutely. I've seen you do it before. Not on issues this explosive. But you have a reputation of wordsmithing every public communication to minimize anything negative and maximizing anything positive."

"That's why we have a communications office," *the mayor is getting heated up now.* "You know it's my responsibility to make Fort Christian as attractive a place to live as possible. What we say about our community has impacts much further than either of us can see. And that comes down to simple word choices, in anything we communicate. If everything is negative, people flee to the suburbs. If everything is wonderful, they move back. My job has been to make sure everything in Fort Christian is wonderful, because if I say it and people believe it, then everything will become wonderful, eventually."

"You can do that in your advertising campaigns, and your speeches to visiting groups at the convention center. But when it comes to the death of a citizen at the hands of a city police officer, that's never going to be wonderful, Mayor Richards. Not for the victim's family, not for the officer, or his family, and certainly not for the citizen who died because of a decision that officer made."

I give her a moment to respond, but she does not. I continue. "The only way the people of Fort Christian can and will feel safe is if you do exactly what I suggested in the editorial. You can't sit on it. You can't defer and blame council. You can't even say there is no precedent because you've had citizen committees review and recommend actions to the city council forever."

"Those are advisory boards, who study a specific policy or investment priority to advise the council of which among many alternatives will be best for everyone."

"Consider this independent review an advisory board then," I push back. "They should look at all the evidence gathered by the internal affairs team, interview those involved. A representative sample of citizens should be given the same opportunity to do a deep dive and publish their findings and recommendations."

"But they wouldn't be law enforcement professionals trained to look into events such as occurred."

"And that's the point." *I don't seem to be getting through.* "What's the official name of the police union?"

"The International Brotherhood of Police Officers, Local..."

"Did you hear what you just said? International Brotherhood... What does a brotherhood do? It protects those who are in the brotherhood. What is a report from a small group of the brotherhood going to do? Protect the officer involved." I stop for a moment to see what she does, but then I continue. "I will predict they will come up with some lame excuse as to why it was necessary for their brother to kill an unarmed man whose only offense was that he's Black."

"You're deliberately being provocative," the mayor pushes back, which is exactly what I want her to do, because until she recognizes the truth of the matter, she's going to go along to avoid insurrection amongst her police members with an election coming up. She needs their votes.

"Then what was his offense?"

"Bo Madison, according to the report, was disorderly and under the influence and in the heat of the moment it appeared he might harm a police officer or store clerk."

"If that's the case, then what are you afraid of? Let the citizens see the evidence and confirm your version of what happened."

"You're implying only Black people can be peers of the victim."

"Read me the section in the editorial," I instruct her.

"Such a commission should be made up of peers of the victim as the internal affairs investigation has been made up of peers of the officer involved."

"Where does that say only Black people can be peers?"

"You were saying the internal affairs team is overwhelmingly white police officers."

"One token Black you recruited out of Arlington because no senior officers in Fort Christian are Black, except the commissioner who you sidelined."

"He supported the recommendation when it was enacted,"

"Under duress. No one wants to sit on the sidelines when his team is in crisis, but that's exactly what's happened here. We both know who pushed this through after you selected a less qualified candidate to be commissioner."

"Would you say Dwight Eisenhower was a less qualified candidate to lead the invasion of Europe in the Second World War?"

"What are you talking about?" I'm completely lost.

"Dwight Eisenhower wasn't the most experienced or most senior officer when Franklin Roosevelt named him Supreme Commander. But he had other qualifications that made him more able to forge a coalition than those who would normally have been in line for the job. That was what Roosevelt needed and got by selecting Eisenhower."

"Are you saying Nathaniel Brown brought things to the department Michael Hauptman wouldn't have?"

"This is off the record." *Mayor Richards is apparently going to explain something I've long wondered about.* "If you print anything I'm about to say or even intimate it, I'll deny everything and you'll lose all access to me. Got it?"

"Go on."

"Michael Hauptman was a terrorist. Not in the sense of someone who was trying to overthrow the government, but in the sense that he put fear into the people because they had no idea what he would do next. People make plans based on predictability. If I know the laws are going to be enforced, I know what I can and can't do. But if a law is not enforced, but suddenly is, to punish one person, but no one else, then you can never be sure when you're going to do something Hauptman decides to punish. You do what you've been doing right along and he pulls out a law that hasn't been enforced in who knows how long, to punish you because he wants to. Who knows why? And afterwards he may or may not enforce it. What are you supposed to do?"

"If that was the case, why was he everyone else's choice?" *Something here doesn't make sense to me.*

"You don't get out enough," the mayor accuses me. "You talk to the people who think they've got him figured out. Whether it was special favors they did for him, accommodations made for his family, maybe they thought if he was commissioner, I'd have to sit on him more and keep him off the streets. I don't know why anyone wanted him in that role when Nathaniel Brown was available, knew what Hauptman was doing, and was courageous enough to take on the hard issues that needed to be addressed."

"Maybe the hard issues you wanted addressed, but clearly he didn't address at least one that has now come back to haunt you both." I have to go for the jugular when she's skating around the real issue.

"I talked to Nathaniel when I put him on suspension," the mayor admits. "I asked him how this happened? He admitted he didn't see it coming. And in thinking about it, what happened doesn't make sense to him. He is convinced there is something we don't know, something we don't see on the video that explains it. But whatever it is, he's not sure anyone could have prevented it without having a key piece of information Nathaniel did not."

"Sounds like an excuse."

"Only because you don't know Nathaniel. He's been beating himself up over this since it happened. I doubt he's slept. And he won't let go of it until he knows why, and the appropriate action is taken."

"Appropriate action... what are you saying?"

"Doesn't matter to him what the internal affairs report says. He will pursue the truth to the end and ensure justice is done."

"Because a Black man was killed?" I ask to understand what she's suggesting.

"Wouldn't matter to Nathaniel. Black, White, Asian, Muslim, Latino… whatever. Someone died on his watch. He has to make sure it doesn't happen again. That can only happen if justice is done."

"He was your pick. You have to defend him," I point out she can make nice speeches but that still doesn't give her a pass on what I think she needs to do.

"He was confirmed by city council. He may have been my recommendation, but he sold himself to the other members. Until now, no one has brought Hauptman up. What are you responding to?"

"You and I both know the only reason the suspension resolution was even suggested was because one member of council in particular doesn't think the commissioner is able to separate himself from the department he served in to be objective in matters like this. Now I know you worked against the resolution, but ended up voting for it only after Nathaniel endorsed it as an appropriate action, in events such as what just happened."

"I doubt he thinks it was such a good idea now," Mayor Richards reflects more to herself than to me.

"Why?"

"I talk to him every day. Several times a day, really. He's frustrated because he can't do anything. He can't talk to the investigations team, can't talk with the officers involved. He wasn't even the one to suspend Officer St. James, and that's part of his responsibility. He feels like he's not able to do his job and is eager to get back to work."

"You're not going to bring him back, are you?"

"What do you mean?" I hear the surprise at my question in the tone of her voice.

"You suspended him for what happened on his watch…"

"I suspended him to give the internal affairs department a free hand to conduct the investigation without interference or guidance from the commissioner. I intend to bring him back the minute they file their report."

"I'd advise against that," I'm the one surprised now as I had a totally different impression of what was going to happen next.

"Let me get this straight. The editor of the Morning News is advising the mayor of the city what she should or shouldn't do. What gives you any more credence than any other citizen? You've not been elected by anyone. You've never served on an advisory board. You gather information that depending on which political party you are talking with are either facts or not, but in any event, you publish them and offer recommendations to the citizens of the city for their consideration. I would expect to hear from my constituents if they agree or disagree with your counsel."

"And have you?" I'm not used to being scolded like this.

"Obviously I have or I wouldn't have made this call."

"And what are they saying?" I hope they are supporting my editorial.

"Generally, they agree that if the officer involved is not held accountable, the city should take further action. Whether that comes from asking the attorney general's office to empanel a grand jury, or simply fire the bastard, which is the term that has become their favorite moniker for him, they want to see consequences."

I can't listen to excuses any more. "Why don't you just fire him now. Bo Madison is dead."

"I understand your feelings since you were close to Bo."

"He was my team mate at UT. But rather than play professional ball, he served his country because he believed in what the country stands for. That's bullshit, but I couldn't convince him otherwise, even though I tried. And when he returned? Well, Uncle Sam used him up and spit him out. He was never the same. Shrapnel in places that made him less of a man. Nightmares he couldn't run away from of his buddies blown up right next to him. How does anyone get over that?"

"I'm sure you've been doing your own investigation," the mayor's voice changes. "What do you think happened that night?"

"I think it was murder." No question, but I can't prove it.

"Then help me prove what happened," she suggests to me." Do your investigation, but instead of a citizen's committee reviewing what the department found, go to your sources."

She considers her advice to me. "If you get people on the record. Bring out the truth and by that I'm talking the unvarnished truth. Can you do that Daniel?"

"I have been working on the truth since I got the call from Bo's sister," I respond. "I'm doing this one myself. Anything on the subject you see me publish was written by me. Others are working the sources and gathering as much information and proof – another word you're not likely to see in the internal affairs report, but I'm looking for the proof of what I think happened."

"But are you able to be objective, something we have assumed Nathaniel can't be, but for all the wrong reasons?" the mayor asks as if she doesn't believe me.

"Are you asking if what we find doesn't support my theory will I publish it anyway?"

"You've been telling me I have to do what's right. Given your closeness to Bo, can you?"

"I spent many nights holding Bo so he could put the images in his head aside and finally go to sleep. I won't let go until justice is done."

CHAPTER ELEVEN:

gBeto Dahomey Brown, Attorney General, State of Texas

Nathaniel has been morose since our neighbors came over. I didn't expect it to have such an impact on him, but then again, I'd forgotten Bo Madison broke his rushing record at the University. *Clearly, he remembered and was likely personalizing aspects of this case I can't begin to imagine. He's probably saying to himself, 'there but for the grace of God go I.'*

How would I be feeling if Nathaniel had been the one killed by a Fort Christian City Police Officer?

And Mick St. James? Why did he have to be the one? I thought that was all behind me. As much as I regret what happened, and what I did, not a day goes by I don't wonder what if I'd made a different decision? How would my life be different? I'd certainly not be here with Nathaniel, not be attorney general. By that measure it was the right decision. But now I have to wonder, since I only have one side of that to consider.

"What are you thinking?" Nathaniel apparently has noticed I've gone off to some other place in my mind. He's sitting across from me in our family room. He was reading reports on his laptop. *I'm assuming he's trying to keep up with what's going on at the department so he can re-engage as soon as Mayor Richards reinstates him.*

"Wondering what I can do to help you."

"I'm fine. A two week all expenses paid vacation at Brown's resort in Fort Christian, Texas? What more could I ask for?"

"How about I make us a nice dinner? Open a bottle of vino. Lower the temperature in the bedroom. We don't want to set off the fire alarms when we heat it up in there later."

"You've got this all backwards. I'm supposed to take you out for a nice dinner somewhere, buy an expensive vino, as compared to the swill we normally drink at home, and then bring you home for a close encounter of the first kind in the chilled down bedroom."

"I'm good with that," I offer to keep him thinking pleasant thoughts.

"Yeah, well, not tonight. I'm knee deep and need more time to think it through."

"Knee deep in what?"

"I really can't talk with you about it in case you end up prosecuting."

"No facts, just your gut reaction," I'm trying to keep this at a level where it won't be a problem for him. "Is this case coming my way?"

"From what I've seen, I will be surprised if you don't end up with it in your lap."

"What are the implications for you?"

Nathaniel takes a long moment to consider, "For me. Personally. It makes me look incompetent at worst, and inept at best."

"No way you come out okay." I push to see what he really thinks, since he's not been talking with me about it. "And the internal affairs report? What's it going to say about you and your leadership of the department?"

"They're annoyed with me. They thought they were going to get a big pay raise through under me and that hasn't happened. They thought I'd go to the mat to get them more advanced weapons and intelligence systems. That hasn't happened. They thought I'd basically let the union discipline everyone, but we know all they would discipline anyone for was lack of paying their dues. I won't be surprised by anything they say because they're looking for an opportunity to remind me, I'm only in this job because they let me serve in the department long enough to be considered qualified."

"Happily willing to bite the hand that feeds them..." I suggest.

"The world of a police officer is different than the world of anyone else..." he begins, although I've heard this particular diatribe before. "The world as I know it could end any day of the week at any time of day or night. Some whack-o decides to shoot his way out of a bad situation; I come home in a body bag. There's no reasoning with some people. Nothing you can do or say that will keep them from exercising their god-like power to pull a trigger. Take a life. End the existence of someone who thought today was just another day. That's the reality for police officers. You can't take anything for granted. You have to hold your loved ones tight, because you never know when you're not coming home to them."

"You're preaching again," I remind him.

"Haven't had an audience recently. Sorry if I'm boring you."

"Why don't you just go teach? The threat goes away for us. You'd make nearly as much money if you took over the Law Enforcement Futures Institute at the University. Walter said he'd support you if you wanted it."

"I don't need the governor to talk to someone on my behalf," Nathaniel seems to be at loose ends, not sure what he wants, probably hoping the worst possible situation doesn't occur, and hoping the mayor will let him just go back to work.

"He talks to people on my behalf all the time. That doesn't seem to bother you."

"You're elected," Nathaniel begins. "I'm appointed. There's a big difference. You're accountable to the voters. I'm accountable to the mayor and council. And we both know the council has never been a big fan of me."

"Don't you think you've changed some minds?" I have to press him to think of the situation differently.

"We both know a certain councilman will never be happy about me being in this role. That's why I'm sitting here when I should be downtown helping resolve the situation."

"Chill," is all I can think to say. "One member of council is not going to put you out of your job. You said yourself; his presence probably makes you work that much harder, which is a good thing. You do remember saying that, don't you?"

"After enough alcohol I'm liable to say most anything." Nathaniel pushes back, unwilling to admit the truth.

"Okay. I hear you," I shift tactics on him. "Who do you think Childers put on the IA team?"

Childers is the lieutenant in charge of the internal affairs team. He would decide who was going to work the investigation.

"It's all white men. Older men with more than twenty-years in the department. With the one exception. The officer who came in from Houston. He's Black, as I remember, but also not a voting member."

"You can hope he volunteers to help write the report since so many officers prefer to dictate rather than even fill out forms," I note.

Nathaniel shakes his head, "Ziegler. He likes to write. If anything, it's likely they put him on the team to do just that. He's good at listening and capturing the essence of what people are saying."

"Is he going to write what the other members and Childers tell him to write, or will he use independent judgment to select words that may be less inflammatory?"

"Ziegler?" Nathaniel seems surprised I would raise this issue. "He's gonna be totally objective. No editorial. Show me the facts, baby. And if you don't have facts… guess what? You're not gonna get the story you're hoping for. Deadlines? Only so much bullshit. If the story is truly great, it will find its legs. The trick is still being here when someone reads it."

"What are you afraid is going to come out?" I ask.

"Nothing of substance. More nuance than anything else. Some people in the department got moved to new beats. If they were getting paid in whatever sense, they may be unhappy about how we reorganized things. May have taken them out of the lucrative payoffs."

"Just means someone else is able to benefit from the largesse of punks on the street who are working all kinds of scams to separate someone from their money." I summarize.

"We're cleaner than most departments and for that reason I tend to be upbeat that things will get back to normal with only the changes that have to be made. And then I think more realistically. Someone died on my watch. Things can't go back to the way they were. The way they were permitted something like this to happen. And it can't. Not ever again."

"What does that mean for you?" I push him.

"Means I've got a lot to consider, a lot more to plan out and even more to do."

"What would have to be in that report to keep you from returning?" I ask since he doesn't seem to be considering this as even a possibility. Not that I think this will be the outcome, but I need to make him see the whole picture, which I don't think he is.

"Keep me...?" Nathaniel confirms this has not even been a consideration for him. "Nothing I can think of. The mayor and I talk every day. She can't wait for me to get back."

"Nathaniel," I hate to break his bubble, "She's not the one who would keep you from returning. What might be in that report? Something that could give her no choice? Something that could cause her to have to release you? There must be something. You need to think about it."

Nathaniel puzzles on my challenge to him. The silence grows and the concern on his face tells me he is thinking through things he's not been focused on to this point. "If this is all a set-up..."

"Meaning what?"

"If the union decided they would get a better deal from someone else..."

"The union?" I'd not considered this but clearly it seems to be a concern for him. "They might set you up? They'd really do that to you?"

"If someone thinks I'm preventing the members from putting more dollars in their pocket, I can see that person going around and talking to everyone. Would that cause anyone to set me up? Kill someone just to get rid of me? Why not just shoot me? That's probably still an option, but I'm having trouble thinking the union leaders would set me up this way."

"They're your friends," I can't conceive of anyone killing someone just to get more money for the union members when they're a police department.

"When you see the side of life police officers do, life seems cheap." Nathaniel reminds me.

"You think it's possible," I note.

Nathaniel looks sad, "Anything's possible, but I hope not."

"Apart from your fellow officers, is there someone else who might be trying to set you up?"

Again, Nathaniel reflects on my question as if he'd not considered this. "I suppose any of the organized crime groups might want me gone, but I have no idea which one would cut a deal with St. James. I just don't see him as wanting anything to do with them. He may have killed someone in the line of duty, but I don't think he's corrupt."

I wonder about LaMance's question about why these two people? "What if there's another explanation. One you haven't considered?"

Nathaniel looks at me quizzically. "You know something I don't?" but then he nods, "Of course you do. That's your job. What should I be considering I haven't?"

I wonder if I should say anything or let him figure it out on his own. "What do you know about the shooter and the victim?"

"I know St. James as well as any other cop on the force. What's it been? Twenty-five years or more? But what do you really know about someone you see, but seldom even have a conversation with? Not that much. He's an acquaintance. Not much more. Now on the other hand, Bo Madison? All I know about him is he broke my record and passed on a pro career, even though he probably would have been picked up by somebody needing another strong runner to spell their money guy. Kind of the role I would have had."

"You're framing this wrong," I have to tell him. "Forget about football for a moment. Recently. Last six months, what do you know about Bo Madison?"

Nathaniel sits back to consider my question. He shakes his head. "Don't think I've heard anything about him in the last six months."

"Did anyone at the station mention him?"

Nathaniel shakes his head again. "I didn't realize right away it was the same person. Last time I heard about Bo was he was in Afghanistan or some place over there being the hero. Fighting the good war for all of us."

"He's been back for years. What does that tell you?"

"That I don't know anything about him. What he's been up to or why he would become a target."

I let Nathaniel consider my questions for a moment.

LOVE

"You're right. I've been making assumptions without asking the right questions."

"Are you asking the right questions about St. James? Or are you so focused on your own situation you're not being a cop?"

That gets his attention. He stares at me as if he was on the witness stand and just made an admission he didn't want to. I've seen this look too many times before. He shakes his head as he continues to think about my observation. He rises to get a glass of wine. "You want some?"

I shrug not sure if I want some now or it will be better to wait for dinner, although I generally sip my way through preparing a meal. "Sure. Red please."

Nathaniel pours the two glasses and hands me one as he takes a sip of his. "Why is it you're insightful when you drink the first glass and brilliant when you reach the third?"

"Because the audience, if drinking along, is only hearing the echoes of what is in their own mind by the third glass." I offer by way of explanation.

"Is that the problem?" He wonders looking at the glass he is swirling. "I'm acting like I'm in an echo chamber, only hearing my own thoughts? Not listening to those who have insights I don't?"

I look at the legs of the wine in my glass now. "It's an easy trap to fall into. Not just for government officials like us, but people everywhere. They tune into the echo chamber of political rhetoric and block out all other thoughts, thinking those that agree with their own must be correct. As a result, the world grows small. It's easier to comprehend. The choices become black and white with no nuance, no other side to the debate. And that's why we find ourselves demonizing anyone who doesn't look like us, who doesn't belong to the same social circles, who didn't go to the same school or play on the same teams. We've been whipsawed by that echo chamber here over just the last few days. You playing off Demetrius White who bumps you into Bo

Madison who broke your record and now lays dead in the morgue because one of your cops shot him for no discernable reason. You sit here unable to do your job because someone didn't trust your ability to be impartial. That person clearly doesn't know you, and yet made a judgment that has ramifications beyond what either of us can influence. All we are seeing demonstrates how little control we have of our lives, and we are forced to make decisions whose long-term consequences we cannot see. And yet they come back to haunt us."

CHAPTER TWELVE:

LaMance Freeman, Deputy Attorney General, State of Texas

As I carry the file to gBeto's office as I have on so many occasions, I wonder if this time will be different. Will this time lead to a clear direction, as opposed to so many where I get sent off to find out something more suggested by the file notes, but not clearly determined?

She's in her office with the door open as usual. She's entering something into her screen, although I can't see what. I hate to interrupt her concentration, particularly when she's really into whatever it is like now. I stop and wait at the door.

"I know you're there. Come on in. I'll only be a minute." gBeto always seems to know when I'm there, even if we haven't made eye contact.

"Take your time. We're only trying to solve a possible homicide," I offer to get her attention, otherwise experience would indicate I could be waiting for twenty or thirty minutes for her to finish up.

My statement must have not registered as she doesn't look up or slow down her typing. Whatever she's working on has her full attention. But then she surprises me by stopping, quickly re-reading what she's written and then sending it off into the ether. "Email to Nathaniel?" I suggest.

"Walter," she responds. "That's out of the way, so what do you have for me?'

I lay the file on her desk. "What we know of the individuals involved in the cop shooting."

"Bo Madison and Officer Michael St. James." I take the file and open it to see the cover page. I glance up, "Should I just work my way through or are you planning on giving me a guided tour?"

"You want highlights?" I ask.

"Might help with my time crunch, rather than calling you for an explanation of anything and everything I don't understand."

"Highlights: Bo Madison. Born in Selma, Alabama. His parents moved to Fort Christian when he was three. Likely has no remembrances of that part of his childhood. Grew up downtown in an apartment over a dry cleaner. Was mixed up with drug dealers at a young age, became a mule for them delivering product to the pushers. Found the money was good but he was a target for rival gangs and was beaten nearly to death on two occasions. That was enough. He went on a serious body building spree, gaining like fifty pounds of muscle and discovering he was incredibly fast. A high school teacher recruited him for the football team, and that was when he discovered who he really was."

"A record setting half-back for UT. Why did he pass up a pro contract?" I ask trying to fill in pieces that didn't come out in the Demetrius and Nathaniel discussion.

"He had a half-brother who joined up. Became a Ranger and was sent into combat. He got letters from him the whole time he was in college, about the brother's experiences, having complete strangers become more like brothers than your actual blood brother. Said if we didn't stop the Muslims from killing each other, they would someday come for us. It was Bo's duty to stop the westward march of the Muslim hordes. The brother was killed by a landmine blowing up his vehicle only a month before he was scheduled to return. That was the event that pushed Bo over the edge."

"I suppose a dead brother will do that to you," she reflects and considers what she didn't know.

"Bo served with distinction in the regular infantry. Said he didn't want to be part of any elite groups like his brother. He wanted to experience what the everyday grunt experienced. He got it. He was in some really bad fighting. In one firefight, Bo was the only survivor because he was strong enough, he picked up a light machinegun and chased the insurgents away, killing anyone who didn't run and hide. He was awarded three medals for that incident. A note from his commanding officer was Bo probably realized he was dead anyway since everyone else was. He just went Rambo and somehow survived."

"Did he have Post Traumatic Stress Disorder?" She seems to be simply confirming it's in the file.

"Later notes confirm. He was being treated for it."

I note her shake her head, "What else did it say about him?"

"Completed two tours, but elected not to re-enlist. Seems lots of people were hoping he was coming home to play football. But apparently, he had come to the conclusion if he stayed in either he would be killed or those about him would, because of the recurring images that were distracting him at the worst times possible."

"The PTSD," gBeto nods to herself.

"Out of the Army, not playing football, he drifted from one low paying job to another because he couldn't concentrate on the job. He would apparently be fine for a few days and then he'd be found in the men's room curled up and shaking as if he was in withdrawals, which unfortunately was what was assumed on more than one occasion. No one stepped in to try to help him, but he didn't reach out to his family either. From what I've read, it would seem he was ashamed he wasn't man enough to handle what happened to him."

"And that takes us to the convenience store," gBeto confirms with a brief look up at me.

"That's all we've been able to find on him."

"Any indication if he'd had a run-in with Officer St. James?" she asks.

"No indications. Doesn't mean it didn't happen, but nothing we could find by interviewing people who knew him."

"He was in counseling for the PTSD?" she asks following up on that thread.

"Off and on. Mostly off. He started it twice, but never completed a course of treatment. He was diagnosed as moderately severe, which means if he got through a day without a flashback, it was a good day."

"Did the VA or whoever was offering the counseling work to get him a job, place to stay or anything like that?"

"Not according to the record. He was coming into a walk-in counseling center run by the local veteran's group, but funded by the VA. He wasn't going into the hospital very often if that's what you're thinking. Not seeing a shrink, just a vocational counselor who was trying to help him stabilize enough he could hold a job. But his symptoms only progressed. He was unemployed for most of the last year. There was a note that he sometimes substituted for a bouncer at a local dance club. But he couldn't keep it together long enough to get a regular job there, even though it was only evenings."

She glances through his folder, stops for a second, "He graduated with a degree in Economics, near the top of his class."

"He was a smart guy, who just made a decision from the heart rather than his head, and it eventually cost him his life," I summarize.

"What a waste," gBeto remarks.

"You read on you'll find out the other soldiers who served with him would disagree. They, to a man, praised his unselfishness and willingness to do anything for another soldier or a civilian who wasn't shooting at him. Numerous stories about him helping Afghan families. He pulled a plow in one instance where the ox had been killed and they couldn't plant crops. Turns out they were planting poppies, but Bo didn't know that. Where he gave kids his rations so they would have something to eat. Even organized his squad to rebuild a house that had been burned by the Taliban. Did it in only a day. His life wasn't a waste. He did a lot of good in the short time he was with us. It's too bad we weren't able to help him when he needed us."

"Why Bo?" gBeto asks.

"We have to hope the internal affairs report sheds some light on that because this report won't."

"Officer St. James. What's his story?"

"Couldn't be more different. Grew up in Edge Hill. Didn't graduate from high school, but did get a General Education Diploma about a year later, just in time to be accepted into the police academy. No record of him in high school other than he was passed along from year-to-year, never really completing the studies, but not causing trouble. No extra-curricular activities, no juvenile record. He seems to be one of those kids who floats through the system, leaving no marks."

Does it say who his parents were or what his address was in high school?" gBeto asks.

I take the folder from her and quickly glance through until I find it, "Michael and Sheila St. James. One-Fourteen Broad Street, second floor. Says the father was an auto mechanic and the mother provided domestic services. Took in kids after school, did laundry, cleaned houses those kinds of things. Is he the one you remember?"

gBeto nods, but doesn't answer. *It must be hard to see someone you knew as a kid be facing possible charges, and she will be the one to bring them if required.* "Didn't know he went the GED route. I lost track of him when he moved out of their house after he dropped out of school."

"Did you know he was a cop?" I ask to see how much she does remember, as I still think there's more here than she's saying.

"I can't remember. If his brother ever said anything it didn't stay with me."

"You said his brother was in your class?" I push a little further

99

without pushing hard.

"We were lab partners for chemistry. Nearly blew up the school, but that's another story." I see a smile with that memory. Something I haven't seen in a while.

"Have you kept in touch with his brother?"

gBeto shakes her head, "Nor anyone else with a few exceptions. We all went in different directions. Since I was from the poor section of town, no one thought I'd amount to much. Not many wanted to keep in touch with me."

"It amazes me that people who have so much in common go off in different directions, even though they're all still here in the same city. And yet they make no effort to keep in touch."

"Did you?" gBeto asks.

"Like you, I see a couple girlfriends maybe once a year, but generally not even that. I'm the only one from my class that went to law school. Most of the girls just got married and took menial jobs just to keep the roof over their heads while their husbands worked their asses off trying to make ends meet."

"Why is that? People have such low expectations of themselves? It almost seems they've resigned themselves they can't do more, or they can't succeed, so why even try." gBeto reflects.

"Like your friend Michael St. James."

"He's not a junior?"

I glance at the record again, "Different middle name."

"Didn't know that." gBeto seems to be reflecting on a past she'd rather forget. "What else can you tell me about Officer St. James?"

"His record in the police department shows he was promoted to sergeant after being on the force for ten years, but was reduced back to a patrolman after only six months as he just wasn't able to lead a team effectively, according to his personnel record."

"No details?"

"Looked like notes were removed from the file, probably at the insistence of the union," I note as I have seen that all too often when looking at police officer records.

"Are you sure or are you guessing?"

"There are consistent notes to his file up until he was promoted. For that half year there are no notes. When he went back to being a patrolman the notes resumed. Is that evidence? Yes. Is it proof? No."

"Circumstantial won't cut it in a trial. What else can you tell me?"

"He was cited five times for using undue force in arrests. Each time he was assigned to counseling, which he completed and sent back out. From what I've learned about police tactics, if he was cited five times, he probably should have been cited fifty. Means he was totally insensitive to the person he was arresting and would use whatever tactic made it easiest to subdue the party he was attempting to bring in."

"How often has he discharged his weapon?" She finally goes to the key question.

"In twenty-two years on the force he has discharged his weapon eighteen times, which is the most by any officer on the Fort Christian police force."

"How many times has he wounded someone?"

"Eighteen times," I recite the number that surprised me.

"How many shots were lethal?"

"Seven with Bo Madison."

"He's killed seven civilians?" gBeto seems amazed.

"Yes, although most were when he was on the drug investigations team. Two of them were shoot outs where officers were also killed in the exchanges."

"We have an officer who has killed civilians in the line of duty, lived to tell about it and has continued to kill. Even when not in life-or-death situations," gBeto postulates.

"That's the question we are trying to answer, yes."

"What about his personal life?"

I have to think back a moment, but then it comes to me, "Three marriages, three uncontested divorces for mental cruelty."

"Anything else?" she's fishing knowing there's more.

"Two times one of his wives ended up in the hospital with injuries that could only be explained by physical abuse."

"Did the wife press charges?"

"No. Each time the statements in the file indicated she assumed responsibility for her own injuries, although I think it's safe to assume that wasn't the case."

"Assumptions, indications, nothing we could use in a court room. If this goes to trial it won't be pretty for us. All you've discussed is we have a cop who's had a rough time growing up poor, was undistinguished. He got a GED and a job as a cop where he can be as physical and abusive as he wants because no one has been willing to hold him responsible."

"That includes Nathaniel," I point out. "One of those excessive force citations was last year. A case where Officer St. James wounded two civilians. One of the civilians was holding a girl hostage at knifepoint and St. James shot them both. The girl sued him because he could have killed her with the shot he took. But the department lawyers settled out of court."

gBeto looks away, shakes her head as she exhales deeply. "That was right after he became commissioner. I remember him talking about the situation. He wanted to let the civil case go forward, but the department lawyers talked him out of it, for the good of the department."

"Officer St. James is not going to go quietly into the night."

CHAPTER THIRTEEN:

Sarah White, Director Content, Continuum Media

"When did the mayor have him put under house arrest?" I'm talking with Tic Rogers, even though father would tell me to hang up. I think Tic sees me as being more open minded than father about publishing by-line stories that have a decided viewpoint. Continuum would open up a whole new market for his stories if we would buy them. Now I may be more willing to buy stories and let our readers decide if they want to read them, but father would never let me. It's all about his sense of journalistic integrity. He doesn't see Tic as having any.

Tic is surprised at my question; apparently thought I already knew. "When he was suspended. She didn't make a big deal of it then, but apparently, she was concerned if she didn't do more than suspend him there might be violence in the streets."

"There hasn't been. Apparently, she was right."

"Don't get comfortable," Tic warns me. "It's coming and you'll be lucky if anything is still standing in downtown when it's over."

"Because the rage hasn't had a release yet and it's just building up?" I wonder aloud.

"That is certainly part of it, but there's more," Tic teases me.

"What are we missing?"

"Publish my by-line and you'll have the whole story rather than Politico who's reviewing it for publication on Saturday."

"I can't. It's against company policy and you know it."

LOVE

"When is your old man going to retire so you can make your own decisions?" Tic pushes me.

"I like your work. Like it a lot," I admit. "You have what I think is a fresh outlook and voice, but our by-lines are only staffers and not freelancers. We don't want to publish you one time and have you appearing in Politico the next day."

"A man's got to make the best living he can, and captive to one media company just doesn't pay enough."

"Seeing what we pay I completely understand," *I was shocked how little.* "I wouldn't be able to afford working here if I didn't start up higher on the food chain."

"You know I think you have a future there. I read your article on St. James. I even gave you a credit in my last article for bringing out his past when most of the information about his discipline history is locked up in personnel files."

"I was amazed to learn you can't find information about officer involved shootings from the cop side. Everything out there is about who they kill or wound, but nothing about the officer involved. I don't understand how they can hide behind personnel privacy laws when they're killing people."

"At least we agree on that point. Call me when daddy retires and your policies change," and Tic is gone. At least I got an important tip.

I search the web for the picture Tic referenced. I find it, study it for a minute to confirm what he said, write down the credit and search for the photographer. No other credits. This was apparently his first posting. I search further and find a cell phone.

"Hi, is this Garry Goetz?"

"Speaking. You calling about my picture? How much you gonna pay me for it?"

"Since you posted it already, I'm afraid it no longer has value because anyone can just link to it. Word of advice, you get another picture like that? Call me and we'll talk price. In the meantime, I'm curious when and where you took the picture."

"Who is this?"

"Fair enough," I should have expected this reaction. "You didn't seem interested when you were just looking for a paycheck. I can still credit you with the information and that will increase the value of your next attempt to freelance into the media."

"You still didn't tell me who you are."

"You going to call me before you post your next picture?"

"Yeah, yeah. Who am I gonna call?"

"Sarah White, Director of Content at Continuum."

Silence from Garry Goetz. "Continuum."

"That's right. Now you want a link to your picture or are you going to wait to see if anyone else calls with a better deal? I can get what I want from a dozen other sources I've worked with forever. I'm doing you a favor with the link and credit for the information."

Silence as Garry Goetz tries to contemplate having to continue looking for the payday he was expecting.

"If you change your mind, you can reach me at Sarah.White @Continuum.com." I start to disconnect when I hear…

"Wait," he gathers his thoughts. "Okay. You were the first to call. I'll give it to you. Ace Wine and Spirits over on Main. It's on his way home from the precinct he works out of. I've seen him get his booze there for years. Almost seems like he has a regular order waiting for him or something. Never in there more than a minute. Maybe he calls ahead or something, but last night was his regular pick-up night. I waited to see if he came. Sure enough. Regular like clockwork. Only he wasn't wearing his ankle bracelet."

"How did you know about that?" I need to understand why he took the picture.

"Look, I've kept an eye on him for a couple years now. When he was suspended, I called a friend to get the full scoop."

"A friend on the police force," I try to clarify.

"Someone who knew the whole story. I'll put it that way. And no, I won't give you a name. I was to do that I'd never get shit in the future."

"That person was right even though not many knew."

"The right people knew, and that's about all I'll say about that."

"Meaning the Black community leaders," as long as he's answering I'm asking.

"Them too."

"Why have you been keeping tabs on Officer St. James?"

"This isn't the first time he's done this."

"Kill a civilian," I try to clarify again.

"That too. He shot a friend of mine, who's in a wheelchair for life. My friend is fucked. He can't get a decent job and he's in and out of the hospital all the time for one complication or another. You know what he said to me after St. James killed Bo Madison? Said he was sorry he didn't die when St. James shot him because if he'd known how hard it was going to be…"

"What happened to St. James?" I think I may already know the answer, but just checking to see if he knows what he's talking about.

"Another citation. Like his tenth or something. That's all they do. Put a note in your personnel file and the next person he decides to kill has no idea who's stopping her… or him."

"Your friend's a woman?"

"She was going to be my wife, but she refused to marry me. Said she couldn't be a burden to me because of what St. James did to her."

"She lives with her parents and you visit her every day," I guess.

"Every fucking day. This cop took from me the family we planned together. Took the life from me we hoped for together. And while I'm not going to abandon her because of what happened, I can't remember the last time we laughed together and we were always laughing before."

"Tell me what happened. How did Officer St. James come to wound your fiancé?"

"She stopped to get gas at the convenience store up from General Hospital on South State Street. It was late. Around midnight."

"Was she a nurse?" An assumption now, I doubt she was a doctor because he sounds young.

"Surgical. She'd had one of those days when the procedures are long and the outcome still in doubt when she finally left for the day. Those are the worst, because she just couldn't feel good about all the long hours and effort it takes."

"What happened?"

"A kid... what am I saying, he's older than me. Anyway, this young guy decides to hold up the convenience store. Really? Who does that? They never have that much money it's worth risking going to jail for. But that's beside the point. Apparently, the clerk set off a silent alarm or something because a cop car arrives while she's still pumping gas. Pulls up right in front of the door, but the guy had already left with the cash. He'd gotten as far as the pumps when St. James storms out of his car, sees the guy next to Kelly and pulls his gun, shouting at the guy to get down on the ground. The guy panics. Grabs Kelly as a shield, but St. James shoots, hitting Kelly with the first shot and the guy with the second. He's just out of control. There's no reason he should have

LOVE

taken that shot, either one for that matter. Kelly was on her way home. But St. James didn't even bother to find out whether she was involved or just an innocent bystander."

Garry falls silent overcome with rage and grief all bubbling about inside him.

"I'm sorry for what happened."

"Do you know how much the guy took?"

I shake my head, but he can't see that. I answer, "No idea."

"A hundred and twenty-seven dollars of which a hundred was the change in the change drawer. Everything over a hundred and fifty goes into a safe the clerk can't access. It was all for nothing."

"Unless you have no money for food and have a starving family somewhere." I suggest. "Sometimes people are driven to absurd choices when their kids are starving."

"Not the deal. The kid... guy was looking for money to pay his dealer."

"What happened to him?"

"Kelly's bullet hit her spinal cord. His pierced his lung. He recovered and she didn't. Not like she was before."

"He's in jail?" I follow up since I want the full sense of what's driving him.

"Already out. A hundred and twenty-seven dollars doesn't get you much time, even though he was as much responsible for destroying Kelly's life as St. James. But while St. James has immunity and protection to destroy lives, Ahmad Jackson will self-destruct at some point. If a cop like St. James doesn't take him out, one of his street buddies likely will."

"You keep an eye on Officer St. James," I note. "Where he lives, what he does, even what liquor store he frequents. What else can you

109

DHTREICHLER

tell me that might be of interest to Bo Madison's family and those who want to see justice in this situation?"

"He has an anger management problem. Of that, I'm sure. He gets into a lot of fights. Bars, wives, friends. Seems anyone around him is likely to get a beating, whether deserved or not. I get the impression he has a lot of demons, because he's always chasing them, if you know what I'm saying. Trying to strike out. Drive them away, particularly when he's had more than one drink. I've never seen him have just one."

"You go into the bars to watch?"

"Since Kelly's not much for partying anymore, I'll go by his usual haunts, when I leave Kelly's house, just to see what he's up to."

"But you don't do that for Ahmad Jackson," I realize and seek to confirm.

"I'd be the one to get killed if I followed that dude around. No, not going there. Like I said, he's not long for this world, regardless of what I might do. But St. James? Different story. Someone's got to bring him down. I don't see anyone else standing up to do it. Guess it might as well be me."

"You don't really care about another story as long as you get this one right," I bait him.

"You're right about that."

"What do you do when you're not playing detective?"

"Me? I'm nobody," he tries to put me off.

"You obviously aren't particularly to Kelly and now Officer St. James. What do you do?"

"I'm a medical school dropout. I was in my last year before residency when this all happened. I couldn't do what it took to finish, so I got a certificate to take pictures…"

"X-rays?"

LOVE

"Radiology. I can read the film, but they don't let me, because I didn't get the paper needed."

"For Radiologist," I confirm. "Is that what you wanted to be?"

"No. I wanted to be a surgeon, have Kelly in the suite with me, saving lives together. That was my dream. Neuro was what I planned, but not anymore. Now I'm just like everyone else, trying to get by, while life drags me off in another unplanned direction."

"What time did you take the picture of St. James?"

"Look at the picture. I had the date and time stamp on just so no one could accuse me of surfacing an old picture."

"You thought this all out," I realize as I glance over my notes. "I think you might have a future if you decide justice is more interesting and important than taking pictures of patients."

"That an offer?" Garry Goetz almost sounds interested.

"What are you going to do if we find enough to lock him up?"

"That won't be an issue. You do your job; you'll find more than enough. You dig into St. James and Bo Madison you'll find more than enough. But you can't just go look at the public sources. You need to get out and talk to the people on the street. They know. And that's another reason people are waiting. They want to see if you're doing your job, if the police do their job, and whether the judicial people do theirs. Everyone is waiting and watching and getting ready if you don't."

CHAPTER FOURTEEN:

gBeto Dahomey Brown, Attorney General, State of Texas

Walter Rutherford never has a lock of hair out of place, or at least that seems to be the situation, and today is no exception. As his assistant, Janine, ushers me into the Governor's Office, I see the usual mementos. Those from his former life as a corporate executive, and a few from his current role in public service. The big knock on him when he was running, was whether he could take the pay cut. He actually got to see the president more often as a corporate executive than he has since becoming governor.

He is writing something on his computer, doesn't look at me, but finishes his document. That takes a couple minutes. I wait soundlessly, not to disturb him.

When he looks up, a smile comes to him as naturally as if he didn't have to rehearse it. But from what people have told me, that smile was seldom seen before he ran for office. Walter is a pragmatist, an opportunist, and a realist all rolled together. I know I'm not going to get a bunch of nonsense from him when I come to see him. I'm going to get a straight scoop of whatever is on his mind. I expect today to be no different. "gBeto," he gestures to the usual chair, but he rises and comes around the desk. "I would have come see you, but today has been… a little more packed than usual. I hope you don't mind coming over to see me."

"I'm always happy to share a few minutes of your time, sir."

"I want to talk to you about the St. James – Madison shooting."

"We have a name for it now?" I ask since I've not heard anyone else refer to it this way.

"Just internally. I don't make that linkage when talking with anyone outside these walls. But as I'm sure you're aware, the Morning News ran an editorial about an independent investigation. As you can imagine more than a few people have called and sent notes to me expressing their opinions." Walter lets that sink in, looking for any reaction from me, but none are forthcoming.

"Normally I would defer to the mayor and let her decide what to do. But I've had several conversations with Jenny in the last few days. She is feeling she will incur a morale problem in her police department if she does anything before the release of the internal affairs report."

"Which, by the way, they are dragging out longer than usual," I note for his benefit.

"Jenny mentioned that. Apparently, the investigators are having some trouble reconciling sworn statements that appear to be contradictory. Yet no one is willing to modify their statement."

"And I take it the independent officer from Houston isn't willing to sign off until they do."

Walter looks away and considers how to answer my question. When he does that, I know the answer will be artful and obfuscated. "Jenny indicated a lack of consensus. Unusual, given most of the officers have conducted hundreds of prior investigations together."

Well done, Walter. You outdid yourself with that one. "The mayor isn't planning to respond to the editorial or the community groups advocating an independent citizens panel," I seek to confirm although I'm sure I know the answer.

"Jenny asked if there was precedent for me to create such a panel."

"How far back did you have to go to find that one?" I smile knowing how Walter thinks.

"Sixteen-ninety-three. We had a colony-wide commission on witchcraft as a result of the Salem witch trials. You know Britain passed the anti-witchcraft laws in 1641. At that time, we were subject to British Common Law. Some could say it really doesn't pertain to today. But since our whole system of common laws is based on the British Common Law I disagree. What do you think?"

I smile at Walter because I know what this is all about. More than anything, he wants to know if I have his back. "You make a good point about our laws being based on British Common Law, but frankly sir, I don't think that argument is really necessary. As governor you have the authority to establish whatever commissions and independent citizen advisory boards you deem necessary. It is only common courtesy for you to defer to the mayor of a city where the incident may have occurred. But if the mayor has informed you she does not intend to establish such an independent board, you may, if you have what you believe to be cause."

"What would constitute cause?" Walter wants to tie this down.

"The editorial. In and of itself could be cause. But there are other media reports assuming the internal affairs report will not recommend any substantial changes in the department or punishment to the officer involved."

"That would be sufficient?"

"I would be willing to support your action if questioned by either the judiciary or the media."

Walter nods, clearly pleased. "That like a get out of jail free card?"

"More like you never go to jail card," I suggest with a head nod.

"Then let's talk mechanics. I'm going to appoint an independent citizens committee to look into the Fort Christian Police Department and more particularly Officer Michael St. James. Now I know this is going to be difficult for you given Nathaniel's role. I want you sequestered from the panel even though your office will run the investigation and present findings to the independent commission. Any problems so far?"

"None whatsoever," I affirm knowing where he is going.

"Who would you have leading this?"

"LaMance Freeman. She's the Chief Prosecutor in my office. It makes sense the senior most person should take this on."

"I want LaMance filing her reports directly with me. She should copy you so you know what's going on, but she will be taking her direction from me. Any problems with that?"

"I completely understand why that's important."

"I trust Nathaniel will survive this inquiry. However, it is likely his reputation will take more than one ding. I've just never seen anyone escape unscathed. You may want to prepare him for that. Let him know this is not focused on him. But we... I, recognize there will be collateral damage, no matter how many good things he's done since he took over the top spot."

"We've talked about how social change travels by fits and starts," I respond. "Things can go along for decades or more without sufficient support materializing. And one event, no matter how small, can catch the attention of enough people, who decide 'enough is enough.' And while you may have been making incremental changes that make things better, they all get swept away in a moment when the right people say now is the time."

Walter nods. "I understand what you're saying. Hadn't thought about it in those terms, but it makes sense. It describes what I think we may be seeing."

"No issues here. Nathaniel and I will be prepared for whatever happens. The most important thing is that justice is done."

"That's why you're attorney general. On my side it's more about what systemic changes do we need to make to avoid these situations in the future."

"Sir, if you would permit me? I'd not recommend using the terms you used. I understand the systemic change part, but it should be to build a just and equitable system."

"Since it's just the two of us talking here now. You know I'm not a lifetime politician. I'm not schooled in political correctness or sensitivities. You talk about a just and equitable system. How does that eliminate racism?"

I nod impressed he's given this more thought than I feared he had by his first statement about avoiding these situations. "Is that what you think is needed? Elimination of racism?"

"Well, I don't know. For a long time, I thought we'd eliminated inequality only to find not so much. While the law is equality, the fact remains a whole lot of people don't agree. They don't act that way when given a chance to make a choice. Is that because of learned behavior from parents, relatives and friends? Where does it come from? I hear people talking about institutional racism, but I don't know what that means. It all comes down to people making a choice to exclude someone. Making a choice not to admit someone to whatever. It all comes down to a personal choice as far as I can see. The City of Fort Christian doesn't make a choice, but the people who live there do. It's not the institution, it's the people."

"That's very insightful, sir," I observe to make sure he's following me. "But where institutional racism comes from is traditions. That's the way it's always been. Racism is the tradition. The message goes out loud and clear. You don't mess with the tradition. Where did you go to school sir?"

"Harvard."

"They had traditions there when you attended, I'm sure."

"They did," he confirms.

"And those traditions weren't voluntary. You were expected to respect those traditions."

"Yes," he knows what I'm saying now.

"Institutional racism was part of the Harvard tradition, whether Blacks, Jews or any other minority, since most of the Harvard endowment money came from White graduates. Had to, because the numbers of Black or Jewish grads are small in comparison. The tradition of a legacy admission supports admissions that were similar numbers as in the past. More Whites than any other ethnicity."

"You were Yale Law." Walter seeks confirmation.

"Harvard didn't accept me. Yale was the next best place to go at that time."

"Again, proving your point. I see what you're saying. I just never thought of it in those terms. Thanks for educating me on institutional racism. What do I need to do to eliminate it in state government?"

"That's a big ask, sir, but I'm glad you did," I'm surprised at the turn of this conversation. "You would probably have to ask everyone who works for the state to retire all at the same time. You would have to get rid of all procedures. Then you'd have to go hire all recent grads who represent all ethnicities, and all religions, and all social levels. You'd have to put them into a blender and mix thoroughly. You'd have to cut off all communications with their families. Make sure they don't watch the news. Then you'd ask them to develop new policies and procedures to do their work that are absolutely equitable and just. An example might be that if the state employee never sees the person who is seeking services. They can't judge them. They don't see addresses, so they don't know where they live. They don't have access to financial data so they have no idea if someone is rich or poor. You'd have to have people monitoring what they say and do to ensure everyone is treated equally. Even then I'm not sure you'd get it all."

"Are you saying it's all a matter of tradition?" Walter seems overwhelmed by my response and what it would take. "Handed down from one person to the next? People aren't the problem; it's all the people who came before us and established those traditions."

"People are the problem," I clarify for him. "As you noted, acts of discrimination are choices people make. People can choose inclusion. People can choose diversity. People can choose equity and justice. But way too many don't."

"Because people get to a point where they get comfortable with their life," Walter realizes. "They've figured out how to get by or better."

"That's a big part of it, as it see it. But there's more. The world is constantly changing. Sometimes the change takes place over centuries and sometimes overnight. When you get comfortable, the slow changes can be accommodated. No big deal. But when rapid change happens, people who have a comfortable life suddenly see it go away. Whether it's the offshoring of manufacturing jobs, or coal miners who lose their jobs because of solar energy or gas power plants, or auto workers who see their jobs go to Mexico. People are afraid someone else is going to disrupt their comfort. But that doesn't address all the people who never got comfortable. All the people who send their kids to school not to learn, but to make sure they got a good lunch, because they don't have enough money to put three meals on the table for their kids. What about them? They see the system we've established, the traditions if you will, is rigged against them ever getting comfortable. They don't get the good teachers in school. They don't get the remedial education to stay in grade. They don't get the enrichment other kids do, because they never went to the museums or took vacations their better school peers got to."

"You grew up poor," Walter notes. "Why did you make it?"

I take a deep breath, searching how to answer this question. "I grew up worse than poor, we were dirt poor. But a teacher saw something in me. She opened doors that got me into better classes and eventually into college. A professor did the same. He got me into law school. People who were just doing their jobs, who weren't racist, who didn't assume I'd never amount to anything, took a chance on me. It made all the difference. I felt I had to do well for them. They put their

LOVE

reputations on the line to give me a chance. I owed it to them to deliver."

"And you have. Attorney general, lecturing the governor on something he should have already known."

"I'm sorry, sir. You ask questions, I have opinions, even if I may not have all the facts."

"What should I do to end racism in my government?" Walter comes back to the basic question, even though he had the chance to avoid it.

"I can't give you a complete answer off the cuff like this. I need some time to think it through, but it starts at the top. First thing would be to put out a memo to all department heads detailing your policy is that equity and justice are primary concerns. That means every citizen is treated the same without exception. Now that will not mean we lower service to the affluent, rather it means we will provide the same excellent service to everyone, even the chronic complainers and those who are seeking special treatment. And then you have to make examples of people across the government who do. Reward them. Recognize them. Hold them up as shining examples of what you and we should expect."

"Do I punish those who do not?" Walter is trying to understand what I'm suggesting.

"No, you simply advise them they will need to find employment elsewhere, since they seem unable or unwilling to exhibit the necessary characteristics of a State of Texas employee We are all civil servants. As servants we are expected to provide exemplary service to all who require or request it."

"Do we give a second chance to those who test my resolve?"

"No. This is not baseball. Either you are willing and able to do what is expected or you're not. If you have to test the system, then you clearly are not. You may experience high turnover for a while. You may play directly into the fears of those who don't want to see change occur. But we don't determine the rate of change in society. The lesson of the pandemic is there are many things beyond our collective control that affect us and who we are. They force unwanted and unexpected change. We have to learn to be flexible, adaptable and responsive if we wish to maintain the comfort levels we achieved in less turbulent times."

Walter nods his head, "I asked you to come by to accept what some would see as a humiliation. The need to stand by and not help your husband. The need to stand by and know he will take personal hits that may be unwarranted. But you accepted that all with grace and turned the humiliation into an opportunity to advance something that is core to you – equity and justice."

"They are core to who I am," I agree.

"I'm going to have to consider your recommendations about an equity and justice policy. If you would flesh them out. Send along your thoughts, I would appreciate it. Not likely I'll be able to do much with it right now, but maybe soon. In the meantime. That economic development task force is ready to get started. I need you to drive it for me. It will be a good diversion while all the other events play out around us." Walter rises to tell me we are done for today.

CHAPTER FIFTEEN:

Anne Rutherford – Political Not Quite Dowager

GBeto looks tired. Walter said he gave her a rough time, but she handled it well. Walter is always cryptic like that. I hope my husband doesn't learn from his brother. "Here's the tea," I recognize Rose who is bringing in the pot. We are situated in my living room, under the massive painting of John, my husband's father who started the family business that supports us all to this day. *Never could get in to spending money to memorialize oneself like that.* But the elder Rutherford was related to Rutherford Hayes who was named after one or another of my husband's ancestors. *I can't keep people straight who have been dead more than a century.*

"You like yours without cream or sugar as I remember."

gBeto nods, still seems to be recovering as she is normally much more engaged than this.

"Take a moment and gather yourself. We have important things to discuss. I will need your full attention."

"I take it Walter is not happy with my lecture."

"Walter is a babe in the woods when it comes to politics. No. He needs to hear about things he either hasn't considered or considered too little."

"You have talked with him since our little chat?"

"I talk with my brother-in-law every day. Probably more than he talks with his wife, but that's because he is governor because of me and not because of his wife."

"And I am attorney general because of you, and those you rallied to my cause." *gBeto is always grateful if not always strategic.*

"Good. Now that we have finished expressing appropriate gratitude, we need to discuss your political future."

gBeto frowns. "Does Walter want me off the ticket altogether because of Nathaniel?"

"Walter doesn't know what he wants, which is typical of him. If he had to make a decision all by himself it would invariably be the wrong decision and he recognizes it. We've had that discussion. He didn't want his lieutenant governor, who has proven to be exactly what he needed. In hindsight he will admit it was the absolute best decision he could have made. But he didn't make it. I did, and told him what he had to do to get elected. And I was right. Only after the election did he stop fighting everything I had to say to him and start to listen."

"I didn't know that," gBeto remarks before sipping her tea.

"Some day we are going to be able to get rid of the middlemen of government and just get elected ourselves. Until then we will elect clueless men and let them think they rule the universe."

I see an eyebrow raise as apparently gBeto wasn't expecting that analysis. But I've never been one to hide my brilliance under a bushel, although if I'd been a couple inches shorter it wouldn't be hard to hide under a bushel. "We have important things for which we must lay plans starting today. Now I know Walter has given you a full plate, but unfortunately politics requires you to be elected to do all the things Walter thinks important. It's not too soon to get started."

"Maybe I can get Nathaniel to help with some things as he has some unexpected free time right now."

"Good idea. Nathaniel can help with the fund raising and organizing the committees to contact voters about yard signs and speaking opportunities."

"He helped with those activities last time. He may even remember some of the people he worked with. Be good for him to be talking to someone other than the mayor."

"You're not a fan of Jennie Richards?" I wonder about the tone of her voice.

"Not that. He provides insights to the mayor about the information he is getting from sources other than the internal affairs team. They aren't supposed to talk to him so they don't. That really frustrates him as he knows he could help, and isn't permitted to."

"He did a tour in internal affairs, if I remember correctly."

"He did, but that was eight years ago," *gBeto seems to be reflecting on that time unhappily,* "He's done his share, knows the sensitivities, and knows how to get to the truth. I think if anything, he's afraid this group may not get there, because he's not sitting on them and keeping them focused on what really matters."

"Didn't he put the best person in to lead it?"

"Depends on what you mean best person," gBeto's tone says it all.

"Why haven't I heard about this before?"

"Every organization is a collection of tribes," she starts the long route to an answer, "They have their own leaders, their own rituals and their own values. Sometimes it's really hard to move from one tribe to another. Nathaniel had to choose between someone from the internal affairs tribe, all of whom are hated by the rest of the officers, and someone who might have more integrity but wasn't from that tribe. The latter would be unable to get the department to do the basic work. He did the prudent thing. He didn't mess with the tribes and picked the natural leader in the group he had to deal with, who would have been a total disaster if he'd had to put him somewhere else. Unfortunately, sometimes you arrange people in less-than-ideal positions to get the best overall effort. As a result, he has who he has, but he clearly would have preferred someone else."

"And you were okay with how he solved his problems?"

gBeto seems to reflect for a long time, "Sometimes we talked about it and sometimes he just did what he thought best. A lot of times it would end up a short discussion before he'd get exasperated with me. Just cut me off, by saying I needed to be there to understand. He was right. Anything in the abstract will work. It's when people get involved that the best laid plans… just seem to fall apart. And it's only in retrospect you see what was there all along. But the conflict over every little thing keeps you focused at the wrong level."

"Good, now that you've got that off your mind, we can return to you." I reset expectations.

"What is Walter saying?"

"Walter told me that with the current situation it would probably be better that you not be considered for anything other than attorney general this round. Probably wouldn't support you for the position if you weren't already in it. But that's when I started talking sense into him."

gBeto looks crushed even with my comment at the end. "Maybe…"

"Maybe you should wait and see what was decided," I suggest. "You have a tendency to want to internalize blame, when you're not the one who killed anyone. You're not the one who was too lenient in personnel matters and failed to more aggressively discipline a rogue cop. Yes, I'm talking about Nathaniel. It's a good thing he's not running for office, because he wouldn't stand a very good chance of being elected dog catcher this week. But I digress."

Again, gBeto seems to pull in, trying to accept the blame on herself.

"Now stop that. Right now. Your husband has broad shoulders. He can carry the blame for his own actions, or lack of them. That's not your problem at the moment. You're running around acting like you're the guilty person here. You're not. So, stop it."

gBeto looks like a scolded child. Maybe I'm laying it on a little heavy. I don't get to act like a mother very often. Maybe I go a bit overboard when I do. Particularly when it's a wayward protégé of mine like gBeto. "What do you have to say for yourself?"

"I don't know what to say. I mean I'm trying to do the right thing, but I'm not sure anymore what is right, and what's just running away."

"There's hope for you yet. You've recognized what you're feeling. Everyone wants to run away when personally attacked. Your feelings are natural. But what you've got to accept is no one is attacking you. No one is openly attacking your husband, although that is going on behind the scenes. He brought that on by agreeing to that silly suspension rule. Okay, he made a mistake. Get over it."

"What would you have me do?"

"Your job. That's all. No one is asking you to do anything else. And when you do your job to the best of your ability there's no one better. You have a sharp mind. Use it when someone gets out of line. You know the law. Use that to your advantage. Cut the legs out from under anyone who hasn't done their homework. You're going to find more in that situation than who have. You carry moral weight as the chief law enforcement officer. Everyone knows what you're supposed to stand for. If you do, no one can attack you for doing what the people elected you to do. Got it?"

"What you're telling me is I'm in a really strong position to influence outcomes as long as I follow the law."

"If you're seen as arbitrary or inconsistent in anyway, you're finished. But that's not you. If anything, you're too black and white. You stay away from the grey bands as much as possible. Everyone knows that, who has watched what you do. You don't like to interpret without precedent. Walter was saying you were debating 1683 witch trials for a precedent. You instantly said it wasn't necessary, because the law supported the authority he needed without it. You know the law. Most people don't."

"I should focus on doing my job and getting ready to run for re-election." gBeto summarizes what she thinks she's heard.

I give that 'mother's not upset with you' smile I haven't had to use in a while. "Not entirely. Yes, I think you focus on your job and get ready for re-election. But I convinced Walter you're still the strongest candidate for lieutenant governor, even though he wanted to start talking to someone else. I told him if he won't stick with you, I wouldn't stick with him. Then he'll be sitting at home watching Fox News re-runs with all the other old fogeys. He didn't like that much." I almost laugh at the remembrance.

"Wait. Walter still wants me for lieutenant governor? With all that's going on?"

"He's giving you a shot to sell him and the people of Texas that you're the best person. But that means you have to be perfect between now and the convention. Why do you think you're co-chair of that economic development council? That's to give you credentials outside law enforcement. That's to give you visibility in another context in the minds of the people. Walter sees that as the centerpiece of his last term in office, if he's lucky enough to be re-elected, and that's no sure thing Even with you on the ballot with him. Walter is giving you a trial by fire. He wouldn't do that for anyone else."

"He wouldn't do that if you weren't making him," gBeto pushes back, apparently not sure she's up to what I've bitten off for her to chew.

"How long have you been working for my esteemed brother-in-law?"

"Three years," gBeto responds without thinking.

"Three years. And in those three years or the year you campaigned together for office; did you ever see a time when Walter Rutherford did something because someone made him? Did you ever see an idea he espoused that was not his own? Walter chose you to head up that economic development council without any input from me. He did that because he believes you will not only learn from the experience, raise your public profile as a result, but also because he knows what comes out of that council will be right for Texas. All of Texas, and not just the usual suspects."

"Don't you think it would be better if I only have to think about getting one thing straight?"

I shake my head, "Sometimes gBeto. Do you think Walter can think about only one thing at a time? He has to take care of today's business, plan for next year, plan for the rest of his term, plan for re-election, plan for that term, help other candidates get elected, find new candidates to run who will replace him, when his term is up. Candidates who will support that governor in marching towards the good life we want for everyone. So, no. You don't have the luxury of only focusing on one thing."

"You're saying it just gets worse," gBeto shakes her head as if wondering why she ever let herself get this far.

"I'm saying it only gets better. When you have authority and power you can achieve great things. One without the other leaves you in limbo, seeing what could be done, but not having the ability to deliver it. That's what we're trying to achieve. Matching authority with the power needed to get things done. Now in the area of law, you've walked into something that was totally foreign to you three years ago, and now you own it. Took you what? Six months to figure things out? But now it's second nature. Being governor's the same..."

"Governor? I thought you were pushing me for lieutenant governor."

"A stepping stone," I point out for her. "You get to be governor by being lieutenant governor. When you get to be governor you know what to do, because you've been in the room on most discussions for the last four years. And it's time we stop outsourcing what we want done to men. You are important to the change I've been working towards my whole life. A woman governor who can open the doors for other women. To wield power directly at least half the time, rather than by exception."

"Were you already thinking about governor when you recruited me for attorney general?"

"Walter's only in this job because I needed someone trustworthy to open the doors for you. I've tried to groom a lot of women candidates. Some wanted the job, but only out of vanity. Some wanted the job because they felt an obligation. You were the first woman I met who really had no self-awareness of who you could be. You only wanted to help the people you could, not realizing you have the ability to help many more than you ever thought possible. I can build a party around you. You're the first person I've met I can truly say that about."

"Why are you telling me all this now?" gBeto is still fighting the truth.

"Because you won't believe it until you see it. If you don't start preparing, you won't see it. I have a problem of building up your confidence. I have to make you believe in yourself, without spoiling who you are."

"Which is?"

"Someone who's not in this for yourself. You will always be the reluctant warrior. And I've studied history. The best generals are always the reluctant ones. Unfortunately, all the great generals have been men. But that's finally starting to change. Anyway, generals who came to a battle, cognizant of what he was asking his soldiers to sacrifice, always stood with them and not behind them. Led them into battle rather than sending them into the carnage that was about to happen. The great generals thoroughly defeated the enemy on the battlefield. Then they extended a hand in friendship when the battle was done, so everyone could return home and rebuild their lives."

"You see me as a reluctant general." gBeto has clearly never thought of herself as such.

"Many of those great generals came from backgrounds not much different than yours. They were self-made. They rose to prominence by their actions and their words. Actions first, with the inspiring words

128

driving those actions. I've heard you when you're passionate about something. I've heard you when you don't believe in the outcome. You are transparent. You are real. And you don't, for a single moment, think of your own well-being first. I'll have to work with you. At this level you can get away with that. But not at the next level. You have to weigh political consequences, because if you don't you will be out of office so fast it will take your breath away. And if you're out of office and those you supported are out of office, it will take a decade or longer to build back to the point where you left. We can't afford a lost decade. We can't afford to hesitate. We either move aggressively to grasp the authority and the power, or we go home and shut up, because then it's someone else's game."

Damn it. I've given her too much. She's not ready to accept who she is yet. Just got to keep reinforcing the truth. Show her the milestones along the way. She looks bewildered. Damn.

CHAPTER SIXTEEN:

LaMance Freeman, Deputy Attorney General
State of Texas

How do I tell gBeto her husband doesn't have control over the department he leads? I close the folder I've just finished reviewing and look out the tiny window of my well-worn office. My window on the world that I find every day is not the world we think we live in. The view may be of Waters Street in downtown Fort Christian, a typical urban street and maybe the drama playing out is a typical urban drama. Where people of all races and religions and sexual orientation seek to establish their own identity in an uncaring community.

That word always makes me stop to think. *Community. What is a community if not a place where people grow up, live and work together? A place where family creates tensions among people who experience rapid change, as they mature and the rest of the family accepts change at a much slower rate, hoping to hold onto the self they established years ago. That is the original conflict we each experience. Differing expectations where our elders try to slow the rate of change in the young and the young seek to rebel and establish their own identity apart from the parents and grandparents.*

At least that's the way it has been in my family as I grew up. Although I'm trying to be enlightened about it, I can already see I'm trying to let Keisha, my daughter, become who she is going to be, but if you ask her, she'll tell you I'm smothering her. Keeping her from experiences she desperately wants, but I know have the potential to change her forever and not necessarily in good ways.

Is that what happened to Officer St. James? Did his parents simply not engage him? Did he learn his life lessons on the street, the urban streets like Waters Street? Where all kinds of people pass the next day of their life, hustling to make a living, both legally and illegally. Encountering each other with cultural and racial frames of reference that crash into each other, sending confusing signals about intent and needs and expectations?

I see that if no one is interpreting these encounters, explaining that intent and perception may not be aligned, one can develop hostile reactions to the stereotyped other. If they wear a Hajib they will flee from a white male, because their religion says they should not be seen by anyone other than a husband or family member.

If a Black man is hanging out on the street late at night the presumption is he's scoping out how to rip off some White guy or sell drugs to him. If he encounters a Latino, that man is likely willing to do any job the White guy will, but for less money and likely will work harder to get the job done. And that makes the Latino a threat. Someone who will take the White guy's job if he isn't diligent, isn't smart and isn't careful.

And after that experience did Officer St. James decide the only way for him to survive on those streets was to have power over all the others? And that power and authority came from becoming a cop? Knowing all the other cops would have his back as he wielded that power and authority ruthlessly, carelessly, punishing all those others who had established themselves in ways that either debilitated him through drugs or directly competed with him for jobs. He got to be in charge. Got show them he was superior to them because he could punish them if he chose. Got to take them from their families by arresting them for one infraction or another. Got to send them away if he wanted to remove someone he saw as a direct threat. And he got to kill someone who may have challenged him in some way, or posed a threat to his authority.

From what I'm reading, I can see that may have been what happened with Bo Madison. Officer St. James saw an opportunity to bring down someone who had a bigger persona than himself. Someone who had been a star running back in college, been a hero in the war; but was now struggling to re-establish himself on the streets of Fort Christian.

I stand up and walk over to my tiny window on the world. Look out on Water Street. Watch the people who are going about their daily business, whatever that might be. *Are they concerned for their own safety? Concerned that those who are employed by the city to protect them, may actually be only wanting to control them? Herd them into a non-threatening routine? That's not what they are employed to do, but seems to be the result of who we hire to do a different job, the job of protecting us and our lawful rights from each other.*

A White man passes a Black man on the street below. They do not seem to see each other, hurrying along to their individual destinations. They do not stop and inquire about the day of the other. Is it good so far? Are they happy and healthy? Is the family good? Those are the things members of a community would stop and talk about. Show a concern for the other, rather than hurry away afraid the other may harm them in some manner. How did we get to this point? How did we establish communities of fear, rather than mutual support?

Maybe we just let our cities get to be too big. Maybe it's just not possible to get to know everyone, to remember a face when there are hundreds of thousands or even millions of people all around you. But all it really takes is lowering your own protections long enough to make contact with someone else. To be personal. To be real with them. To show you're interested in them. Open and willing to help if you can, in some way. That's all most people need from each other. Knowing that if something happens, you can reach out to the other and they will be willing to help, rather than turn you away.

I hear the door to my office open. I turn to find gBeto peaking in. "Am I disturbing you?"

I shake my head and return to my desk. I don't sit but do look down at the folder I'd just been reading. "Was trying to make sense of it."

"What?" gBeto comes in and closes the door behind her.

"Why a cop would kill an unarmed and unthreatening man. Any man. Black, White or Brown."

"You answer that question please share your insight," gBeto responds earnestly. "In the meantime, have you worked up the file on Michael St. James?"

I note she refers to him by his name rather than his title of Officer. She hasn't separated him from the person she knew growing up. I wish I could get her to tell me what she isn't about that time. I feel there's something there she won't touch, but I doubt I'll ever know, unless the media somehow digs it out and tells the world. And if that happens, it likely won't be good for gBeto, who clearly would prefer to forget it. "It's right here. Just finished reading through myself." I push the file across the desk.

gBeto looks at the file for a long moment before picking it up. Almost like she really doesn't want to know what we found out by going back through his records. Talking to friends and people who work with him. I'm starting to think we probably should be talking to some of the people he has arrested in the past. Get their side of his personality. "I'm sure the one thing you're wondering, is whether he broke house arrest."

gBeto looks up from the folder as if surprised. "I thought the photo was old."

"Actually, has a date and time stamp on it," I point out. "Copy in the file. Easy to read."

"Could it have been added later?" gBeto isn't happy to learn Michael St. James isn't playing according to the rules.

"Our experts say this is the real deal."

"He was there?" gBeto puzzles what that might mean. "What does the ankle bracelet say."

"That he wasn't. Says he never left his house."

"Have you been able to reconcile what's going on?"

"You may want to sit down," I gesture towards the chair she

usually sits in when she comes to visit. I sit down behind my desk. I see the dread in her eyes although she is trying to hide it, as she takes the seat more gingerly than usual. "This has implications for Nathaniel, so you need to just set that aside and listen."

gBeto won't look at me now. Apparently, that is what she was dreading. Maybe I'm misreading this. Maybe it's not her experience with Officer St. James, maybe it's what she's expecting to come out in this whole affair that will affect her husband's career.

"The official report is he was in his home the whole evening despite the photo. The official explanation is it must be faked, as to the time and day. But one of the officers Scottie interviewed away from the offices gave a possible explanation. Unfortunately, we can't use it because it's speculation, but this officer said it is possible to get the ankle bracelet off without it registering."

"I thought that was supposed to be impossible. That was why we rely on it." gBeto is the one trying to reconcile this insight. "Did he tell you how?"

"No. Just said he knows officers who have gotten it off in the past. Said this was no big deal, since St. James didn't go kill anyone while he had it off, which apparently happened in at least one instance. The officer who was on house arrest got it off and went and killed the key witness against him. He was not charged with the murder of the witness because the system records showed he was nowhere near the victim. All charges against him were also dropped because the key witness couldn't testify."

"The police officers have figured out a way to protect themselves from the law they're sworn to uphold." gBeto is starting to understand why I asked her to sit down. "I wonder if Nathaniel knows."

"You may want to ask him sometime. Since he came up on the force, I would assume if this officer knows about it, likely Nathaniel knows too."

"And hasn't done anything about it," gBeto shakes her head in incomprehension or regret.

I decide I need to get her to move beyond the implications for Nathaniel, "Scottie said the officer was willing to share that the liquor store in the picture is where St. James gets his. Now this is where we have another problem. Scottie interviewed the owner of the liquor store. He told her that St. James hadn't been in to purchase any alcohol from him since the shooting. But the officer told Scottie that St. James doesn't buy any alcohol. He worked a deal to provide protection for the store if the owner would give him a bottle of Jim Beam a week."

"The store owner was covering for St. James is what you're telling me."

"Nothing we could use in court," I remind gBeto. "Seems the owner was telling the truth. St. James hasn't been in to buy anything since the owner is gifting him what he wants, in a quid pro quo."

"Why do you keep saying we can't use it in court?"

"The officer Scottie interviewed told her point blank he wouldn't confirm anything he was saying, even under oath, because he'd never be able to get another job in policework if he testified against another cop. Didn't make any difference that St. James makes the whole department look bad. He just wasn't willing to trade his career to hold a bad cop accountable."

"This isn't just the Fort Christian department we're talking about here," gBeto realizes.

"No. And that's why you can't personalize this just to Nathaniel. I'm sure he's doing everything he can to clean things up. But it's like a tribal thing. Police officers standing together against the hostile world that would just as soon see them all dead."

That gets gBeto's attention. "Would you have us just putting one cop after another on trial to try to hold each one who crosses the line accountable, or do you go after the root cause?"

"Until recently we didn't even go after one cop. Last year ninety-nine percent of police officers who killed someone in the line of duty were not prosecuted. You couldn't even get information on the officers involved, although there was public release of the victim's information. Seems to me the fix is a change in the laws to remove the supreme court decision that provides protections to officers who either perceive a threat to themselves or someone else and use lethal response to address the issues. I read recently that before that decision, threats to officers, or others, were cited in reports filed after lethal shootings about thirty-five percent of the time. After the court decision it doubled. Tells me the officers figured out how to get away with murder."

"Are you saying we have to get the supreme court to reverse itself?"

"No, but we need to change the laws they were interpreting. Make any death a mandatory suspension without pay, a full independent investigation to determine the facts of the matter. Any officer who has more than one lethal encounter in a year is unable to serve in a capacity that requires her or him to carry a weapon for five years. I don't know. Make it near impossible for anyone who has a lethal encounter to have another."

"But what about officers who are involved with drug dealers or major crimes?" gBeto is trying to understand my thoughts on how to change the root causes. "They may find themselves in situations where they are forced to protect themselves and their fellow officers by using deadly force. What about them?"

"We can't let things get to the point where life is cheap. If we have an undercover cop who breaks up a cartel or gang and it ends up in a shooting affair, maybe the cop needs time away from assignments like that to regain perspective."

gBeto nods but goes on, "We don't do that with soldiers. We put them out there for a year or more and expect them to kill anyone perceived as a threat, whether they are or not. Then we bring them home and tell them they did a great and needed job, but we don't need them to do that anymore. Isn't that the same thing we're talking about with the elite squads in our police?"

"I think the issue is the people who have been in combat are the people who sign up for the elite teams in our police. And they do it because they see the mission the same, even though it's not."

"What do you mean?" gBeto still isn't following me.

"When our soldiers go fight, they are defending the country against people who want to kill Americans. For them it's kill or be killed. Simple. They're not trained to be a beat cop. They're not there to enforce laws. They are there to keep people from killing us. When someone returns, are they able to make the distinction that the people they are encountering now have constitutionally guaranteed rights? That they are only to use force when directly threatened? And that should be the exception and not the going in premise?"

"We have perpetuated a culture of militarism in our police force, rather than selectively applying military tactics and weapons in the rare occasion when we are encountering organized outlaw forces bent on committing major crimes," gBeto summarizes what I'm thinking.

"We can't arrest every officer, nor can we shut down the department and start over," I continue the line of thinking. "Even though more and more people are calling for us to defund the police. But I think we are at a point where we have to have a conversation about alternatives. There are a lot of good and dedicated cops who put their heart and soul into helping and protecting people.

"But it isn't just a few bad cops. Everyone stands behind the rogue cops. No one stands up to them and forces the issue. No one is accountable because the police unions will fight to make sure there is no disciplinary action. Make sure the members can continue doing their jobs and make sure the city or state continues to supply them with the latest military grade equipment. They can essentially fight a war on the streets of our cities, something that should be unthinkable."

"But what about riots? Who helps restore order?"

"Why are we having riots?" I push back. "Not because the people are happy with the way things are. The riots come from inequality, from injustice, from people perceiving they have nothing to lose by going out on the streets. Destroying the symbols of the oppressors. Why am I telling you these things? You know them better than I do. You hear all these things from Nathaniel, who's spent his whole life trying to solve just these problems."

gBeto nods, "Many lifetimes,"

"What? Is he reincarnated? A cop from another era?" I have to ask having not understood her comment.

"No," a sheepish smile from gBeto, good to see a change in her expression. "He has spent his whole life anguishing over reconciling the difference between the ideal and reality of policing. He once said it seems he's been at it at least three lifetimes. What he was really saying was a lifetime trying to learn how to be a good cop. A lifetime trying to ensure everyone experienced fairness and justice and another trying to affect the reality, so the ideal could be realized."

"And that's why it's important that he get back to work, get past this whole affair with Officer St. James, and be given the opportunity to bring about fundamental change by the mayor and council."

gBeto looks at me for a long moment, picks up the file and returns to her office.

CHAPTER SEVENTEEN:

gBeto Dahomey Brown, Attorney General, State of Texas

"Daniel Porter, Editor of the Fort Christian Morning News, and the four ministers of the Fort Christian, predominantly Black churches, are waiting to see you." Elsie, my administrative assistant announces at my open door. I knew they were coming, even have it on my calendar. *I can guess why they're here, to tell me they can't sit on things much longer.*

"Show them to the conference room," I begin.

But Elsie was expecting this, "They're already there waiting for you."

Elsie is nothing if not organized and intuitive. "Okay."

As I enter the room, all rise. I squeeze around the table in the old attorney general's office to shake each man's hand, even in this era where such is usually not considered hygienic. They don't seem to have a problem shaking my hand.

"Gentlemen, I appreciate you taking the time from your busy schedules to come share your thoughts. I assume you want to talk about the Bo Madison case. And if that is the situation, I have to let you know first off, I can only discuss publicly known aspects of the case since it is a continuing and ongoing investigation." We sit.

I look up at the picture of Walter Rutherford behind where the desk was when I took office. When I decided to occupy smaller quarters, to send a clear message that people in this office are equal in importance and status. That message has had mixed success.

"Madam attorney general," Daniel begins. "You are correct. We're here to discuss the Bo Madison case with you. There are things about the community response to it you need to know."

Thus, the four ministers of the Apocalypse? "I can only do my job properly when members of our community come forward and share relevant information as you are today. Again, I want to thank you for being here."

"If I might start things off by summarizing what you will hear from each of the others here today," Daniel Porter begins. Daniel has assumed the role of leader of the Black community, only because none of the ministers has been able to convince the others to follow him, not for lack of trying by each of them. "The internal affairs report is taking much too much time. Bo Madison was laid to rest on Saturday. Here it is Thursday, and still no indication from the mayor as to when it will be made public. Members of the various congregations are getting restless. Some are saying the mayor is deliberately slowing down the report hoping other events will distract the Black community so we won't properly register our dissatisfaction with the outcome."

"First of all," I interrupt. "Let me make a few things clear. I've spoken with Mayor Richards. I have been assured the report will be forwarded to council members in the next few days. Once they have had a chance to read it, the report will be made available to you, Mr. Porter, for you to publish relevant sections."

"But not in its entirety?" the Reverend Lomax of Mt. Zion AME church inquires as this has apparently been a topic of discussion with his congregation members.

"When I talked with Mayor Richards, she said the report would be released in its entirety, however, the appendices with specific personnel records would not be released as it would violate privacy laws." I inform the Rev, although I suspect he won't like that answer.

"We're talking about a report about a murder," the Rev Lomax responds immediately.

"With all due respect Reverend Lomax, that is for the courts to determine, not you and not me and not the members of your congregation." I push back, but try not to sound too defensive.

"But we all saw the videos," he is getting worked up. "There was no doubt about it."

"I saw the videos as well. But as I said, it is not for you, or me, or your congregation members to decide. We operate under a system of laws that delegate the responsibility to determine guilt to the court system. Now if members of your delegation are selected for jury duty and are assigned to a case against the officer involved, which is still to be determined, then that person may have a vote on guilt or innocence."

Daniel inserts himself at this point, "We understand the legal framework. But what I think Reverend Lomax is trying to communicate is there is a presumption of guilt out there from the videos that have been widely shown. There is anger that is about to boil over if the internal affairs report whitewashes this as nearly every other internal affairs report has over the years. We have no expectations that anyone in the department has suddenly grown a conscience."

"Then I interpret what you're saying is I need to be aware of the community's perception both that the officer is guilty of murder even without a trial, and that there will be violence in the streets when the report comes out, if it follows in the tradition of earlier such reports. Is that what you're trying to tell me?" *I'm trying to keep this all under control, but it seems these men are expecting me to do something I have no authority to do, which is to intervene with the mayor.*

"I am amazed my congregation has kept it together this long," Rev Lomax responds.

"Have you had a similar discussion with Mayor Richards?" I ask, wondering.

"She's a White lady. How's she supposed to understand what my people feel?" Rev. Lomax hides nothing. "She's part of the problem as far as my people are concerned."

"You've not voiced your concerns to her or the members of city council," I seek to confirm.

"We've not had a sit down like this with her, no." Daniel replies for the group.

"Why not?" I ask. "She's directly responsible to you for the city police department. I will only get involved if charges are to be filed."

"Governor Rutherford said he's asked you to look into the situation, even before the report is released." Rev Lomax blurts out. "Apparently he's not confident the internal affairs report will result in justice being done."

"The governor has asked me to begin an investigation, but it is a preliminary effort, not a preparation to file charges." I inform them. "We want to make sure justice is done. If our findings confirm whatever the internal affairs report shows, that should give comfort to everyone that the right determination was made regardless of the outcome."

"But what if your findings don't agree?" Daniel inquires, "As I assume is most likely."

"I am not making any assumptions. My most seasoned investigator is working on it, and LaMance Freeman is conducting the first level reviews. She will also be reviewing the internal affairs report when it becomes public. She is the lead prosecutor in the department. I hope that reassures you that we are not taking the events lightly. We have the best possible people reviewing what is known and continuing to gather more facts."

"If this goes to trial, who would be the prosecuting attorney?" Rev Lomax apparently has the most contentious congregation.

"That will be up to LaMance Freeman. As the lead prosecutor, she makes the assignments."

"Could she assign herself?" The Reverend Clyburn of First Baptist Church asks. He's been quiet up until now, but likely only

LOVE

because Rev. Lomax has decided to be vocal.

"She could, but that will be up to her," I am trying to make sure they don't point out a conflict for me given Nathaniel's position in the department.

"What are you doing to make sure justice is done?" The Rev. Lomax again.

"I am making sure the best people in my department are given a free hand to find the facts and take the appropriate action."

"In other words, you're not doing anything to help," Rev Clyburn sounds like he suspected this all along.

"Reverend Clyburn. How long we known each other? Since you came to Fort Christian. When was that? Five, six years ago?"

"Seven in May," he responds less angrily.

"In all that time have I ever not given you a straight answer?"

I see him consider my question for a moment, even though he clearly knows the answer and is just jerking my chain. Very quietly he responds, "Not that I recall."

"Have I ever not done exactly what I said I would?"

Now he scratches the back of his head, "If you give me a minute, I'll likely remember something."

"If you do, please tell me because I have no recollections such as that. I have pursued every criminal and every party seeking to twist, bend or reshape the laws of this state to create advantage for themselves against everyone else who lives here including you and your congregations. If Officer St. James committed an indictable offense, charges will be brought. He will go to trial. If not, then your congregation and Reverend Lomax's congregation and those of the rest of you will have to accept that justice has been done, in accordance to the laws of the State of Texas. That should be enough for you and your congregations."

"If it's a whitewash and you do nothing, then we know they got to you," the Reverend Lomax shoots at me once more.

"If the report establishes a threat to either the officer, other officers or a third party, then he would be within his rights to use deadly force to prevent harm. I know that's not what you want to hear, but it is the law of the State of Texas, as confirmed by the supreme court. I can't change that and neither can you."

"But we all know that wasn't the case here," Rev Lomax comes right back at me.

"You would deny the right to a trial by a group of his peers to this officer because you believe his guilt is explicitly shown on the videos that you and your congregation can use your judgment in lieu of a court appointed jury."

"There is no doubt," Rev Lomax is getting exasperated. "You've seen the videos. Why do we have to wait for justice?"

"You're advocating for mob justice," I pronounce.

"You may want to call it that, but it's justice just the same." Rev Lomax looks at Daniel who clearly sees where I'm going.

"When do you not advocate for mob justice then?" I push back at him. "And who gets to determine who the mob is? Would you want a group of White supremacists running around lynching Black folks all because they happened to be on the streets after the sun goes down? If you're out on the street then you must be guilty of something because I see you out when the criminals all come out. Just because no one has filed charges against you yet, doesn't mean you're innocent. Is that what you want?"

"You're painting an extreme picture." Reverend Lomax responds not quite sure if he should retreat or push on.

"No, I'm painting a picture of what it was like living in this

144

country not long ago. Within the lifetimes of people we know."

"You're saying we're better than them, because we won't do to them what they did and are continuing to do to us, every day." Daniel reasserts control of the discussion.

"Daniel, I know you're going to write an editorial about this as soon as the internal affairs report comes out. I know you're going to be wanting to make sure the viewpoint of the Black community is heard. I applaud that because all minorities need a voice in our society. And you're likely to report that I've not gone out of my way to ensure that justice is done.

I would ask you to reconsider making any statement about what I've done, what I'm doing or what I'm likely to do, because so far, the only authority I've had in regards to this case has been to respond to Governor Rutherford's request that I commence an investigation. And I have done that. I reviewed the information we have gathered so far. I've made suggestions, which the investigator is free to follow or not based on what else she finds. While we have a preliminary report now, it is just that. We will continue to gather as much information as we can find. Then we will compare it to what the department puts into their report. Most of the work is yet to come. It is too early for me to comment on the case beyond what we are doing."

"No insights that would describe whether a strong case exists?" Reverend Clyburn this time.

"As I said, since it is an ongoing investigation, I can't comment on specifics or findings so far."

"Are you going to be sequestered by the Governor?" Rev Lomax asks the question I expected right up front.

"He has asked that I let my staff run with this as much as possible," I confirm.

"Our White governor has taken the other Black advocate off the case, just as the White mayor took the Black commissioner off the case." Reverend Clyburn clearly isn't happy. I have to clarify this quickly.

"Nat- uh, Commissioner Brown supported the suspension of the commissioner during a deadly force investigation to ensure there is no undue interference," I inform them. "As the person ultimately responsible, he wanted to make sure the recommendations are free of direction, shading or any other attempts to minimize unacceptable behaviors."

"But the inmates are running the asylum in his absence," Rev Clyburn choses to describe the situation.

"I can't comment on your description, as I don't have the level of familiarity with the individuals in the department needed to make such a judgment." I hope he understands I'm saying he doesn't either.

"Nathaniel Brown is the only commissioner who's even tried to limit the effect the police union has been having. And even he's only had limited success." Daniel is preaching to the choir, but I can't say that, so I say nothing.

"Governor Rutherford has not taken me off the case. I am reviewing everything we are gathering. I'm asking hard questions of my team. We will ensure justice is done, whatever that means in this case. You just have to be patient. Your congregations need to be patient. Soon we will know how we are to proceed. Will this case be the end of such events in Fort Christian? Unfortunately, it is not likely, since we are only dealing with one person in this case."

"What are you saying?" Daniel jumps all over my comment, which I instantly realize I should not have made.

"I am hopeful the internal affairs team will look at not only the circumstances of this particular use of deadly force, but the systemic issues that may have led to it."

"Could you be a little more explicit?" Daniel thinks I may have given him something.

"Not at this time," I glance at the four ministers. "Is there anything else you would like to discuss?"

"You're saying you've not been sidelined by the governor, but you're letting your best people run with it. And what happens if we don't like the outcome of their efforts?" Rev Clyburn asks.

"I am the attorney general. I am responsible for the outcomes of our enforcement of the laws of this state. I am also accountable to the people of the State of Texas for the actions of my team and myself. If you are unsatisfied with what we do in pursuing this matter please come back for another discussion. You may even bring Daniel if you need an interpreter," I hope they laugh and they do. "You are always welcome here. Your thoughts are important to me, but the law is what I must enforce."

CHAPTER EIGHTEEN:

Estella Velasquez, gBeto Dahomey Brown's Campaign Manager

"Do I have to get you back in the mud wrestling pit and thrash you again, just like I did when we were freshman roommates at the university?"

I see gBeto laugh as we sit across from each other at Sunflower Café, a sandwich shop around the corner from her Water Street offices. "You were ten pounds heavier and a whole lot stronger than me then," she responds.

"You were rail thin as a freshman. Good thing Nate has fattened you up a bit."

"Thank you for introducing us, without your expert guidance then as now, I'd probably still be single to this day."

"Doubt that very much. One of those Wall Street lawyer types would have plucked you out of law school, and taken you away to New York."

"Well, there was…" she teases me because she had more than one proposal of marriage in law school, even though she was solidly with Nate, who stayed in Fort Christian after graduation to take a job with the police department.

"And Nate would have come to your rescue in his police cruiser. Would have driven it all the way to Austin from Fort Christian if he'd had to."

"You know, you're the only one I know who still calls him Nate," she muses. "Even I've taken to calling him Nathaniel."

"That's because you're both bigshots now, living with the rich folks over on Snob Hill."

"If I'm a big shot, it's because you got me elected in the first place. Don't go acting all innocent on me."

"And that's why it was important for us to have lunch today, of all days," I start into my spiel. "You need to reach out to a few key donors and start the money train."

"Who are they going to put up against me?" I'm surprised she doesn't already know, but with all the press on the shooting, I guess she may not be doing her usual round of conversations with key people.

"Hugh wants another shot at you, but I don't think they're going to give it to him," Hugh Stevens is in private practice, but does a lot of contract lobbying for Exxon. "The election was close, but you were both unknown quantities then. That's no longer the case. You have a track record, with a high favorability polling. Hugh's been out of sight for three years now."

"If not Hugh, who?"

"Susan Atwater seems to be the name I'm hearing from more than one person," I toss out to see what reaction I get.

"Susan? She's still in her first term as Tarrant County District Attorney."

I see gBeto consider Susan, who she has worked with in her current role.

"Why would she want to risk what she has for an uncertain shot?" gBeto asks.

"I think she may be smelling blood in the water over this officer involved shooting in Fort Christian. Since your office will likely prosecute rather than hers, maybe she thinks you're going to take all the negative press, particularly as they examine Nate's role in the whole thing."

"Nathaniel didn't contribute to the problem," gBeto responds defensively.

"But he didn't prevent it. So, he's going to be hung with it no matter what happens." I instantly see her head go down, *oops, didn't mean to do that*. "Hey, we're talking politically here, nothing more."

"I'm afraid for him," gBeto admits. "No telling how it will get spun. There are indications a faction of officers has been organizing, looking for a reason to get rid of him. He knows them too well, and isn't giving in on demands they've made. He once told me the union steward told him they'd be better off with someone less familiar who would want to buy peace, where Nathaniel's willing to go to war with them, because he knows how far the union will go before backing down."

"That's tough," I note. "Your own people working against your success. You'd think they would be happy one of their own was finally given a chance to lead the department, rather than always bringing in someone new, who doesn't know the community or the officers."

"But Susan's track record is really light. No major wins, or anything she can brag about. Just solid conservative management of the department. Is that what you see?"

"If the shooting blows up in your face, she'll still look good in comparison," I point out. "It's never about who will be the most qualified, or person who is best for the job, but who isn't in the doghouse at the moment. Whether it's because of a careless statement, or past indiscretion. Doesn't matter. Someone finds a way to spin things, you can walk on water and suddenly find yourself drowning."

"How do we put Susan in the doghouse?" gBeto asks.

I smile before taking a sip of my tea. "I'm working on that. She easily won in Tarrant County because she'd just won a high-profile tax evasion case when working in the Federal Prosecutor's office. Her name was mentioned in the New York Times, multiple times, just before the primary. That was all it took, because the incumbent retired and the seat was open."

"She's never run against an incumbent."

I shake my head hoping she sees what I do, but also hoping she sees she's still going to have to do the fund raising and go shake hands and kiss all the babies just like she did last time. I know campaigning isn't what she lives for. She seems to think of it as a necessary evil. She's probably right, but that's the only way you get a chance to prove yourself. Plunk yourself in the line of fire and see if you can quickly devise a strategy that will let you live to fight another day.

gBeto nods in understanding of my main point. "You have a list for me to contact?"

I slide the list across the table, "Same folks as last time with a few additions. People we vetted to make sure they were sympathetic to the cause. They will be expecting a call from you, as they've already been touched at least once."

gBeto looks over the list. I see her nod that I've recorded how much each party gave last election. I know she sent personal notes of thanks to each and every one of them. The names must look familiar to her. We offered to write them all out for her. All she had to do was sign them, but she refused. Said if the person was generous enough to give gBeto money, the least she could do was personally thank them.

"You working the issues?" gBeto asks, likely knowing I have.

"I have your base issues. Things you wanted to get done this term, but have just been too busy to get to putting all the other changes in place. Been thinking your slogan should be 'finish the job.'"

"That would imply I'm not going to run for office after this next term. Is that a good thing to put out there? Means anyone thinking of running will be comparing their philosophy and approaches to whatever I'm doing. Means I'll have to constantly defend myself in the press. Not sure I'm up to or wanting to do that."

"If you don't like it, we've got time to work something better."

"Think it would be best." gBeto dismisses that discussion.

"What are you hearing from Anne?" I decide I need to see if she will give me any insight that would address the constant rumors about her.

"Walter seems inclined to keep me on the ticket unless I really screw up. Got that directly from him."

"Anne's not saying anything?" She's the real power behind the Rutherford family and political strategy.

"She confirmed what Walter told me. Said I have a bright future if I don't screw it up."

"Sounds like the Rutherfords," I acknowledge. "Get out and meet people. When it's time to get out the vote, they'll take your call and maybe even a ride to the polling station."

I decide to sip my tea. See what's on her mind. But she doesn't pick back up on the conversation. She must be preoccupied by something else. Likely the shooting as that is having a massive impact and it's not always positive.

I finally ask, "Are you committed to making this race?"

She glances up at me, "Why?"

"I don't see or hear the fire I did last time. I know the public exposure on the recent events has to be having a toll on you, but frankly this is the most disconnected I've seen you. And I'm confused as to what that means."

"No, no. I'm in. Both feet. I am tired, but it's not just the one case. Lots of things swirling. I'm finding things that lit me up last time don't seem as important now. The system works, even though I questioned whether it did. Bad guys get sent away. Good guys are exonerated. Families stay together. Things seem to be working, and maybe that's all

I can hope for."

"Sounds like you've been trying to lift the hard stuff and are now getting frustrated you can't lift things all by yourself. You need to build coalitions, trade support. Get something done rather than just try another case that really doesn't matter, except maybe to the tax collector in the treasury."

gBeto looks at me piercingly. "What's worth trading away? Your integrity? Who you are? Or are you suggesting trading meaningless support for a policy you really don't care about to get one passed that you do?"

Now she has me worried. There's more going on than she's telling me. I have to assume it has to do with the shooting case, as that's the only high-profile case she's on at the moment. "Nothing's worth trading your integrity over. You can't walk away from who you are. If you compromise on that even once, you'll never recover. Never get back to the arena to fight another day. You get to go sit on the sidelines and watch the circus, because at that point that's all it is. You can't influence things from the sidelines. Can't make things better for others. That's who you are. Someone who's trying to make things better for others. Afterall, you made me a better mud wrestler."

gBeto looks at me for a long moment before what I just said sinks in. Then the smile appears, as she takes another sip of tea. "You taught me all the basics."

"Maybe that's what we need to do. Challenge Susan Atwater to a mud wrestling match. Keep the hose on so the mud just gets more and more slippery. Then you can hang that nickname on her: Slippery Susan. That should work. Just do that and we can save all the time and effort looking for donations and having debates."

"I like the way you're thinking. The way this fall is shaping up I'm not going to have a lot of time for debates or anything else." gBeto seems to be fading back into her immediate problems and not focusing on the campaign.

153

"Should I start looking for a replacement candidate for you?" I toss out to see how she reacts.

"Replacement?"

"Well, you don't seem to have much interest in your own re-election. Maybe I need to talk to LaMance. Last time we talked, she was still interested in moving up someday. Maybe I should suggest now is the time."

"LaMance could easily do the job, but she's never run a campaign."

"Neither had you until last time out," I remind her. Got to do something to shake her up as this lethargy just isn't going to make it.

"Are you thinking of running yourself someday?" gBeto asks seemingly from out of the blue.

"Me?" I have to stop and think for a moment, "I know what I do really well. I'm an organizer. I get things organized and then execute them according to a plan, but flexibly. When the opposition pulls some rabbit out of a hat, I can quickly pivot to make sure we still win at the end of the day. That's me. Crisis management with a year vacation between. I don't know I'd manage an honest job where you have to punch in at eight and head home at five with an hour for lunch. I don't work according to a clock. I get started when I get up. Five am somedays and ten on others. Some nights I'll work right through until dawn if that's what it takes. Other days I'm outta there when there's nothing pressing. Always something to do, but if no one's waiting on it, they'll get it before they need it. That's me."

"Whatever happened to what's his name? Josh, was it?"

I don't want to go down memory lane with all the losers I've spent a night. "I realized I don't need no guy. Besides they all stink until you get them in the shower, and then all they want to do is get in your pants. Don't think I'll be half of anyone anytime soon, if ever."

"Josh is long gone?"

LOVE

"I saw him last week, but only to wave from across the street. Got to maintain social distancing you know."

"That's sad…"

"Are you saying I'm sad?" I shake my head. "I'm not sad, I'm as happy as anyone gets. I got my health; I got excess weight. I can survive any drought, famine or plague, I got my freedom and I got my best friend from college, who I got elected to be State Attorney General, a position I never even knew existed until you ran for it. What do I got to be sad about?"

There's no significant other in your life. No one you care more about than yourself and no one who cares more about you than they do themselves."

"That's not true. I care about you more than I do about myself and you care about me more than you do about yourself. I know that. Only reason you'll take an hour out of the middle of the day to come have lunch with me when you don't even do that for Nate. You both work downtown, but you never have lunch with him and you're fucking married to him."

"Good analogy. You're not sad, I'm the one who's sad you don't have someone…"

"Knock it off. If I want someone in my life like that, I'll fix it. Believe me I can fix it. Just need to carry a bar of soap with me to scrub them down before I bring them home."

"You talking about a dog?"

"You weren't specific."

gBeto rolls her eyes, finally laughs. "Now I remember why you're my best friend. You can always get me to laugh when even Nathaniel struggles with that from time to time." gBeto considers her own comment for a moment then looks back up at me. "What kind of dog are you considering? A big shaggy dog you can just cuddle up with or a rat terrier who will be talking at you non-stop and always trying to herd

155

you towards it's bowl so you'll feed it?"

"Since you put it that way, likely need one of each. Cuddling is always important. In my line of work, I probably need a dog always talking at me. One that will make me stop talking long enough to listen to others."

gBeto tosses down her credit card, I toss in mine and she picks up the donor list. "I'll start working on this tonight. When you get the issues list done, lets have another lunch. Think this next month or so I'm gonna need some comic relief just to keep me sane."

CHAPTER NINETEEN:

LaMance Freeman, Deputy Attorney General
State of Texas

gBeto asks me to come down to her office.

Apparently, Fort Christian Mayor, Jenny Richards, is having a press conference to release the internal affairs report. When I get there, the door is open. I poke my head in as she isn't at her desk. I see her adjusting the volume on the television on the wall across from her desk. "You wanted to see me?"

"It's time. Now we'll at least have direction."

I nod and pull the chair around. I push the door closed to not disturb everyone else.

"The mayor give you any indications?" I ask.

gBeto shakes her head.

The mayor takes the podium and addresses the media present. I see the back of a dark-haired woman in the front row. I wonder if that's gBeto's new neighbor, *what's her name?*

"I have officially received the report of the Fort Christian Police Department's internal affairs Investigation into events involving the use of deadly force in the arrest of Bo Madison by Officer Michael St. James on the night of March 17th."

Mayor Richards opens the report to the executive summary page from what I can tell. "The investigatory team reviewed all physical evidence; all reports and videos filed from that evening including videos obtained from bystanders. They collected interviews from over one-hundred and twelve individuals who were either present at the time of the events, or were knowledgeable about the events in some manner. Following are the findings: Officer Michael St. James responded to a call from the owner of a convenience store at approximately one-fifteen am on the 17th of March. The complaint was that one Bo Madison had caused damage in the convenience store, by destroying unpaid for merchandise in response to a denial by the clerk to sell him beer. Mr. Madison left the store without harming the clerk, although he went outside and sat down on the curb, leading the clerk to believe he may return and potentially harm him for his refusal to sell alcohol."

"When Officer St. James and his partner Officer William Tissot arrived, they discovered Mr. Madison sitting on the curb with his head down, as if contemplating something. Officer St. James approached Mr. Madison and inquired if he had in fact damaged merchandise, and then refused to pay for it. Mr. Madison did not respond to the inquiry, but rather rose to his feet, rather unsteadily indicating that he was either inebriated or under the influence of some sort of drugs. Officer St. James attempted to discern the actual cause of Mr. Madison's behavior, but this only caused Mr. Madison to push the officer away and turn back towards the convenience store. The officer attempted to stop Mr. Madison from re-entering the store and was unable to discern whether the intent was to harm the clerk or do other damage in the store. Officer St. James called to Mr. Madison warning him to stop and return for questioning, an order which he did not comply with."

"Officer St. James used a taser to get Mr. Madison's attention, which it did. Mr. Madison turned around and charged Officer St. James, which led to the officer firing his weapon, striking Mr. Madison lethally with three bullets to center mass as he had been instructed in weapons training. This is the most complete summary of the events of that evening as pieced together by the internal affairs team and through questioning of both witnesses, and Officer St. James and Officer Tissot, who was present throughout."

One of the media people present has apparently raised a hand. Mayor Richards responds, "I see your question, and I will answer it in good time. I would like to finish reviewing with you the findings of the internal affairs team, and their recommendations, before I take any questions. Are you good with that?"

Apparently, the journalist is and the mayor continues, "The internal affairs team has found that Officer Michael St. James violated multiple procedures in his conduct that night. When he came upon the ultimate victim, the only offense noted by the person who filed the complaint was that he destroyed some merchandise and had not paid for it. Something that could easily have been handled in small claims court, rather than through what turned into a violent encounter. The clerk indicated he was fearful Mr. Madison might attack him, but in fact he had not and while worried that he might return to harm him, there had been no indication prior to Officer St. James arrival of any threat against the clerk. When the officer approached Mr. Madison, the victim did not respond. This was clearly not a threatening situation for the officer that would cause him concern for his own safety, and yet he drew his weapon and a taser. This would be a direct violation of department procedure and protocol."

Mayor Richards turns over the report and glances around the audience before continuing to read the findings. "Officer St. James approached the victim in an antagonistic manner and tone of voice, accusing him, rather than asking if there was some problem. Officer Tissot should have entered the store while Officer St. James engaged Mr. Madison, but he did not, electing to stay to help Officer St. James subdue Mr. Madison if necessary. This was a clear indication there had been a coordinating discussion between the officers before they encountered Mr. Madison."

"Officer St. James did not attempt to confirm the condition of Mr. Madison, rather relying on the untrained observation of the clerk that he may have been either drunk or under the influence. What was ultimately determined in discussion with Mr. Madison's doctor at the Veteran's Hospital, is that he was having a severe PTSD episode, which had been in progress for several hours at the time of the encounter. The doctor had received a call from Mr. Madison to that effect two hours prior. The doctor had advised him to use relaxation techniques to stop the flashbacks. Try to go to sleep. If he couldn't relax sufficiently to stop the episode, he might want to consume a moderate amount of alcohol, which apparently led him to the convenience store."

"Now while Officer St. James was unaware of the PTSD episode, he did not seek to understand the behavior of Mr. Madison, and in fact, Officer Tissot could not confirm that when Officer St. James shot Mr. Madison that he was in fact charging the officer to do him harm. He may have simply been seeking to escape from whatever images were in his head."

Mayor Richards shakes her head, "Officer St. James violated department policy by attempting to tase Mr. Madison when the latter was simply walking away from him. Department protocol is to talk with the suspect and determine his intentions. That was not done. Officer St. James then addressed Mr. Madison using repeated racial slurs, which also violated department policy. When Mr. Madison turned on Officer St. James he did not question his intent, but simply opened fire as Bo Madison continued to approach the officer. Another violation of department policy and procedure. Shooting the victim in center mass also ensured death, while a leg or extremity wound would have served the same purpose, if the victim's intent had been ascertained as threatening to the officer, another officer or a civilian."

Mayor Richards, has to stop for a moment to gather herself. "Despite the numerous violations of department policy and procedure, the internal affairs department finds no premediated intent. The officers reacted in the heat of the moment, perceiving a threat unto themselves and potentially the clerk, which caused them to not follow normal procedures, and thus react with lethal results although not intent. For that reason, the recommendation is that Officer Michael St. James should be terminated by the Fort Christian City Police Department and his license and certifications also terminated with no opportunity for reinstatement."

Mayor Jenny Richards gathers herself up and looks out to the audience. Upon the recommendation of the internal affairs department of the Fort Christian City Police department I am terminating the employment of Officer Michael St. James, and also recommending to the state certification bureau the termination of his licenses and certifications as a law enforcement officer in the State of Texas."

She nods to an officer just off stage, "I am also submitting this report and all appendices to the State Attorney General's office for review and potential prosecution if warranted. The State Attorney General's office shall have complete and open access to all notes, recordings of interviews and deliberations by the internal affairs team in their review. I am now willing to entertain your questions."

"Guess we saw that coming," I glance over my shoulder at gBeto who looks like she swallowed something very unpleasant.

"I want to hear the questions," gBeto responds almost annoyed.

"Mr. Holt," The Mayor recognizes the Fox News reporter in the front row.

"Mayor Richards, I counted eight violations of policy, each more egregious than the violation prior. Three shots to center mass when a leg or arm wound would have been procedure for a threatening situation. That had not even been confirmed. Prior coordination between the officers was noted, how can the internal affairs team say this was not premediated, or not the intent of the officer?"

"I have read the report, Mr. Holt, but I have not listened to the transcript of their deliberations, so I can't answer your question."

Tic Rogers continues with a follow-up question not waiting to be recognized, "From the description of the incident, do you believe the conclusions are accurate and the recommendations all that is warranted?"

"That is for the State Attorney General's office to determine. I have acted on their recommendations. That is all I am permitted to do. Either accept the recommendations or not. I believe the actions I have taken are justified based on the report."

"You're kicking it upstairs," Tic Rogers continues.

"The city council is not a judiciary body. We have no authority to judge the officers involved or impose a sentence. We have taken the most extreme personnel action we are permitted to under the law. We have concluded he is not fit to serve in law enforcement in this state ever again. We have seen to it that happens."

The dark-haired woman in the front row raises her hand, "Mayor Richards. Eight violations of procedure. How could that happen? I mean one violation of procedure would normally result in a suspension or remedial training or something. And Officer St. James has been on the police force for several decades. How does someone just completely go off the rails like that?"

"We will have to wait for the State Attorney General's office to make that determination." Mayor Richards clearly doesn't want to handle that question.

"Then the report does not address motivation." The journalist continues her line of thought.

"No."

"Does it indicate any recommendations for changes within the department? Fail safe procedures to make sure something like this can't happen again?"

"No."

"Is city council intending to look into it further?" same woman.

"We will when we have the full report from the State Attorney General's office. If they recommend we change procedures, we will take that under advisement."

I glance back at gBeto, "Looks like our scope is increasing."

Tic Rogers raises his hand again. The mayor recognizes him, "Is Officer St. James free since he is no longer in your employ? He was under house arrest, although he seemed to have found a way around that. Is he still under house arrest?"

"I am waiting for instructions from the State Attorney General's office before we remove the ankle bracelet."

Then I see Daniel Porter rise to his full height. "Mayor Richards."

He is greeted by silence, finally the mayor responds, "Yes?"

"You have said repeatedly today that the city has done everything it is authorized to do. If I had walked up to Bo Madison and shot him three times center mass outside a convenience store, I would not be sitting home with an ankle bracelet waiting for the State Attorney General's office to give you instructions. I would be sitting in a jail cell waiting to be charged. Why is a police officer given special treatment? Why isn't he sitting where any other citizen of this city would be sitting and facing the same prospects?"

"You are not a sworn officer of the city, Mr. Porter. You are a civilian. The laws apply to you differently than they do sworn officers as determined by the laws of this country and affirmed by the supreme court. While I understand your frustration…"

"Outrage, Madam. Outrage."

Softer response, "I understand your outrage, Mr. Porter."

"No Ma'am, I don't think you do. Bo Madison was my friend. My friend is dead. That is an objective fact regardless of what the supreme court may wish to interpret. All men are created equal. That is an observation of the founding fathers. If I am to believe the founding fathers, then I should be treated exactly the same. And yet, you have just stated I would not. You have shaken this country's founding principles by the actions you have taken today. You would cause every American to question whether the intent of our founding fathers is being observed in the country they founded two hundred and fifty years ago. Are you saying that the ideals of this nation have not endured as Abraham Lincoln feared? Are you saying we do not have a right to equal treatment under the law? If your course of action is to win out, then we are all the poorer for being Americans."

"I think you need to make a call to get her off the hook," I suggest to gBeto.

I watch as she dials a number and watch on television as the mayor at first ignores her cell phone ringing in her pocket, but she doesn't know what to do with Daniel Porter. She removes the phone from her pocket and looks hoping for salvation, sees the number and answers. I hear gBeto's side.

"Tell Mr. Porter that the State Attorney General's office will be picking up former officer St. James at his home in thirty minutes and transporting him to a state correctional facility where he will be held without bond, pending arraignment for charges that will be specified in court tomorrow."

We watch as Mayor Richards repeats, almost verbatim, gBeto's statement. We watch as Daniel Porter turns to look at the camera, realizes we are watching, and nods to gBeto. "I thank the State Attorney General for taking swift action to see that justice is done in this instance and ensure that no man or woman is treated differently under our constitution and set of laws." Daniel Porter takes a seat.

"I too thank the State Attorney General for taking swift and decisive action in this case, and commend her for not specifying the charges until she and her team have had an opportunity to review the report of the Fort Christian City Police Department internal affairs team. I would ask, however, if possible, could she return our one and only incarceration ankle bracelet? We never know when we may have need for it, and would prefer not to have to contact the department of corrections to find out what happened to it after former Officer St. James is transported."

gBeto apparently texts the mayor who looks down at her phone and then back up to the audience with a smile. "The State Attorney General has just given me assurance we will get to keep our ankle bracelet. And she reminded me I need to inquire as to whether it is operating properly given certain reports that have surfaced."

The dark-haired woman in the front row then raises her hand, "Mayor Richards. Given this case has been transferred to the State

Attorney General, does this mean you are reinstating Commissioner Brown?"

I notice gBeto watching now with rapt attention, phone in hand.

"Thank you, for your question. The answer is no. Questions have been raised by the events. They were not addressed by the internal affairs report. I feel compelled to spend time with the leaders of the department to evaluate more fully what the commissioner could have done and what he can do at this point to ensure we have no further incidents like what has recently occurred. Until I am satisfied, with a clear roadmap to address deficiencies in the department, the commissioner will be placed on administrative leave, rather than suspension."

CHAPTER TWENTY:

Anne Rutherford, Political Dowager Almost

Everyone is here except gBeto, who for some reason has been delayed. Probably talking to Nathaniel about the surprise announcement. I'll give her another few minutes. "Cindy, how is everything at the hospital? Are my friends on the board providing the equipment you need for your specialty?"

Cindy Ho is a slight dark-haired woman whose hair is always pulled back into a tight bun. As the head of Neurosurgery at Dover General she is highly respected both in her profession and the community. She talks with all the docs and most of the business leaders frequently. She is always a great sounding board for political considerations. "We are looking at a few things we've suggested might make sense near term. But for the most part, the robotic surgery equipment still needs another turn or two of maturation before I'll be wanting to have it perform my surgeries."

"But it is getting closer?" I ask.

"For general surgeries they are fine now. It's the fine incisions in brain cells that worry me. Yes, they should be more capable than a human surgeon of being precise, but a machine only does what it's programmed to do. There is not sufficient uniformity in the brain formations that I'm ready to just sit back and turn it loose."

Aamaal Mojazza listens politely, the head of the criminal division of the State Attorney General's office, she works for and is a major supporter of gBeto. She has only recently joined our little strategy group. A clear thinker, she also brings a fresh perspective about the growing minority communities across the state. "Aamaal, I take it you're knee deep in the investigation of former officer St. James?"

Aamaal adjusts her headscarf as she turns her head to look at me, "Yes. Things are very busy right now." She glances up at the clock and then offers, "I suspect gBeto is on a call with the governor. He's been calling her every day looking for an update."

"Walter understands just how sensitive this whole thing has become. I understand his need to closely monitor what's being done."

"I'm sure she will be right along."

LaMance Freeman is sitting next to Aamaal. She looks worried. "Do you need to be somewhere else, LaMance?" I decide to ask directly. I seem to startle her.

"No, no. Just multitasking. Getting things mixed up in my mind. I use my work computer to keep things straight. When I'm somewhere else, I can't refer back to see how things relate. I'll be fine as soon as I get back in to work in the morning."

"Estella, has gBeto sent you anything?" Since this is a political strategy session, it really is Estella's meeting as the campaign manager, but gBeto is the candidate. We can't go too far down the road without her.

Estella shakes her head as she scrolls on her phone.

"Well, we might as well get started while we're waiting for gBeto. I want to thank each of you for carving a few minutes out of your very busy schedules. The purpose of this meeting is to advise gBeto on how to handle the issues of the day, to enhance her re-election prospects. And each of you bring a unique perspective that will be essential to realizing that goal. You've all met Aamaal this evening. She will be a great help in providing additional perspectives we need to ensure gBeto is addressing. With that brief introduction I'll ask Estella to conduct the meeting."

"Thanks Anne," Estella glances at the door and shrugs. "Sometimes we have to just keep moving and not look back. I think tonight may be one of those nights, but no worries. I'll brief gBeto after the meeting if necessary. I'd like to start out by asking several of you for your impressions of how gBeto is handling the upcoming trial. I think we've all been surprised that the city has been quiet. The kind of demonstrations that have become common elsewhere haven't occurred here, at least not yet. Although I understand there is significant anger that is being kept in check by the leaders of the Black community."

Cindy starts, "You know, I don't have much time to watch the news. My impressions come from conversations with colleagues, the support teams at the hospital and patients and their families. What I've been hearing so far, is people seem to trust that gBeto isn't going to let this go the way other shootings have. A White cop kills a Black kid or adult and walks. The fact he's been incarcerated since the report was released took some of the pressure off. The fact that she stood up and did it publicly was also important. For the moment I think she's in a good place."

"I would agree, although I'm talking to the political people, not the average voter," I begin. "The people I talk with are calculating every word, every nuance, every potential vote defection. But what seems to be working at the moment is that gBeto is acting and not talking much. That seems to be something a lot of people like. We've had politicians who are only words, and the words are either hollow or flat out lies. It's refreshing when someone just goes and does what needs to be done without having to stand up in front of everyone and explain the obvious."

Aamaal nods agreement, "People in my community are watching, but just like gBeto, they aren't saying much. They disbelieve anything has really changed. They think, or maybe fear, somehow the court will find a loophole and he will go free. Everyone seems to know what happened was wrong. Everyone fears something like it could happen to them or their child. The fact Bo Madison was dealing with PTSD, and the officer didn't even take the time to try to understand what was happening to him, was unforgiveable for many of us. We came from those battlegrounds. We saw what Bo Madison saw. We felt the pain he experienced, and have the visions he tried to erase from his memory.

LOVE

We understood and maybe that made it just that much harder for us to accept what happened to him at the hands of a man who should have gone to fight for his country, but instead chose not to."

"LaMance?" Estella asks.

"It's real hard for me to be objective since I'm the one carrying out her instructions on this. I ask people in the Black community what they think. I get answers that seem to be a lot like what Aamaal just described. Fear, incomprehension, disgust and resignation seem to be the things I hear and see more than anything. And what do they think about gBeto? I don't get much that's negative because most people who know me, know I work for her. They're real discrete about saying anything negative. I don't know, but like Cindy said, people seem to be giving her the benefit of the doubt right now. Anything goes south and they'll be out in the street in a nanosecond. That's the feeling I get, although no one is saying anything to me about it directly. And that's to be expected 'cause most everyone knows I work closely with the police on nearly every case I prosecute."

"What about you Estella?" I ask since she's not volunteered anything yet.

"What am I hearing? Crickets. People aren't talking. I don't quite know what to make of it. Normally people are blowing off steam, talking it up, taking shots, expressing their disbelief and their expectations of an unchanging world in the face of all the change that is taking place at such an accelerated rate. Crickets makes me nervous. Makes me think the water is slow boiling in the pot, and any nudge will turn up the heat and blow the top."

"You're not at all comfortable." I try to summarize what I thought I heard.

"For gBeto? No. I'm not, because I don't know how people are seeing this. If she sends the son of a bitch to prison for the rest of his unnatural life, there will be people who think he should fry instead. If they fry him there will be people who think he should have been released. Others think losing his license is as a bad as Bo Madison losing his life? I don't get that, but that's just how some people think. That's why the crickets make me nervous, because those folks aren't letting off steam. Does that make sense?"

"And you think they're going to punish incumbents? Is that what you're saying?" Cindy asks.

"I don't know. When people stop talking, that's not a good thing for politicians. You don't know which way the wind is blowing. It's like we're in a dead calm. Everyone is waiting for the wind to pick up. When it does, we'll finally know which direction the people are heading. Which way we need to go. But until then, we got nada and I don't like that."

"What do we do in the meantime?" Aamaal asks. "I'm new to all this,"

"The only thing we can do," Cindy offers. "Prepare for any contingency, putting the most time in the direction we think we should be going, but preparing to pivot on a dime if we need to. And that means not being too committed to our preferred course of action, not being too public about it, but being more suggestive if you know what I mean."

"I agree with that," LaMance offers. "And I think that's where we are, really. We've been consistent in what we are doing, but we've been looking at a lot of options. Not studying them or anything, but looking at them. Trying to figure out 'what if something takes us in that direction'. I think we're okay."

"You see, that's where we differ," Estella speaks up. "My experience is people drink their own bathwater until it's too late. Candidates who fail are those who don't do everything they can possibly think of and more. Candidates who don't take anything for granted. You're telling me you think the people are with gBeto. Well, they were three years ago. But that's a point in time and a lot has happened in the world, in their lives, to each of us, but we're not factoring that in. We're thinking people know her better now. Think people like what they've seen. That's not necessarily true. We've liked what we've seen, but we're five people out of the millions who have the opportunity to vote. Unfortunately, we won't have any idea who those people will be until after they've left the ballot box. We can do everything we can to get our people to the polls, and still, that will be a small number of those we will need to carry this election. If we don't approach this election every single day as if we are behind in the polls, on election day we will find we are."

"The voice of experience," I pronounce. "We need to take that into consideration, but we also need to be smart about this election and not get out ahead of ourselves. Research suggests that some people, and I would presume that includes most of the people in this room, have already made up their mind who they are going to vote for. Some of those will have decided they want gBeto regardless of who the other side puts up. Some will never vote for her, generally because of a party affiliation other than ours. In most cases they are against her because of some ad, or gossip or singular event that has stuck in their minds about her. Our job is to touch all those folks lightly. Let them know we are a big tent and we are welcoming of their support should they wish to provide it. Our task is to provide hard evidence to everyone else that gBeto is the better choice. And until we are sure of the other candidate, that is hard. Incumbency goes a long way because we have a record to point to. But it only takes us just so far, because in that record people will find things they like and things they hate, no matter what we think. We have to make sure people see the good things they want to see."

"Any time you want my job..." Estella kids me with a big smile.

"Okay," Cindy moves us on, "What do you want us to do?"

"Talk to everyone you know," Estella responds. "At this point it's more of a listening game than a selling game. Find out what they like and dislike about the job gBeto's done. Try to go deep if you can. What specifically bothers you about her, about the decisions she's made, about the public statements, how she addresses an audience, how she answers questions. Anything that goes into forming an opinion about her."

"Already doing that," Cindy responds. "Who do I give the

download to?"

"Me for now, until we get our research director on board," Estella responds. "Mark Roberts who did that for us last time has gone onto the Governor's re-election team. I need to find someone else who is as good. That's an issue. The other side grabbed my next choice already. I'll likely have to go outside and bring someone in. I don't like to do that, but sometimes you don't get a choice."

"What else can we be doing?" LaMance inquires.

"Issue research," Estella responds. "When you're talking with people, what are the issues they bring up? What are the hot buttons, if you will? What are the topics that will drive the choice of candidates? We have some research on that a polling firm did for us last year when we were trying to get a sense if we had an issue on electability in the upcoming election."

"What did it show?" I ask, not to change the subject but to give everyone an insight into what she means.

"A year ago, it showed gBeto had the highest favorability rating of any elected official in the state," Estella says proudly. "But she was still new in the role, had steered clear of personal controversy and was seen as someone who is authentically interested in equally applied law and order, what I still think is the primary hot buttons for this upcoming election. However, that was a year ago. A number of cases have been tried under her, a number of decisions made and new laws put into effect. The first interpretations of those new laws are going through the courts now. Those are the places where discontent can hide. And the elephant in the room is how the general public is perceiving her handling of the pending trial of former officer St. James."

"And there are lingering questions about the fact the mayor still has not reinstated Nathaniel," I point out knowing neither LaMance nor Aamaal would bring it up out of loyalty. "People are assuming there is something wrong there. Assuming he either knew things about the officer, about the culture of the department, knew something, or did something or maybe even failed to do something that could have saved

LOVE

Bo Madison's life if he had simply acted."

I see everyone look down, including Estella, "And your reactions confirm there's an issue there. We will have to confront it early in this effort. It may... and I know none of you want to hear this... but it may be better if Nathaniel simply resigns, because then it wouldn't be a lingering distraction."

gBeto enters the room and addresses me as she takes her seat next to me, "That won't happen. Nathaniel did everything he could to get rid of former officer St. James, but the union fought him every inch of the way. And the union ultimately decided they needed to get rid of Nathaniel, which is why he's still on administrative leave. They keep raising issues for the administration to go chase down. Only when all the evidence is brought forward, there's nothing there implicating Nathaniel. It's all the union manipulating the situation hoping to get a more pliable commissioner."

"This is the first I've heard of the union..." I begin.

gBeto responds before I can go further, "And you won't hear any more about it, because Jenny Richards needs the union to support her in order to get re-elected. I hate to be that blunt about it, but it happens to be the case. The union put a lot of money and manpower into her first election. She cut a deal with them, and that deal was she would appoint someone from their ranks. What the union didn't count on was she would pick Nathaniel, who wasn't their candidate. And who it was doesn't matter anymore. But their current efforts are aimed at getting their candidate in and Nathaniel out."

"How does this play?" Estella asks, confirming she was unaware of what was going on behind the scenes.

"I'm trying to convince Jenny that she can win without the police union support. What she's afraid of is if she doesn't go along with them, they will convince the other unions to back her opponent. They have a history of punishing mayors who try to confront them, and they've successfully brought the other unions with them when they have. But I think the trial is going to bring out the role they played in protecting a dangerous person for decades. And it will also show they have played the same role protecting other cops who feel they can get away with murder any time they want. That was what Nathaniel was trying to change, and that's where he got crosswise with the union."

"Was the union the reason that suspension ordinance was passed by council?" Cindy asks.

"Suspension of the commissioner?" gBeto seeks to clarify.

Cindy nods.

"They wrote the original draft and sold it to council," gBeto confirms. "Nathaniel went along with it at the time because he was trying to get the right from council to terminate any officer who the commissioner determined to be a threat to public safety. That was how he intended to send former officer St. James into retirement. Only the union was successful in blocking that companion piece leaving Nathaniel exposed."

"The key to reinstating Nathaniel to help your re-election is convincing the other unions to support the mayor's re-election, if the police union actively works against her and you," I summarize.

CHAPTER TWENTY-ONE:

gBeto Dahomey Brown, Attorney General, State of Texas

As the women get up to leave, Anne leans over to me and asks, "Would you stay for a few minutes? I have a message I need to deliver."

I nod, "Need to talk with Cindy for a moment, but I'll be right back."

I approach Cindy who is finishing a quick conversation with Estella, "Thanks for all your help, I really appreciate all the people you have talked to on my behalf. The only reason I'm in this job is because of you and the rest of the girls who have stepped up to support my candidacy."

Cindy grasps my hand, "We have to stick together if we want to lead change."

I give Cindy a hug and as I move away, she says quietly, "How do we separate the union support?"

"The police union has always been a fair-weather friend," I observe for her. "We just need to show the others we have their back. It may mean singling out the police union, but they started this with their irresponsible behavior."

"Are you willing to say that publicly? Take them on directly?" Cindy seems to be afraid of alienating one of our core constituencies. I understand her concern. We normally wouldn't think of taking them on.

"I'm hoping the courts will do that for me, although normally they wouldn't make any statement about the role of a union in protecting the rights of its members. But in this case, they may well note the part they played in keeping former officer St. James on the street."

"Is that in writing anywhere?" Cindy asks knowing how hard it will be to do anything about the situation if it's not.

"I'm going to make them think they can control it by referencing his fitness report, which is in his personnel file. I plan to subpoena it and hope the court supports my request. Make the union think they can control it there."

"Because they will say it's a protected document," Cindy notes. "Amazing to me how similar the issues are in city government and hospitals. Seems every decision comes down to walking the fine line between protecting someone's rights and ensuring only competent people are delivering services."

"It's always complicated when you're talking about someone's paycheck, and the ability to feed a family. No one wants to do that to someone. But we also have to balance it against the larger public."

Cindy nods, "Sounds like we have our work cut out for ourselves. I'm pleased you at least have a strategy in mind. Now the question is whether that strategy will work or we find ourselves on the outside looking in after November."

"With your help and insights, I know we can make our case to the voters. Hopefully they're listening."

Cindy touches my hand again and nods as she heads for the door.

I say my thanks to each and return to Anne as Estella closes the door behind them, "Sorry…"

"I'm sure my brother-in-law had important matters to discuss with you," Anne responds and I'm surprised she knew Walter had called just as I was getting ready to leave.

"The governor only calls when he needs to have a better understanding of matters of importance." I respond, but there is something in her tone of voice, almost a cautionary undertone.

"This may take more than a moment," Anne turns to take a seat

LOVE

and I follow.

"Sounds ominous," I respond to recognize what I think I'm
hearing and let her know she can get right to the point, which Anne
usually does anyway.

"I had a conversation with Walter you probably have not," she
begins. "And it's about the case you are building against former officer
St. James."

Anne has never crossed this line before, relaying a conversation
she had about a case I am prosecuting. She is always to the point, and
she is incredibly well informed. But she has never discussed the
specifics of a case with me, although she has pointed out that some
cases have potential political implications I need to consider. *Where is
she going now?*

"Walter expressed concern that groups seem to be forming on
both sides of the question."

"What's the question? It seems to me we have indicted him based
on evidence that he may not have acted to protect himself or his fellow
officer when he killed Bo Madison."

"You are looking at the evidence and I have not," Anne takes a
step back. "But from what I understand, and even your statement seems
to confirm, you lack evidence to conclusively prove your case."

"It goes to intent. What was the officer's intent?"

"And that is where your case hasn't been made, am I correct?"

"We are still gathering evidence that may establish intent, but you
are correct," I admit still wondering why we are having this
conversation. "At this point in time we do not have conclusive evidence
of intent."

"You are walking a fine line," Anne observes, hoping I will see
the situation as she does. "By arresting him as you did prior to reading
the internal affairs report you raised expectations, particularly in the

177

Black community about what would happen. From a political perspective the worst situation would be where you go to court and lose. If this man is set free after what everyone has now seen a dozen or a hundred times in that video, the streets will most certainly erupt in violence. This close to the election that will not help anyone's re-election chances, and that includes the governor."

"I agree. But the court will decide based on the law and the evidence…"

"What are your thoughts about obtaining unquestionable evidence of intent?"

"About what would constitute intent?" I'm not sure what she wants to know.

"What would convince a jury he intended to kill Bo Madison before he did."

I nod understanding Walter's concern and why he's not raised the issue to me in the context Anne has. Her concern is about the election impact of how I'm doing my job. Walter can't discuss that with me because it could be construed as applying political pressure on me to affect the election, which would be unethical for me and him."

"As I've informed the governor, my team continues to talk to individuals with knowledge of the incident, of the former officer's statements and his behavior. We are taking statements, identifying potential witnesses we may ask to testify, and gathering any physical evidence that may help."

"You still have a hole in the case." Anne puts it bluntly.

"More than one," I admit. "But at this point in any investigation that is not uncommon."

"Are you expecting someone will come forward who is willing to testify? Someone credible enough it won't be dismissed?"

"Expecting may be a stronger term than I'd normally use," I

clarify for her.

"What do you do if you don't have clear intent?"

"I'll review all the evidence, the statements, the likely witness line-up and the ghosting we will do of the defense. I have a whole team that's looking at the probable evidence the defense will present and the likely witnesses and what they will likely say. We will walk through the whole case as we expect it to play out. Now there is a high probability the defense will have something we haven't identified. Some piece of evidence, some witness we don't know about. But at the moment we think the primary defense will be that we haven't proven beyond a shadow of a doubt, prior intent. That's why we are almost singularly focused on how we close that gap."

"And if you can't close it, what do you do?" Anne comes back to the same question I've been wrestling with and discussing with my team every day.

"I won't know the answer to your question until I do the final walk through with the entire team playing out the various scenarios."

"I am certainly not in a position to advise you on the merits of your case," Anne begins, and I know I'm about to finally be told what Walter is thinking, "But I have a question for you. Will it be better for everyone concerned to drop the case if you are sure to lose it than to go into court and have a jury reaffirm that the judicial system favors White people over Blacks?"

I never expected to be asked this question. But I have thought about it every day. "If I drop the case with my public actions to date, then my political career is finished. If I go to court and lose the case, my political career is finished." I summarize where I find myself in the context of the question, she could ask that Walter could not.

"As someone who has watched the politics of this community for a number of years, I would agree with your assessment," Anne is now dead serious. I've not seen this Anne before even though I knew it was there. "And that means your only choice is to find the evidence and win the case."

CHAPTER TWENTY-TWO:

Mayor Jennie Richards, City of Fort Christian, Texas

Daniel Porter sits in the front row of City Council Chambers with what I call the four wisemen. The ministers of the predominantly Black churches in Fort Christian. I nod to them as they each take their seats. I'm not sure what they are interested in discussing, since I've done all I can about former officer St. James. But I'm sure they have some grievance they wish to file with the city. We will listen and decide what we can do.

I call the meeting to order, take the roll and approve the minutes of the last meeting. "With approval of the minutes we have arrived at agenda item three: Voice of the Community. Does anyone have issues they would like to discuss with council this evening?" I intone.

Of course, Daniel Porter is on his feet and quickly approaches the microphone as if he were ready to fight anyone else who wanted to speak first. "Mayor Richards and members of city council. I am here this evening with the leaders of the congregations of the four predominantly Black churches in Fort Christian. Together we constitute the Black Fort Christian Coordinating Committee. The combined congregations represent more than sixty percent of all Black families residing in Fort Christian. And for that reason, we believe we can accurately represent the prevailing sentiment of the Black community."

"You have informed us of how you have determined your legitimacy in the past, Mr. Porter. There is no need to revisit how you justify your claims. What would you like to discuss with council?" I respond.

"Police Commissioner Nathaniel Brown remains on administrative leave." Daniel intones.

"He does," I confirm.

"While our members were concerned that a Black police commissioner was suspended when a White officer killed a Black man, we gave the city a chance to show it was going to improve the work performed by the internal affairs organization in the recent investigation through your ordinance. I would like to go on record as saying the Black Fort Christian Coordinating Committee supports any action by city council to repeal that particular statute. We do not see where the police commissioner did or would have had any negative effect on the process the department used to investigate the incident and produce a set of recommendations in the report released by council."

"Excuse me, Mr. Porter. Are you saying city council should repeal that ordinance?"

"Yes, ma'am. We believe it is better for the leadership of the department to exercise leadership rather than let lower-level functionaries issue a report of such consequence."

"Your recommendation is noted," I inform him and motion for him to proceed.

Secondarily, we believe the city has not been transparent as to why the commissioner has not been reinstated. If the city believes the recent investigations have uncovered malfeasance on the part of Commissioner Brown, then the city should take immediate action to terminate his appointment. However, if the city has not uncovered any malfeasance, or dereliction of duty, then we would expect the city to reinstate Commissioner Brown. He needs to exert some semblance of control within his department. The lack of strong leadership at the top is most disconcerting. The absence of strong leadership at this particular point in time has made the situation unacceptable to our congregations and constituencies. We expect more from you mayor, and members of council. You represent us, but none of us would agree with how you have voted recently. None of us would be willing to work for the re-election of any of you, given your washing your hands of a significant responsibility."

"Mr. Porter, your declaration of political intentions is interesting information, but totally irrelevant to this discussion."

"Is that why you choose to ignore our complaints?" Daniel Porter reacts to my comment. "Because you have written us off? That is not acceptable either. We are your constituents and you represent us, whether we voted for you or not."

"We are not ignoring your complaints. We put them into consideration with all other suggestions. In community advisory meetings the best suggestions rise to the top. We don't make those determinations; your congregation members and readers do. There are always opportunities to be appointed to those boards. I would suggest your ministers talk to their congregations and seek volunteers to engage with the city in that fashion."

"We have made a note of your suggestion madam mayor, but in this instance, we would like to call the question, so to speak. Let's end the debate. If you have any cause to maintain Commissioner Brown on administrative leave, we recommend you terminate his contract and go find someone who will have your confidence to make changes in the department. Changes that will ensure no officer will ever take the life of another Black man in this city."

"Is that your demand, Mr. Porter? That Black men are no longer to be held accountable for criminal activity in this city?"

"That's not what I said, madam mayor..." he begins backtracking awfully quick.

"Then what is your demand?" I have to ask.

"That no Black man be killed by a police officer, since the officers of this city seem to have difficulty determining what is a criminal offense and what is not."

"A more reasonable demand, Mr. Porter, but also not one I can support as mayor. We have what I would describe as a robust policy about officer involved shootings. We have recently enacted the very policy about how the department shall handle such events you are

LOVE

advocating we repeal. We are now in the process of witnessing how that policy plays out when invoked. I would recommend to council that we make no adjustments to the policy until the current events play out fully and we can evaluate whether it served as a constructive process or impeded clarity and due consideration of all events and known facts. Then we may ask you to come discuss potential changes in a work session, rather than open meeting. In a work session we can have a more complete dialog around the subject and have more time to thoroughly consider all facets."

"Is it the position of this administration that the will of the people is of no consequence? That the voice of the people is not your concern? That the only recourse to your blatant unwillingness to consider our recommendations is to take our complaints to the streets where others may join us in demonstrating the powerlessness of this government to impede the will of the people in this matter? Is that what you're saying madam mayor?"

CHAPTER TWENTY-THREE:

Nathaniel Brown, Commissioner of Police
City of Fort Christian, Texas

I inspect the dining room table I have just completed setting. Candles lit. Wine glasses filled. All the appropriate silver where it belongs. And all that is missing is the main course, which is still in the oven. It's been a while since I went this overboard for gBeto. I really ought to do this more often, but only if she opens up and that is yet to be seen.

The seafood medley is done, as I smell the odors coming from the open oven. This should be perfect with the white wine I found yesterday. The wine was what gave me the idea to make an intimate dinner rather than the quick bites we tend to have most evenings. A slow meal. A long conversation, rather than the usual gobble down followed by us both going to our respective corners to prepare for the battles of the following day at work. It had driven us apart until I was suddenly at home with more time on my hands. Suddenly able to do more than the bare minimum in the hours not in the office. I should have tried to take more time, but work always seems to be more important than an intimate moment alone.

I carry the hot dish into the dining room and call, "gBeto!"

No response. *Guess I need to go find her.* I go to the office where she normally is this time of day, but she's not there. I check the bathroom and the bedroom in case she is still changing from the day at the office. *Nope, not there either. Where is she?* I walk back through the kitchen and see her just sitting in one of the chairs in the backyard, looking off in the direction of the sunset. I open the door and decide it better to go to her than call her in.

LOVE

As I approach, she looks up at me. I can tell it wasn't a particularly good day. She's trying to decide on the next course of action. I decide to set that aside, "I have a nice meal on the table…"

"What is it?"

"One of your favorites. Not a Tuesday dinner," I explain to her.

"It's not wine Wednesday."

"I'm serving a white. Does that whet your appetite?"

I see her set aside whatever it was she was thinking. "White hunh?"

I have her curious. A first step in my plan for the evening. I nod without saying more, hoping that will make her more engaged. I see her attempt to pick up any odors coming from the kitchen, but we are too far away. "You'll have to come inside if you want to know what it is."

"What kind of white?"

"Argentinian Torrontes."

"Seafood," she guesses instantly because that's the only dish we have with that particular wine.

"Is that enough to entice you, or would you rather I put it back into warm until you've soaked up the last rays of sunshine for today?"

She rises and kisses me to let me know she appreciates my ability to read her mood. She passes by on her way to the kitchen. I swat her on her bottom in a playful attempt to get her attention.

"You saying I need to go on a diet?" she asks not seriously.

"I'm saying I like your ass," I respond immediately.

She enters the house before me, inhaling and "Mmmm." Informs me she is liking the smells. I help her into her seat, pour the glass of wine and take my seat before pouring my glass.

"Appetizers, very nice." She remarks as she holds up her glass for a toast. "What's this dinner to?"

"To you. The woman who will figure it all out."

She half lowers her glass to look at me. "You abdicating your responsibility to help?"

"Not abdicating, but as long as I'm on administrative leave, there are only a few things I can do that will really help. I can't talk to you about the case. I can't advise you on strategy. I can't tell you things that aren't in the public domain. This is to the woman who will figure it all out. I know you will, it's just going to take all your resources to do so."

gBeto seems okay with my toast and sips her wine, "Excellent choice. We haven't done this in a while. So why tonight?"

"Just the fact we need to slow things down a bit. We can clear our minds and do what we do best, which is collaborate."

She takes a bite of her appetizer, nods appreciation and then looks at me from across the table. "You're unhappy with me."

"There's a difference between being unhappy with you and disagreeing with a decision you have apparently made."

"What decision is that?" she asks as she takes another bite of her appetizer.

"I think you need to respond to the article about your supposed grudge."

"You haven't responded to any of the accusations the union has made about you," she points out.

"There's a fundamental difference. The article about you was public and available for all to read. The accusations about me have been internal to the city and have not appeared in print. There is now a question in the mind of those who read the article. They have to make up their minds as to whether to vote for you or not. No one has a question about me based on the union's accusations since they aren't public and no one is voting for or against me this November."

"I disagree," gBeto responds, takes another sip of wine and then pushes more of her appetizer onto her fork. This is all just to make me wait and hopefully listen better. "You are on the ballot whether you want to be or not. A vote for me is a vote for you. A vote against me is a vote against you. The longer your administrative leave sits there festering, the more votes against you."

"I understand Dan Porter tried to force that at last nights' council meeting." I point out as I'm not sure if she heard.

"I got the Cliff Notes at work," she advises me. She told me they have a clipping service that sends excerpts of blogs in a summary. They permit her to get a sense for the major issues being discussed.

"Who do you think was behind that maneuver?" I ask her, thinking she's gotten some feedback from colleagues.

"He was. Got to have an editorial this week and you're it. From what I hear he practically had to drag the Fab Four to go with him. None of them wanted to be seen as calling to have a Black commissioner terminated, all afraid they'd hire a White man to replace you."

"Obviously sitting here I'd not heard that."

"You're on the phone all day, don't give me that shit." She calls me out. "What are your sources saying?"

"The Rev Abernathy wasn't consulted. Obviously, he was not happy with them. Said they were just looking to show their congregations they are working for a resolution, since the trial keeps getting pushed back at the request of the defense counsel. And you just keep letting them do it. The Rev thinks you're going to find it pushed out past the election if you're not careful. If that happens the other side is going to eat you alive, according to the Rev."

"It won't go past the elections," gBeto responds. "I've talked with

187

the judge and she's done giving them more time."

"When will the trial start?" I push her to see if she knows or is speculating about the judge.

"We seat the jury on Monday."

"You're going ahead even without the t-shirt saying I hate Black people?"

"The strongest evidence we have of premeditation is the comments he made to Officer Tissot. Who won't testify against his former partner. But we have the written statement he gave that was cited in the IA report. They couldn't ignore it because if the case came to us, we would demand to see it. They addressed it by citing it as a procedural violation rather than a confirmation of premeditation."

"And without confirmation of premeditation, eight counts of failure to follow department procedure and endangerment is not enough for a conviction." I shake my head.

"Not since the supreme court decision," she reminds me. "Why is it exactly you want to be reinstated? This just isn't a job for a sane person."

"We've had that discussion before. You think you're going to lose but you're going ahead and hope something breaks your way? Hope something comes out that will enable a conviction? Has anyone pointed out that hope is not a strategy?"

"You have, darlin'," she nods to me as she takes a bite of the seafood. "This is excellent. Did you add some of the wine this time?"

"I did along with special spices I'm not revealing."

"Tastes like the Italian spices I use sometimes – basil and oregano, mostly."

"Special spices," is all I'll give her. "When you lose the case, what do we do?"

"You're assuming if I lose the mayor won't reinstate you."

"A reasonable assumption at this juncture," I point out.

"And that I won't get re-elected," she continues.

"Also reasonable," I agree.

"But I've come to just the opposite conclusion. And you made me. With your analysis for Sarah. You said that White folks don't want to see powerful Black folks in high offices because they're afraid of the decisions we would make."

"That's what I'm seeing," I admit.

"But if I prosecute a White officer and lose, then all the White folks will come to the conclusion that it's okay for me to be attorney general because I can't upset the status quo. And they'll let you go back to being the token Black police commissioner because you can't do anything either. You weren't even involved in the decision to fire the officer. Rather than getting rid of us, they'll be able to say to everyone, look how progressive we are. We got Black folks in important offices. But all the time they'll be saying to themselves, we got them Black folks under control 'cause no one is going to fuck with the police department and the vigilantes they have giving out protection for bottles of Jim Beam."

I can't answer immediately because I know she doesn't mean what she's saying and have to process her logic for a minute.

"Cat got your tongue?" she pushes me.

"I'm seeing what you're saying, but I don't agree with you. As I see it, once you lose, the White folks will say to themselves, okay. The Blacks had their chance. They couldn't pull it off. They still don't have the numbers at the polls. We don't have anything to worry about. Let's put Whites back in and put everything back the way it was."

"That certainly is a plausible alternative to my thoughts." gBeto responds still searching for another possible future, one that allows us both to ride into the sunset with our heads held high someday.

"But not the alternative you're still working," I suggest.

"And will until the verdict is in."

I never doubted her intent. I just wish I could help her find that one piece of evidence she's lacking to make the case.

We eat in silence for a few moments. "What are you hearing on the campaign side?" I finally ask to re-engage her.

"Everyone's spun up. The machine is cranking through the voter rolls, generating position papers, developing ads both for me and against the unknown opponent. I'm already booked out every night from September 1st to election day. Every Saturday and Sunday will be spent at election headquarters working strategies, developing stump speeches, talking with volunteers and making the calls I have to make myself. I hope you're back to work by then because you won't have anyone home to make nice dinners for."

"Do you have me slotted in to help?" I ask. I did last time but I wasn't the commissioner then and my time was much more predictable.

"I'm an optimist, so no. I expect you back to work and will simply appreciate any time you can make available to help in whatever capacity you can. Are you going to refill my glass, Garcon?"

I leap up and comply with her request. Add a little to my glass, and finish my meal thinking through the conversation.

"It's time for dessert," she suggests. I know what she's saying and frankly I'm surprised she's in the mood, as she seldom is when she's under stress. But then maybe she's thinking this is the best it's going to get until after the trial.

"I have a chocolate tart with strawberries," I offer to see whether she really is interested.

"It can wait," she responds. Evidently, she really is interested in making love. Amazing what a nice dinner, even without a nice evening of mindless social chatter will do. She watches me sip the remains of my glass of wine.

"What?" I finally ask.

"Just waiting. You usually don't make me wait when I voice interest."

"Letting the expectation build for a bit. Afterall, I expect this will be the last time we'll do this until after…"

"I just might surprise you," she's being coy about it, but I know her too well. Stress just makes it near impossible for her to reach an orgasm, and makes it more difficult for me. And if I'm honest with myself I'm wondering how well I'll perform tonight since I still don't know my fate.

"Are you worried?" she asks.

"About what?"

"You know," she responds, "Don't be. We've had a nice meal, good wine, relaxing time to be together. That's generally all it takes for both of us."

"But this isn't a usual time for either of us. The stresses are different, the consequences are different, and our ability to influence the outcome is decidedly different."

"You don't trust our ability to pull this off?"

"We're playing at a whole different level than in the past," I point out. "The stakes go well beyond anything we've had to deal with before. A whole community, a whole state is watching what we do. Can we do what we said or are we just so much bullshit?"

"I'm not bullshit and neither are you," she responds with a twinkle in her eye I've seen before.

CHAPTER TWENTY-FOUR:

gBeto Dahomey Brown, Attorney General, State of Texas

Sarah White arrives at my tiny office on Monday morning. LaMance and Aamaal are in court for the jury selection. I have decided it best if I leave it to them and not interfere at this point. Nathaniel has convinced me that if I don't take on the articles attacking me, they will fester right up to election day. Better that I answer the charges than let others exaggerate them.

"Is this where you hide out all day?" Sarah looks around. "This is about the size of my cubby."

"The state tries to make up for the low pay with luxurious working conditions," I joke. Sarah glances around and shrugs at my description.

"Thanks for inviting me over. I was surprised and pleased that you would reach out to me."

"You gave me the heads up it was coming. Gave me time to consider how to respond, and Nathaniel convinced me to respond now rather than let them just continue to point to it."

"What's the story?" Sarah asks.

"There is no truth to the allegations that I have any personal history with Michael St. James that might constitute a grudge or hard feelings of any kind. Yes, I encountered him more than once when I was in high school, but it was through his younger brother, who was my lab partner in chemistry. I have not spoken to former officer St. James since I graduated, and frankly, I'd not even thought of him until his name surfaced in this event."

LOVE

"What was it like growing up in East Hill then?" Sarah completes her notes and goes on to her next question.

"I can't speak to a general experience for people; all I can tell you about is mine. It was the best and worst of places to be. Best because of some of the people who influenced my life, and for me the worst of places to be because we were poorer than dirt."

"What does that mean? Poorer than dirt."

"My parents both worked subsistence level jobs, and the money wasn't consistent. We went long periods with nearly no food and often no or little heat in the winter. The only thing that saved me was my mother teaching me to read at a very early age, and an older cousin who took me to the library nearly every day, because my mother was doing laundry and cleaning people's homes. My mother just didn't have time to look after me."

"You read a lot?" Sarah tries to complete the picture I'm creating for her.

"Anything that sparked my interest. My cousin would tell me things about what she was reading. Of course I had to read it too. I was constantly reading above grade level. But more than anything, it was a means of escaping in my mind the extreme poverty in which we lived. I could be a princess, an astronaut, a judge… I particularly liked reading courtroom dramas. There was something to the procedure that just made sense to me. How lawyers built their cases. I would try to do the same when I talked with my teachers, build a case for the point I was trying to make. It must have made an impression because I was put into the better classes in my school, although I went to the poor school. I didn't get into the advanced placement classes or anything like that. But I did have some dedicated teachers where I went. And that made all the difference. When I was getting ready to graduate, a guidance counselor helped me get into the University of Texas. I got a full scholarship for an essay I wrote on the American Dream my civics teacher asked me to write."

"What did you say about it?" Sarah wonders next.

"I said everyone has a different American dream, because we all experience differences depending on who we are and where we live. But each and every one of us has a dream that is enabled by the opportunities America affords. There was a little more to it, but that was the approach I took."

"Must have been well written for you to get a scholarship," she observes.

"Good enough to get attention, but my parent's income is what got me the scholarship. It was clear I would be washing clothes with my mother if I didn't get a full scholarship."

"It must have been like a whole different world when you found yourself living in a dormitory and eating in a cafeteria every day."

"I'd had free lunches at school forever, but the food was a whole lot better at college. I gained weight and had to go on a diet my freshman year."

"Were you prelaw at the university?"

"No, I had no expectation I'd be able to go to law school. When the scholarship ended, I was going to have to find a job. I majored in English with a minor in accounting. Was hoping I could go to work for a newspaper when I graduated, and if I couldn't get a job there, I'd try to work for an accounting firm. Somebody has to pay the bills and keep a record of it. At least that was what my guidance counselor recommended."

"You went to Yale, didn't you?"

"I did."

"How did that all come about?"

"I befriended a professor who also taught adjunct in the law school. He let me into his Constitutional Law class as an elective. I really liked that course because it just explained so much to me about how our government works. Some of the law students complained that

LOVE

I dominated the discussion and I wasn't even admitted to the law school. After me the university put in a policy that undergrads couldn't take grad courses as electives. It was known as the Dahomey rule. Might still be for all I know."

"How did this professor help you get into Yale?"

"He was a Yale grad, and he sent my course final paper to the admissions officer who had been a classmate of his. With his recommendation I was admitted and offered a full scholarship."

"Let me get this straight. Two teachers saw the potential in you and helped you get into college and then law school. You weren't expecting to go on after high school and then had no plans for law school. Others just saw your potential and took it upon themselves to help you."

"Yes."

"Were either Black?"

"No."

Sarah notes this, "You owe who you have become to two White people who made education not only possible but secured scholarships for you."

"I go back a little earlier than that. They were important, but if my mother hadn't taught me to read and my cousin taken me to the library and tell me stories about what she was reading I would never have been capable of excelling at school. It started there."

"You obviously had to do the hard work of mastering your lessons. If you'd not worked hard on your studies the teachers would not have picked you out from amongst your classmates." Sarah continues her line of thought.

"That's true, but if my cousin hadn't taken me to the library, where I had a safe warm place to study, I never could have done it at home. The house I lived in… it had a dirt floor and a wood burning stove. One room we all lived in when it was too cold to go anywhere else. Once my cousin started taking me to the library I slept at home, but that was about it. School all day, library for the evening and weekends."

"Where did you eat on the weekends if you had your main meal at school?"

"Sometimes there would be something left for me when I got home, but not always. When I graduated, I only weighed eighty pounds. That's why I had to go on a diet after I got to the university. I shot up over a hundred in like a few weeks. It wasn't muscle I was adding. I had to lose it all and then start exercising. It filled me out rather than all settling in as a pot belly."

I smile at the remembrance of my pot belly that embarrassed me.

"And you graduated at the top of your Yale Law School class. You made Law Review and published a couple papers you wrote for your classes."

"Yes."

"What I'm hearing is yours is a story of becoming a self-made woman, overcoming severe deprivations, because others opened doors for you that you fully took advantage of. Is that how I should sum up your life?"

I shake my head, "I didn't think you were planning to sum up my life. I thought you were here to get the facts about my lack of relationship to Michael St. James. Why I don't have any kind of ill feelings towards him dating back to my childhood. Sure, I met him and knew who he was, but I didn't hang out with him or really anyone, because the library was the only warm place I could go most of the time. My mother and cousin awoke the love of reading in me. And I've always had a better time with the stories in my head than with the reality of my situation. At least until I graduated law school."

"I had no idea," Sarah finally sums up her reaction to my life story. "It must have been incredibly hard to grow up with nothing and yet have dreams…"

"I had dreams because I read everything. Tragedies, comedies and all kinds of inspirational stories. I liked the inspirational ones particularly. I tried to see myself in them. Rising above meager circumstances to take my place amongst the middle class. That was all I aspired to be. Like all the other kids in my school. Now don't get me wrong, most of the kids in my school were poor enough to get the free lunch, but most of them had clean clothes most of the time, most of them saw a doctor if they got sick. Most of them had an ice cream once in a while."

"And you had none of that."

I shake my head in remembrance, "I remember the first ice cream I ever had. My uncle bought it for me and one for my cousin. He wasn't much better off than we were, but he at least had a regular job with benefits. They went on a short weekend vacation once a year up to the Red River. My uncle had a friend that would lend him a car for the weekend. I think they slept in the car, but they could buy gas and something to eat in restaurants. I remember wishing I could go with them just once, but it never happened. I'd never been out of Texas until I went to Yale, never been out of Fort Christian until I went over to Austin for university. And now I've been all over. It's like the Wizard of Oz when everything changes from black and white to color. That was what it was like for me when I went off to university."

Sarah looks at her notes, "Nothing else you can tell me about Michael St. James? No memories of him, maybe coming home wearing a police uniform or anything?"

I shake my head as nothing comes to mind.

"How much older than you was he? A year or two?"

I have to think to remember, "It's probably in the file and the best I could do at this point is guess that it was two or three years, but I'm not really sure. Just remember I met him through his brother who'd been my chem lab partner. That didn't go particularly well as we nearly blew up the school with one of the experiments that I messed up somehow. Don't even remember what it was, other than the teacher came by just at the last minute, shut off the Bunsen burner and gave us a stern lecture."

"Did you ace the class?" Sarah asks.

"I did, but it was because my lab partner explained things to me. Guess that's why I never became a chemist or a pharmacist."

"From the looks of things, you're right where you were meant to be," Sarah suggests, as she puts away the cell phone she had taken her notes on. "Thanks for talking with me. I'll get a story out with your side of your history and see what comes of it. Is there anything else you would like to make sure people know about your role in this case they might not know if I don't include it in the article?"

"You might note that while we've been having this nice trip down memory lane for me, the prosecution and defense teams have been picking the jury for former officer St. James' trial. I'm not there. I'm not the one making the decisions about how to prosecute this case. I've been involved in the internal reviews to ensure we believe we have sufficient evidence to make a case against the accused. I have held the team to a very high standard because even though nearly every living person in Texas has seen those videos more than once, we had to be sure he was not just doing the job any cop in Texas would have done."

"With eight violations of procedure and policies how could there be any question?" Sarah asks.

"We are talking a murder charge, which could carry the death penalty. I can't take that lightly. Can't assume we have a strong case even with the videos. When my department is prosecuting a death penalty eligible case, we have to erase any shadow of a doubt in our own minds first."

"It's interesting you say that," Sarah muses. "I saw a quote from former officer St. James over the weekend. Said when the full story comes out you would never prosecute him for doing his job."

"I'm not sure what he could be referring to, and in fact, I'm not, although my office is and will obtain a conviction based on the evidence."

Sarah nods, "That was in another blog from the same guy who tried to sell the story to us first. He has a particular point of view he takes in everything he writes. Generally, it's environmental or social justice kinds of things. I find it interesting he's picked up a story about a White cop who killed a Black man and has championed the White guy. It just seems out of place for some reason."

"Maybe you should ask him," I suggest. "Might give you a different perspective."

Sarah shakes her head and for a second, I know I've seen that head shake somewhere before, but I instantly dismiss it.

"I don't publish stories that take only one side of an argument. If the author isn't willing to present a balanced perspective it's not worth reading." Sarah smiles, "I just have to sell it. Bring the audience with me…"

I hardly hear the end of her response as I've heard the comment about 'selling it' in just that tone of voice before. In high school. Maybe I'm letting this one get to me because it's bringing back memories I don't want to deal with, now or ever.

CHAPTER TWENTY-FIVE:

Sarah White, Director Content, Continuum Media

Tic Rogers sent me a preview of his next blog. I wish he hadn't. It's clear what he's doing, giving me a tease. He wants me to see the story he's working and then what happens when another outlet publishes it. *Arrogant, if you ask me.* But I've begun to see you have to be at least a little arrogant, or at least convinced of your viewpoint to write in his world. Doesn't matter what you write, as long as it's consistent with your viewpoint. Doesn't even have to be the truth, or accurate, or even entertaining as long as it's consistent.

In fact, the more outrageous the claims, the more likely it will generate a firestorm of reaction. And in the freelance space it's a lot more important to cause a reaction than to write something everyone agrees with. If you're just stating the obvious no one cares. And that's why we try to balance our stories. *Give the reader something to think about.* The problem is our readers are not Tic's readers. *His don't want to think. They just want to be angry at the people Tic decides to point a finger at. And wag that finger at. And shout from whatever platform will publish him.*

His blog today was hard for me to read. It's because he has decided to take my nice balanced blog presenting the evidence that gBeto does not have a personal revenge agenda for Michael St. James and attempt to destroy it with a nuclear bomb. It almost seems like he has been setting me up, waiting for me to write something he could react to in order to demonstrate how much more valuable his work is than mine based on public reaction.

Tic didn't wait to see if I wanted to buy it. The blog appeared on the Morning News website this morning. I was surprised Daniel Porter bought it. *Maybe the Morning News is trying to increase circulation, or maybe he's firing a shot at gBeto to tell her she better not take the Morning News for granted since she's up for re-election soon.*

As I'm sitting here trying to understand what's behind the Morning News picking up Tic's blog, Rory, my father's business partner, who sells the ads and manages the business side of things, comes into my office and turns on the television. "Morning."

"What's up?" I wonder why he came down and wants to show me something. We rarely talk about work as he's generally not focused on the content side. *Dad said I'll have to spend some time with him at some point to learn the business side, but the content is more important to really understand.*

"Maybe a tempest in a teapot, or maybe not."

He turns it to the local Fox News station, which I never watch and suddenly I understand why he came down.

The news anchor reads, "Continuum's Sarah White claims in her blog of yesterday that Texas Attorney General gBeto Dahomey Brown barely knew the former Fort Christian City Police Officer when she was growing up. However, on the Morning New's website this morning, Tic Rogers, an independent blogger cites a conversation with the former officer who claims he never should have been charged since the internal affairs report proscribed punishment for not following department procedure. That was all. Professional law enforcement officials did not find criminal behavior. And yet the State Attorney General has brought charges against him for murder. The former officer claims he knew the attorney general much better than she has been willing to admit. Furthermore, he referred to a little-known incident that may explain why she would pursue charges when there is no basis for them."

A locally well-known commentator follows the news anchor. Since I don't watch Fox News, I don't recognize this out-of-shape balding and graying old white guy, who speaks distinctively into a radio show style microphone, even though he's on television news.

"Good morning Mr. and Mrs. Fort Christian. I hope you are sleeping well in your bed at night, thinking the police have your safety all under control. Well, I can tell you, from my vantage point, you probably should be sleeping a little less soundly. For they are at it again. You know who I mean. All those people who want to neuter the police department, make sure they can't possibly do their job. All those people who are conspiring to let the black and brown hordes loose on your street, to break into your home, steal your television to make sure you can't hear the truth anymore, to take your money and valuables, to rape the women in your household, to beat the men into submission. You know who I mean."

A picture of gBeto is displayed with the commentator image moving down to the right-hand corner. "You know who I mean." Then a picture of Nathaniel appears next to hers. "You know who I mean."

The pictures move to the upper corners and the commentator's image comes up larger than either but between them. I notice he has a gleeful expression, almost like someone who is yelling 'fire' in a crowded theater or telling a child 'there is no Santa'. A nihilist who lives in a candy store and won't permit anyone to buy. "Alone, either of these hate-filled racists could make life more difficult for every living person in this state. But together, they can protect each other to ensure no one can stop the devious and world destroying plan they have hatched to make sure your life will only get worse."

I look at Rory as if to tell him he can turn it off now, but he is still listening, slowly shaking his head as if he can't believe what he's hearing.

The commentator continues, "You may wonder what can two people do to me? Well, I just happen to have insight on that. Hot off the press folks. One of Fort Christian's most decorated police officers put it all on the line for you in an encounter with a ginormous, out-of-control rampaging black man, who had literally torn a convenience store apart looking for alcohol to fuel his rage against you and me. He had threatened the clerk who was sure he was a dead man walking. When the police officers arrived, they had to repeatedly tase this destroyer of civilization, who still kept coming at them and still it took repeated bullets to bring him down just inches from the two officers who bravely stood between him and you and your family."

I try to see Rory's expression. He almost seems mesmerized by the fantasy description this man is weaving with only occasional intersection with any fact of the case that I'd read, although more may come out at the trial.

The commentator continues and nods towards Nathaniel's photo, "You know who I mean, tried to remove our hero from the force shortly after becoming commissioner eighteen months ago. He has repeatedly tried to remove other decorated and seasoned officers who have the intestinal fortitude to go toe-to-toe with out-of-control drug lords and worse. The men and women of Fort Christian who make it possible for you to sleep well at night. But our mayor has shown uncommon wisdom. You know who I mean was suspended during the departmental investigation to ensure he couldn't unduly influence the outcome. Couldn't impose his agenda of removing the heroes from our department. The heroes who won't permit riots and destruction to occur in our city."

The commentator nods towards gBeto's photo, "But you know who I mean has stepped into thwart the will of the mayor by bringing charges against our hero. Charges that his heroism resulted in murder rather than the safety of us all. Charges that he should go to jail for doing his duty, for taking action when many officers would have tried to talk to the rampaging brute, which would have endangered his partner and the many civilians who witnessed these events."

Rory stares at the picture of gBeto and seems to be listening to what is being said about her. I don't know how he's able to do that as I'm just not believing anyone has the right to say what the commentator is, but also reflecting that he's only saying these things because Tic Rogers started him down this path.

"You know who I mean is going to castrate our hero, chain him up in a dark and damp cellar somewhere and feed him to the rats. That's what these people do to anyone who stands up to them. That's what these people do to ensure they are able to control you and me and your family and your kids… That's what these people do to take from us everything we have worked our whole lives to achieve. That's what these people will continue to do until every last one of us is working for them. Being paid minimal wages. Without health care, without access to clean water, living in the most polluted areas of our cities. That's what they want for us. That's what they intend to do to us."

A big red X appears across Nathaniel's picture. The commentator glances up and says, "Yessss." Then a similar red X appears across gBeto's picture, the commentator glances up at her picture and say, "Yessss."

The image of the commentator grows as those of gBeto and Nathaniel shrink down a bit. "We must stop their insidious plot. We must drive them from our midst. And this is where you come in. You, today, right now. You must send an email to the mayor and your council member. You must tell them that only they can save our city. Only they can ensure the police are not castrated by this socialist left-wing nut job of a commissioner, who is hell-bent on seeing our streets filled with crime, and rioters and looters. Who is hell-bent on seeing life in our city become impossible so we will leave… go somewhere else, but leave all we have worked for our entire lives… to them. To people who haven't worked a day for any of it. To people who just live off the taxes we must pay to all the governments who claim a share of our labor to hand it over to those who are too lazy to work. To all the people who feel entitled because politicians tell them our country owes them a living whether they work for it or not, as long as they vote for you know who I mean."

That insidious smile returns, "And that's where you come in again. You know who I mean is in charge today. She's the State Attorney General. That means she's the top law enforcement officer for the entire state. She can thwart any plans to restore order, decency and humanity to our community. But her kryptonite is you. She was elected to that position by you. And you can toss her ass out of Water Street in a few months by going to the polls and pulling the lever for the other guy. That's how you stop her plans for anarchy. That's how you ensure her worthless husband commissioner never gets another law enforcement job in our fair state. That's how you ensure your safety and your property is protected and your dreams come true for you and your family."

The commentator looks first at Nathaniel's picture and then at gBeto's picture reaches up with a closed fist and pulls it down as he says, "Yessss. And now a word from our sponsors."

Rory looks back at me as if he'd just been run over by a bus. "Wow! What did you say that spun him up like that?"

"You're blaming me for him?" I point to the screen.

Rory rubs his hands together, then shakes them out like he's trying to get off whatever was just sprayed on him by the commentator. "You don't look like someone who's out to take the world from whoever it is that guy thinks is watching his broadcast."

"I'm not," I assure him. "Where did that come from?"

"Well, the first part attributed you as the root cause of the controversy. I haven't seen your blog yet. What did you say?"

"Just what they said, they were accurate," I admit. "Nothing I would have thought would do anything more than set straight what I thought to be a one-sided story about the attorney general having some kind of grudge against the former police officer."

"They referenced that, but said the officer said there was something to it. Do you have any idea what he was talking about?"

"No, but why are you interested in this story?" I'm mystified. "You never come out to discuss content."

"Josh poked his head into my office…"

"Josh? The intern who's doing grammar checking? What did he say?" *Josh is such a nebbish.*

"That it looked like you'd stepped on a land mine, said it was already on Fox."

"So?" I'm not getting any answers from him.

"If we have sponsors or ads cancel, I need to understand how to re-sell it. Could be a big impact if the wrong people think we're taking sides, or even inciting a riot."

"Oh, hadn't thought about it from that angle," I admit. "Does that happen often? That sponsors or ads get cancelled because of something we publish?"

Rory looks sheepish, "Until your dad put you in this job, I had that pretty well under control. People knew what to expect from us. Knew we were attracting an audience that would be interested in their products or services because of the balanced treatment of the news. We have the thinking audience from all major parties reading us because we're like Switzerland. We don't mean to threaten anyone, we just want to make sure they have the facts to make decisions in their lives."

"But Dad does editorials once in a while…" I point out.

"He's the only one. When he does it's usually a centrist position everyone can get behind as opposed to a hijack by one party or the other."

I have to think what he last wrote about. It was before I graduated. I really wasn't paying much attention because I was knee-deep in papers and finals and getting my life in order so Demetrius and I could get married. "Okay, but what about me. You said you had it all under control until me."

"You're a little more unpredictable in what you write about. You've been writing about this local case a lot, again from what Josh told me…"

"What's wrong with a little local color? All stories are local at the end of the day. We just happen to be in a good place to get source material rather than trying to interpret whether someone else really has the right story."

"I'm not being critical… after all, as you said I don't know anything about content, nor do I really want to, unless it affects my ability to sell ads and subscriptions."

"Do you even follow the news?" I wonder based on his description that he's only here because Josh gave him a head's up. Sure, I know Josh is hoping to get a paying job when he graduates and giving a head's up to a partner is a good way to get noticed...

Rory nods, "If you count the weather. It's a long walk from my apartment, and I need to know if I should bring my umbrella."

"You're not hiding under a rock. Come on. I know you follow the news. Everyone does. That's who we are. How could you not believe in our product? Your customers must ask you about stories."

"They don't," he informs me. "If a story comes up, I offer to put them in touch with the author, that way they can get as much background and detail as they'd like. Makes them feel like they're getting special access to a source rather than just some bozo who happens to work here."

What he says makes sense, but I still wonder why he won't admit he follows some news. "Anyway, I've got to learn how to write content. How to know what words sell the story, what facts are essential so people will believe me, how to balance it. Make sure no one will be offended, as you point out."

"It's our brand. That's what we sell. Balance. Pro and Con. Ying and Yang, Cheech and Chong..."

"Cheech and...?" he lost me there.

"What I'm asking is you give some thought to who are you going to offend with what you're writing, such that they may decide not to do business with us."

"I think I'm doing that... well, not to the extent of who. I really don't know who our customers are, or the big accounts for ads. Maybe that would be worthwhile. If you'd send me a list of our major advertisers and what they sell?"

Rory smiles thinly, "Happy to."

"What's wrong? Don't you want to share that information with me?"

"Not at all. You need it," Rory considers something then continues, "I guess maybe I'm asking too much of you, since you just started. Maybe I need to let you piss off a few customers. That way we'll find out if they're even reading what we publish. You know it's possible we're just a habit for companies. They've been advertising with us for a long time and they continue because they think we're reinforcing sales with their existing customers. But maybe we need to enlarge our audience. Attract new readers, who will be introduced to our customer's products and they'll see their sales increase."

"Maybe I need to look for some controversy. Is that what you're saying?"

CHAPTER TWENTY-SIX:

Cindy Ho, Chief of Neurosurgery
Fort Christian General Hospital

When I got the call from gBeto to come have a chat, I wasn't sure what I was getting into, but Nathaniel greets me at the door with a glass of my favorite white wine. He hands it to me and, "She's in the kitchen, says that's where she thinks best. Probably because she's not a great cook and really has to work at it to figure out a recipe." Nathaniel's smile tells me he's not serious. *I know she's a good cook.*

"I'm here to help her figure something out?" I ask in all innocence, still trying to understand why she called.

"Probably whether I need a lobotomy…" Nathaniel smiles devilishly. "The problem is no one would notice."

I make my way back to gBeto in the kitchen. She has a glass of red and the bottle open, which tells me she's trying to figure out something she doesn't expect to figure out tonight. "Hey, you." I embrace her, clink glasses and take a sip. "Okay, what's the topic for tonight?"

"Thanks for coming," she tears up as if she is struggling and needs someone to reassure her.

"Hey, I'm always available for house calls. Besides, Nathaniel says I might get a lobotomy out of tonight. That's a pretty good evenings work for a neuro."

"For me?" she seems surprised at his offer.

"Actually, for him. I'm running a two for one special tonight, but it's a time limited offer."

"You'll have to tell me if we both need it before we're done," gBeto responds with a hint of irony in her voice.

Cindy takes a sip to reflect on our bantering and then asks, "Okay, since this is a pro-bono call, what's on your mind?"

"Have you been following the case my office is trying?"

"Which one?" I have to ask as I think I know which one she's referring to; I don't want to make a mistake and answer inappropriately.

"Officer involved shooting."

"Oh, that one. Haven't spent many calories on it, no." I respond truthfully not really wanting to get sucked into one that is clearly going to be messy.

"I have a problem…"

"Of course you do. If you had it all under control there would be no wine, there would be no call to me to discuss, there would be no talk of lobotomies."

"In that case what should I do?"

"Not so fast," I respond. "I understand you have a problem to solve, but I haven't a clue about it since at the moment it's not my problem, but you're about to change that."

"No. Not really. I need some professional advice on how to proceed. Not on the legal side, I've got that covered. I need help understanding the psychology of the defendant in this case…"

"Who is not your client. In fact, you're prosecuting him and trying to figure out what?"

"Why he did it," gBeto responds before taking a long sip of her red wine.

I'm starting to get a picture of her dilemma. She wants to put this guy in jail for the rest of his life for killing someone, I don't even know who or why. And that's what she wants me to tell her. Why this guy without any information to help? "Walk me through it."

"Cop comes on a guy who is just sitting on a curb."

"Not relevant," I respond. "I don't care what happened then, but did something happen before they met up that night on the curb? Was either distraught, angry, confused?"

"You're suggesting what happened that night may have nothing at all to do with what happened that night?"

"That's where I'd start, but hell, I'm not a shrink, I'm not a cop, I'm just someone who stayed in a Holiday…"

gBeto gives me a look like my comment isn't helpful.

"What you really want to know is why a cop would kill someone when from the evidence he didn't need to?"

gBeto nods her head just once.

"I didn't pay much attention to the reports," I respond to her head nod. "But I asked myself why. And the only thing that made sense to me was maybe the cop was angry about something. Maybe not personal, he was going to kill someone and what's his name was in the wrong place."

I see gBeto try to process my observation.

"There was nothing in the reports they had ever met," she remembers.

"My impression is there's something there, but I'm a neuro, not a psychologist. I don't have any idea how the conscious mind works. I focus on the physical brain and spinal column."

"You didn't see the blogs today?"

I respond with a head shake, "I don't have time for that. I don't subscribe to any news feeds. I don't watch the evening news. I don't read the print newspapers. I'm what our new neighbor would refer to as a non-digital native. Someone who doesn't participate in the information age. I have way too many scientific journals to read, too many professional papers reporting on peer reviewed research that may help me save the lives of more of my patients. Articles that provide insights my predecessors would have given anything to have had access to. But that's progress. That's science. Discoveries come when they come and not a day before. Yesterday's patient is gone. Can't do anything with today's information to help them. But it can help the person who is in to see me today and I better be prepared to apply whatever that article shares."

"What does that have to do with my murder case?" gBeto asks as if I'd sidetracked her.

"You're not listening," I point out. "You want my help; you ply me with wine so I'll just blab off at the mouth and then with all of that you're not listening."

"I'm sorry. Really. I am. I need the benefit of your insights because I'm coming up short and a day late here. If I don't find a rabbit in my hat, I'm yesterday's news.

I didn't know it was serious. "Okay. This is what I know. White cop kills a Black guy."

"That's it?" gBeto is amazed by my simplistic description of the events.

"gBeto, babe. I love you like a sister, but you got to get over yourself. Not everyone is living in your world. What's a fucking earth-shaking disaster for you doesn't even register in my world. I have surgeries to perform. I'm trying to learn how to save more of my patients than I can with the limited knowledge I have from med school and fifteen years of practice. I have to get better at what I do or my patients who survive will go to the doc who has stayed up. Are you hearing me?"

gBeto looks bewildered.

"You okay?" I have to ask.

"You're right," she finally responds as if waking from a hypnotic state. "I have no right to ask you to solve my problem. You have your own to solve, and they're life and death as opposed to right and wrong in my world."

"Stop with the wounded bird routine."

"What?"

"You're fucking fluttering around, flapping your wings to distract me from the issue, which is you're floundering and you're trying to grasp onto any raft in the sea."

gBeto looks at me as if she has just awoken from a long winter's sleep. It takes a moment, but she finally seems to re-engage with me. "I'm sorry. I shouldn't…"

"Stop!" I hold up my hand right in front of her face. "Don't give me this bullshit you're imagining about how you imposed on a friend and you had no right. What the fuck do you think friends are for? We're supposed to be here when you need to bounce something off us. Do you expect we are going to give you the answer to your problem? Not happening my friend. But I may be able to provide some insight that will help you better understand the question. That's about the best I can do to help you. But if you use that insight, you should be able to figure out who to talk to next."

gBeto puts down her wine glass and gives me a hug. "Now I remember why you're one of my best friends."

"You mean I'm not your best friend, above and beyond all the other women who think they are? Come on gBeto. You can do better that that when I still haven't given you what you're looking for."

gBeto holds me at arm's length. "I'm sorry."

"You say that every time you fuck up girl. What's the story? You think your friends are here to extract your foot from your mouth every time you say something you would be better advised to think about more than you do?"

gBeto turns away, takes a sip of her wine and sits on a chair next to her kitchen island. "You're telling me to get my shit together and stop putting my shortcomings on all of you."

"Not at all," I respond and come sit next to her.

"I'm here to help, but you're not giving me what I need to be helpful."

gBeto looks at me for a moment and then articulates, "How can someone kill someone?"

"You're trying to understand how the cop, in this instance, was able to kill someone?"

gBeto nods. "I don't understand it."

"You don't have a motive," I finally realize.

gBeto shrugs at me without confirming.

I have to think about her question since this isn't my field. "Why does anyone do anything?"

"Too broad, I can't get there." gBeto responds.

"Why did he kill him, was it kill or be killed?" Is the only thing I can think of.

"No. The man he killed was unarmed and not a threat to kill anyone from what we can see."

"Nothing in the moment that would indicate the cop was about to die if he didn't kill the other man?"

gBeto shakes her head.

"That would go back to my first question. Did something happen earlier that would convince the officer if he didn't shoot to kill, he would likely die?"

"We don't know," gBeto admits.

"Then that's where I'd start," I feel greatly relieved that I'm giving constructive advice.

"What if… we can't establish something that set the officer off on the victim? What then?"

gBeto looks at me with a helpless look, as if they have already explored this angle and come up dry. As if she does not expect it's going to resolve whatever it is she's distraught over. She's looking for the next level of psychoanalysis needed to get to a motive, since that's what I'm getting the feeling she is looking for. A motive why a long-term cop would kill someone, when he knows that's absolutely the last thing he should do.

"What the fuck, it must have been random."

"Random?" gBeto apparently hasn't considered this motive either.

"The cop. Has he ever killed anyone before?"

"Yes," gBeto responds immediately. Apparently, this has been something she's considered.

"What if the victim was random. Someone who happened to be in the wrong place at the wrong time? Was the cop ending a long rotation?"

"I don't know for sure, but I think so." gBeto responds.

"He may have been very tired and emotionally exhausted. Have you looked into what was going on in his personal life? A girlfriend who dumped him? Ex-wife hassling him for alimony? Kids who need shoes and school supplies? What was going on in his personal life? Was the killing random because he was just angry and dealing with general things he didn't know how to solve? Maybe there was no inciting incident. Maybe he was just pissed off at life."

"I don't know," gBeto responds as if a deer looking into headlights.

I shake my head as a fact comes to me, I'd not considered. "The victim. Who was he?"

"Bo Madison."

"Was he someone special?" I think I remember something about him but can't remember what.

"Set records at UT," gBeto offers.

"Football or basketball?" I have to know as there's a big difference in how people view the two sports in Texas. And that's where the officer might come in.

"Football. Fullback." gBeto responds. "He broke Nathaniel's records."

"Is that relevant to anyone other than you?" I have to ask as it's not getting to the issue.

gBeto shakes her head, "Just that he was well known locally. Could have gone pro, but chose to go to Afghanistan instead."

"Lots of people knew him," I note. "Did the officer know?"

gBeto shrugs, "I would think so, but don't know for sure."

"Maybe you need to find out the answer to that question first."

"I left it up to my staff. I've not been sitting in on the strategy sessions. I get a summary."

"You want to convict the son-of-a-bitch you better get involved in a big way, because you don't know these simple answers, you'll never win the case in court." I summarize for her.

CHAPTER TWENTY-SEVEN:

gBeto Dahomey Brown, Attorney General, State of Texas

Daniel Porter and the Four Horsemen of the Apocalypse are waiting for me in the conference room that could have been my office. The one where Walter's picture overlooks every discussion, whether I want him to or not. And this is one of those discussions where I'd rather he wasn't looking over the discussion. Particularly since there is clear antipathy towards him amongst those who have come to talk with me, and register a complaint.

As I enter all rise to greet me and I am surprised by the demeanor I see. It's the same for all of them. They don't look like they have every other time we have chatted. I've shown them nothing but respect, although occasionally Daniel and I get into it a bit. But the four Revs? I have always thought I was a champion for the causes they seek to advance, equality and Justice. Rev. Clyburn won't even look me in the eye. What's this all about? I am instantly uncomfortable. "Gentlemen. Thank you for taking the time to come by and discuss matters of importance with me. I can only address your concerns if I completely understand them. Reverend Clyburn… are you well? You seem not yourself today." I'm trying to throw them off. Encourage them to not just let Daniel frame the discussion for them.

"I'm fine Mrs. Brown," the Rev looks at me solemnly. "You look tired, are you well?"

"You've always had a good eye, to see your congregation as they are, Reverend," I respond with due deference. "I am tired, but it just seems to come with the job you all helped me obtain. And for that I am grateful. To be in a position where I can gather facts and act on them."

217

"That's what we wished to…" Daniel seeks to insert himself now, but I turn to Reverend Abernathy. The other leader of this group who can't seem to get the others to see things his way which causes them to defer to Daniel.

"Reverend Abernathy. What did I hear about you starting a capital campaign to expand your Nave? Does that mean you've outgrown that grand temple to the Lord that you built out just what was it? Five or six years ago?"

The Reverend Abernathy shifts uncomfortably in his chair, "Mrs. Brown, you have a good memory, although it was nine years ago we expanded our facilities. But yes. We are bursting at the seams and some Sundays we have members who must stand throughout the service."

"But your congregation loves music. They're on their feet for much of it already."

"That's true, we are blessed with a choir director who gets everyone up on their feet to join in. She is truly a marvel and very talented."

"She is, she is," I smile thinking about attending services there from time to time. "But I assume you prefer to have the whole congregation seated for prayer and your sermon."

"I do, that's true," the Rev smiles until the Rev Clyburn shakes his head at him. However, Rev Clyburn stops when he sees I'm watching him now.

"What will this take your congregation up to?" I ask politely.

"Over two thousand," Rev Abernathy beams, "We have four services now to accommodate everyone."

"You have just been such an inspiration for your congregation, and brought comfort and guidance to them."

The Rev Abernathy nods to himself but doesn't say more as Rev Clyburn keeps glancing at him.

LOVE

"Reverend Lomax, how are things at Mt. Zion?"

I see Daniel Porter out of the corner of my eye resign himself that he's not going to get a chance to steer things until I've had an opportunity to talk one-on-one with the Four Horsemen.

"We're not in a capital campaign now. We updated our facilities about four years ago and the congregation wants us to pay down our loans before we do any more. We've increased our outreach work, seeing more folks in their homes when they're shut in and helping folks find the lord every day of the week and not just on Sunday. You know how that is."

"I do," I respond earnestly, again catching Rev Clyburn frowning. "You have always done the Lord's work for your congregation and all that are unable to attend services for one reason or another. Do you still have your outreach program at the city jail?" I know he does, but want to give him an opportunity to brag about it.

"We've been ministering to an average of twenty-five prisoners for quite some time now, helping them see what has led them to that place and better understanding what the Lord's plan is for each of them. In some cases, we've found lawyers willing to represent them pro bono, just to have an adequate defense."

"Wonderful. You have touched many lives that would be lost if not for your grace." And now I look at Reverend Earvin, who starts talking before I even ask.

"Mrs. Brown, my congregation is always proud when you come to visit us. I understand your desire to visit all the churches in Fort Christian, but we are hopeful you will choose us to be your permanent home when you no longer wish to serve the people of Texas."

"With such excellent moral guides in our city as you all, it is difficult to make a choice like that. Even after I leave office, I may wish to continue visiting each of you to gain from the wisdom each of you share. I know Nathaniel and I greatly benefit from the inspiration each of you bring to us."

And now Daniel is ready, a quick nod to the four Revs and he begins, "Attorney General, the jury has now been seated in the St. James trial. You've stepped back from the trial and your chief prosecutor is handling the it. But we're concerned."

"Justice will be served, Mr. Porter," I try to head him off.

"Our collective congregations are nervous," he tries to continue.

"That this trial will end up like all the others where the White cop walks after taking a Black life... You're concerned the message is White men can kill Black men and there are no consequences," again I try to show I know where they are going.

"That has been the case in like ninety-nine percent of the cases, "Reverend Abernathy offers to show he is on the same page as Daniel. I look into the eyes of the other ministers. I see the same resolve, the same fear, the same resignation that history has forced them to accept.

"I understand. I do. All of it. Why you're here, why you are resigned to an outcome. It's all we've known for all our years struggling to change the reality of our place in this society. But you have to believe me that our time is coming. Today is one step towards a new community. Where equality and justice are the norm and not the exception. Where a Black man's life is as valuable as a White man's. Where equality of pay is expected, not just between men and women, but between Black, White, Asian and Muslim. Regardless of your sexual orientation. Regardless of your age. That all the differentiators we have been labeled no longer apply. That is the reality I am here to create. That is the reality we have talked about wanting since I was old enough to speak in coherent sentences, and even before. The reality we have wanted since the first slaves were brought to this country in the 1600s."

"Ambitions don't change anything," Porter responds to my impassioned message. And even though it came from my heart, I understand. They've heard that message since they were old enough to understand. I'm just another one of the millions of Black people in America who wishes it were different, but is powerless to change the

LOVE

narrative of our reality.

"But that's where you're wrong," I push back on him. "We are changing the way things have been with this case. We are going to show that no one, not even a cop, is above the law. And what I intend to show is that cops have a special duty to serve all people in their community regardless of race, sexual orientation, age or social status. No one is more important than anyone else. We value a human life as just that. We value each other and are here to enable each other's success, not pigeon-hole us. Not relegate us, not celebrate a few who make it while the vast majority do not. All of the statistics I've seen show we, as a race, do not share in the American dream. It doesn't matter how you choose to measure it. We are the left behind people. And that stops now."

I see the Revs have tuned out. Heard this all before. Even Daniel seems bored. I stop and wait. Daniel seems to be waiting for me to continue and seems unsure of what to do since I haven't.

"You didn't come for a spirited defense of my intentions," I confess.

"No, we didn't," Daniel acknowledges.

"Then what's on your minds?" I ask contrite, but not sure why I should be.

"We think you have a problem," Daniel begins. He hesitates and looks at the Revs to make sure they are still with him. "Even if you win the case, with the conflicts you have, we aren't confident the Black community wins."

"Your congregations," I seek to clarify what he means by Black community.

"Every Black person living in Fort Christian and Texas for that matter," Daniel attempts to paint the picture. "Maybe even the whole US."

"Okay. What are the conflicts you think I have?"

221

"Your first loyalty is to your husband, and we understand that." Daniel begins the explanation.

"Nathaniel." I let that sit for a moment. "I promised to love, cherish and obey him, but I didn't promise to place his interests over the people of the State of Texas for whom I pledged my faithful execution of this office. You're already 0 for 1."

"You would prosecute your own husband if he were indicted?"

"Faithful execution of my office leaves me no choice. Would you prosecute your husband?" I didn't mean to point out he is gay, but I see the twitter of the Revs which acknowledge his sexual orientation is well known amongst them.

"I'm not an elected official of the State of Texas," Daniel is angry about my assertion.

"You have a public obligation as do I," I remind him. "You have a bully pulpit to sell your opinions every day if you choose. I do not. You can comment on anything you wish, and there is no obligation to be neutral, impartial or even-handed. I do. You actually have much more freedom to decide how you will use your influence on the people of Fort Christian and Texas than I do. You have the backing of these gentlemen, spiritual leaders of our city and community. Esteemed, beloved, and God's representatives on Earth. What more could you want? You have it all. I have obligations, limited authority and unlimited responsibility. I am transitory because if the voters think I am not executing my office as they see fit, they will install someone new at the next election. That's why I have to win this case. I may never have another chance to change our reality. If I don't win this one? We are no better off than we were four hundred years ago. I am taking this very seriously. It's everything I've worked for since I went to law school. It will either be the beginning of a new age for all of us, or the beginning of the end for me as a champion of equal rights and justice."

"I've come to respect your oratory in a whole new way," Daniel responds. "I didn't know you could be so impassioned. So eloquent. So full of bullshit."

LOVE

"What?"

"You have said, and I'm quoting you now, 'Judge me not by my
words, but by my actions.' We've been sitting here for the last ten
minutes and all you have given us is words. You haven't shown us how
you are going to win this case. You have provided nothing that would
instill confidence in any of us that this time will be different. Is it a
failing of Black people, that when we get power, we have no idea how
to exercise it? That's what I'm hearing. Words. What I'm not seeing is
deeds. I'm not seeing people in the community coming forward to
testify against the former officer. I'm not seeing a well-documented
path towards a conviction."

"Come on Daniel. We both know I would never trot my witnesses
and my evidence out before a trial. It would provide the defense
counsel an unparalleled opportunity to devise a targeted response to my
main points for conviction."

"But you're asking us to believe you, to trust you, that you're
different and won't let us down when ninety-nine percent of the time
people in your position have let us down."

"Daniel, you knew my predecessor. Would you be feeling better if
he were in my chair right now? Would you be more confident that the
losing trend will be reversed because of his dedication, insights and
passion to bring about a just conclusion? Is that what you're trying to
tell me?"

"Just the opposite," Daniel responds. "I... we... think there is a
way to see that former officer St. James is convicted. But it's not your
way."

"Not my way? What are you saying?"

"We, unanimously agreed before coming here to ask you to
resign."

I am not processing his statement. It doesn't make any sense to
me. "Resign."

"From looking at everything that is public about this case, and talking to the congregations, we unanimously believe there is a better chance to win this case if you step aside as attorney general and let your deputy succeed you."

"LaMance?" I shake my head unbelieving, but realizing I shouldn't be surprised by anything. I rise and open the door. "LaMance!" I call. In a moment she appears, eyes as wide as quarters.

"Yes?"

I motion her in and close the door behind her. "These gentlemen have told me they wish me to resign and name you attorney general, in the midst of one of the biggest cases you've ever prosecuted. Were you aware of their request? Did you propose it to them?"

LaMance looks like she would rather be anywhere else in the world than here. "Yes…"

"You were aware of their request and you proposed it to them?"

"To Daniel Porter but not the others," she panics. "We don't have a winning case. That's what I told him. And the jury won't be sympathetic since the mayor removed Nathaniel and prevented him from influencing charges. He shares some blame for not making it impossible for something like this to happen. It… the optics of it… just don't look favorable for a conviction if you're seen as protecting him. You have to step down to let me win the case."

I turn to the ministers and Daniel, "Have you ever voiced this opinion to me?"

LaMance shakes her head, "You wouldn't listen to me, but the editor of the paper and the ministers of the major Black congregations? You have to listen to them. Your core constituency."

"No," I turn to face her. "My core constituency is all people who live in Texas. That includes them, the readers of the Morning News and the four church congregations, but there are millions more who live here. They are my core constituency. I have to seek and obtain justice for everyone."

"gBeto…" Daniel starts.

"I will not step aside, now or ever. The people of Texas trusted me to do my job and I will faithfully execute the requirements of my office until the people of Texas chose not to return me. Does that answer your question, gentlemen?"

Rev Clyburn is the first on his feet. "You are letting pride get in the way of justice." The others follow him out with Daniel last.

"When you lose the case, you will be sealing your own re-election defeat. You had a chance to go out with honor, but now… I can't write an editorial supporting your re-election."

"Good-bye Daniel," I close the door behind him and turn to LaMance. "I was elected. I appointed you and you serve at my pleasure. I'm no longer pleased. Leave your letter of resignation on my desk when you leave tonight." Her expression tells it all, but *holy shit, now I have to prosecute Mick St. James.*

CHAPTER TWENTY-EIGHT:

Sarah White, Director of Content, Continuum Media

I see the lights on at gBeto and Nathaniel's house. It's now about seven pm. She must be home by now. Demetrius wants me to fix him something for dinner, but he's just going to have to wait. I need to talk to her, need to understand what's going on. There's something underlying all of the angry media, all of the vitriol. And yet her explanation doesn't match the officer's. *The only way I can come out looking like anything other than a foil for Tic Rogers is to get the facts and shut him up.*

As I walk towards their back door the lights go on outside. In a moment, Nathaniel is opening the door. "Hey neighbor. Looking for a glass of wine and some company?" He's dressed in plaid shorts and an old ratty University of Texas football, t-shirt. Must be from when he played there. "Is that shirt old or what?"

Nathaniel looks down, "Not as old as me, but getting close," he smiles back. "Actually, this was a practice shirt. It's got a lot of sweat, blood and laundry detergent in it's past. I wear it sometimes to remind me how much work I've put in to get where I am."

"Sounds, like a true perspiration-al shirt," I kid him.

"You want to talk to gBeto?" he's apparently decided I'm not just on a neighborly visit. Probably because Demetrius isn't with me.

"If I could…"

"Absolutely, what are neighbors for if not to talk to each other?" Nathaniel waves me in as he calls, "G! We have company."

Nathaniel closes the door and walks over to the refrigerator.

"If you have a white, I think might prefer it today," I interrupt his exploration for a red.

"White?" Nathaniel puzzles for a moment, closes the door to the refrigerator and glances around the kitchen. "I think I have a Super Tuscan next in line."

"Not a white but I like Super Tuscan…" I confirm as he goes to find the bottle. In only a moment gBeto appears in the kitchen door, apparently still dressed for work as she's barefoot, but wearing a nice white blouse and charcoal pants. The multicolored pearls around her neck seem to pull both articles of clothing into them.

"Hi," she greets me. "Didn't expect to see you again so soon, but I am happy to see you. Nathaniel's getting you a glass, hopefully he'll bring one for me too."

"And one for me," Nathaniel responds as he re-enters the kitchen from the storage room where they must keep most of their wines. "You'll like this one."

"Come on in, we can sit in the family room while he struggles with the cork. A record setting running back, used to running past three-hundred-pound football linemen all intent on bringing him down and you'd think he could extract a cork from a bottle of wine? Not so much."

"It's just because I refuse to use those motorized gizmos. I prefer the lever openers they use at the wineries." Nathaniel informs us as I follow her out of the kitchen. "It's more authentic."

"Nathaniel will have our glasses shortly," she sits and I do, across from her in the comfortably furnished family room. I notice the colors are soothing. Apparently, this is a place they come to relax. A place where the room just comforts you with the colors and abstract art on the walls. A fireplace dominates the room, but there is no fire tonight. Too warm. No need to warm us with the display of colored light and heat.

"I really appreciate your willingness to meet with me and help me understand... what's happening here. I admit I have no idea. I'm just an observer, who's trying to make sense of everything even though much has yet to come out in court. I don't know what the verdict would be if it were made based on what we all know. But I'm sure you have a good feel for it, or you wouldn't be going ahead with the case."

gBeto doesn't respond to my characterization of the case. Apparently, that was asking too much. I need to temper my expectations. "What I really came to talk with you about is we had a chance to interview the former officer..."

"You interviewed him," gBeto responds as if she weren't expecting this.

"We did. Two of us from Continuum. We have a highly experienced commentator who gives us stories by the name of Randall Smith. He joined me at the city jail, and together we had a conversation. I'm sure if I'd gone in there alone, it probably would have been a disaster. But Randall, he knew how to steer him, how to call bullshit, how to lower his expectations that we were going to change anything."

"Must have been a real learning experience for you," gBeto observes.

"It was. I'm grateful I have people like Randall, who can keep me out of trouble. Show me what's important, how to maneuver away from making statements that will come back to haunt us."

gBeto nods but is still trying to figure out why I'm here. She must have a million things to do and yet she's making time for me, and I'm nobody important to her. And to her credit she doesn't ask what the officer said to me. She probably expects it will be better if I just tell her. "The officer..."

"Former officer... since he was fired by the mayor personally. That's a real distinction. Not many cops get that kind of attention."

"You don't like him," I realize.

"Didn't say that. I was simply referencing the fact that the… former officer… was fired for a reason. He was not a good cop. He didn't follow procedure. He took a life where the evidence has not supported the need. It's not that I have any feeling about the former officer as a person. I don't know anything about him that isn't more than twenty years old. I don't know what's happened to him in all these years that would make him capable of taking a life. That's all."

"Is that the question you're trying to answer?" I am surprised at the way she phrased it.

"The fundamental question, yes."

"Then you don't believe he acted out of fear for his own life."

"I can only comment on what we see in the videos."

"And you don't think they support he was acting in the line of duty," I push.

"If I did, I wouldn't have brought charges against him," gBeto responds evenly.

"The officer has a different take on what's happened. Why you're prosecuting him."

"No doubt you're going to give me his take on the matter, but for me that's not the issue. He can attribute anything he wants to me. I'm not the one who pulled the trigger three times with his weapon trained on center mass of an individual who was not threatening to him in a life-or-death manner."

"Is that your opening statement?" I have to ask as it sounds rehearsed.

gBeto shakes her head but won't comment on some aspect of my question that apparently got through to her. I don't have any idea what it is.

"I talked to my father about this case. Do you know what he told me I have to do?"

gBeto responds by shaking her head just once, very slowly and keeping her eye on me throughout. She continues to think about something she's not willing to share. Am I stepping over the line by taking advantage of my being her neighbor? Have I made her uncomfortable that I'm using that relationship to my advantage?

Nathaniel enters the room with two glasses of a glorious red wine. "I hope the blood of the gods will help you solve all the issues before us."

"Blood of the gods?" I'm not sure I'm following him although I think he's talking about the wine.

"Sangiovese, the grape in this wine was named the blood of Jupiter, who was the supreme Roman God." Nathaniel informs us. "Didn't you know that?"

I shake my head, inhale the bouquet, and swirl the red liquid in the expansive glass he served it in. I look at the color, appreciating it but having no idea whether it means it's a good wine or not. I just enjoy the taste and the effect that helps me sleep, not recognizing how it enables a looser conversation.

"What are you discussing this evening?" Nathaniel decides to join the conversation. I assume he knows as much about what is happening as gBeto, but I like talking to her one-on-one. Will this change the dynamic somehow? I'll have to continue and see if it vectors us off somehow.

gBeto responds, "Sarah was going to tell me what her father suggested she needs to do to get to the real issues we're dealing with."

I sip the wine and nod approval before setting the glass down. "My father told me I have to set aside any feelings I have about the matter and only consider the facts I can establish. And that's been the hardest part. Establishing the facts. For example, I can't establish the facts around why you are still on administrative leave, Nathaniel. It makes no sense to the casual observer. It makes no sense to most of the informed observers I've discussed it with. And yet here you are, still on leave and not able to help with the investigations that will either convict or not an officer in your department. That makes no sense to me and really, any of the informed observers with whom I've spoken."

"Observers not in the department," Nathaniel responds as if he's trying to steer me to a conclusion.

I have to stop and think. He's correct, none of those I spoke to are in the department.

"Are you suggesting people in the department would have a different take on things?" I ask trying to understand what he's saying to me.

Nathaniel glances at gBeto who is stoic, shakes his head and continues. "The mayor has given me an explanation for her choice not to reinstate me. If you wish to understand her motivation, I would suggest you consult with her."

gBeto seems accepting of that answer and she looks down at her lap.

"I will have that conversation with Mayor Richards tomorrow at ten, which is when I'm scheduled to meet with her. Is there anything in particular I should be listening for?"

"Her choice of words," gBeto responds.

"Meaning I'll likely have a better understanding of her motivation not by what she says, as how she says it?" I respond, to confirm what I think she's saying to me.

"Think wide, not narrowly," Nathaniel responds. "She's under enormous pressure. The problem with politics is no one will tell you the truth. Everyone is posturing all of the time. No one decides to vote against someone because of an action they have taken, something they have said, or even a gesture they make to someone. It's not concrete. People are always interpreting behavior rather than waiting to see the outcomes of what they do."

"How would you describe what you've done as commissioner?" I hope he will be forthcoming but can easily see he may not.

"I've tried, through incredible obstacles, to reform the department to serve all citizens and visitors with the same courtesy and respect they are due. To seek equality and justice in any event we respond to. I've tried to promote competence and rid the department of those who have their own agendas. Unfortunately, although that is exactly what I promised the mayor, it has not proven to be acceptable to those who are really determining public policy in this city."

"What do you mean by that?" I can't leave it that ambiguous.

"The ordinance says I should have returned to work when the internal affairs report was delivered to city council and the mayor."

"And you weren't." I note.

"Draw your own conclusion. It's probably as valid as mine."

"And you aren't the real target," I observe waiting for them to ask me about my observation.

gBeto bites first. "You referenced a claim the former officer made. What was it?"

I shift gears, not sure if I have all the answers I was looking for from Nathaniel. It is clear he's not entirely happy where we've left it. But I need to determine if the former officer is baiting me, or there really is something to his claim. I have the best chance of anyone in getting to the truth, but others including Tic Rogers will have their take on the matter in Politico or the Morning News blogs or somewhere that will create even more questions about the ability of Continuum media to get the real story. I look at Nathaniel and ask, "Did the former officer ever claim your wife held a grudge against him for something he did when or just after he graduated from high school?"

Nathaniel shrugs, "I've known him two decades or more. He's never said a word to me about gBeto. Not even when she was elected. No congrats or anything. He knew we were married. What's he saying now?"

"That she left high school for a year. Something happened to cause her to leave. Whatever that was, explains why she wants him put in prison."

"He said that to you?" gBeto focuses in on my every word. "That my year away explains why I want to see him punished? Even though that was nearly three decades ago, and he screwed up now." gBeto shakes her head as if she can't believe what he said.

Nathaniel looks at gBeto as if this is all news to him.

gBeto looks at Nathaniel in a way that confirms she knows it is all news to him, looks down into her lap and thinks about whether she should respond or not.

gBeto looks at me, "Will I be reading this tomorrow in your blogs and then every other blog in the nation?"

"Tell me what you have to say and then I'll have to make a decision," is all I can say.

gBeto takes a deep breath, "I did leave high school for a year. I went to live with my grandmother on a small farm just across the border in New Mexico. I home schooled for that year and helped my grandmother, who had a health issue. She passed away; I went home."

"You took a year off to help your grandmother who was dying. What does that have to do with the former officer?"

"Taking care of my grandmother had nothing to do with the former officer," gBeto responds with a harsh tone, looking at Nathaniel. "That whole year had nothing to do with the former officer."

"Then why is he saying it does?" I have to ask.

gBeto looks at Nathaniel, "I've never discussed this since. Nathaniel, you don't even know. By the time we met, it didn't make any difference. It was just easier to go on as if nothing had happened."

Nathaniel crosses over to gBeto and sits next to her, "What is it babe? What haven't you told me?"

"The former officer wasn't involved but likely learned from others what happened. I can't imagine why he's bringing this up now. It won't help his case, but maybe he thinks he can influence me."

"I cannot counter his assertion unless you are willing to share more," I decide, but she is really reluctant to discuss whatever happened since she has not even discussed it with her husband.

"He is trying to ruin my credibility… I am damned if I tell you and damned if I do not. But I trust you will use good judgement." gBeto hesitates, "That year I was pregnant. I delivered a child who was adopted at birth. I've had no contact with the child or the father since."

"Was Mick the father?" Nathaniel asks stunned by this information.

gBeto looks at him, "No."

CHAPTER TWENTY-NINE:

gBeto Dahomey Brown, Attorney General, State of Texas

I recognize Margaret Flannery from across the room of the Susan Komen Breast Cancer Foundation fund raiser. We are in the crystal chandeliered Capitol Hotel ballroom, where many political events have occurred for more than a century. I can't even begin to remember how many times I've been here for one event or another. This is just the most recent. Margaret apparently sees me, brightens and comes over.

"Attorney General Brown, we are pleased you would take the time from your busy schedule to come support our cause," Margaret Flannery takes my hand and squeezes.

"I understand you're the Chairperson this year," had to reach to remember that tidbit.

"I am. Thank you for remembering. But this is one of those events where those of us who are coordinating the efforts of many are insignificant in comparison to the efforts of those who work so hard to raise the funds and enable the research that will save thousands, if not millions, of lives."

"You and your husband have always been benefactors to our community and those in need." I say as a way to thank her.

"Is there anyone I can introduce you to?" Margaret Flannery looks about the room.

I shake my head, "I'm here to support the cause, and hope I can be an inspiration to others who feel they may not have the time. If I can make the time, particularly now, hopefully they will as well."

"Sarah has been giving us just glowing reviews of you and your husband. You've been kind to her, helping her adjust to life in a new neighborhood and giving her insights that have been just invaluable to her budding career."

"Nathaniel's unending trivia about wine?" I suggest?

"I'm sure that will be helpful when she begins entertaining, but no. What you've shared about your work to enforce the laws of the state, seek justice for all and equity under the law."

"She's done a good job of explaining things if you can remember them, but I don't know that I've done anything other than make her blogs targets for those who have negative opinions of me and my motives. For that I'm most sorry."

"Don't be," Margaret responds. "Sarah has become determined to tell your story. She wants to ensure anyone reading the many malicious blogs will understand the truth to the matter."

"I hope she learns quickly, because there are many who would be just as happy to see her fail to enable their own success."

"You've just given me the clearest description I've heard of the industry my husband has sought to lead for the last twenty-five years. Thomas is not about to let his daughter fail. He is coaching her and reading everything she writes before it's posted. She's learning fast. But she has an innate feeling for right and wrong, truth and lies, and those who are trying to spin things for their own advantage without regard for those who will suffer from falsehoods spread to the masses."

"I'm sure your husband is about the best mentor she could have, with what you both have accomplished," I think the conversation is nearing an end.

"There's good and bad with what Thomas is doing for her," Margaret continues, surprising me.

"I don't think I know what you're saying," is all I can think of to say.

"Sarah's very bright, but she's always been alone." Margaret hesitates for a moment before continuing. "We couldn't have children right away. And then she came along and has brought joy into our lives. She is exactly what we were missing for many years. But that makes us old to her. She sees us as not understanding what she's going through. Pushes us away sometimes, and others, she's there... the same little girl we raised, needing help or support or just someone to reassure her she's loved."

"I can't speak from experience as a mother, but I think all kids are like what you describe. They see us as old, but only because we grew up in different times, with different pressures and different expectations. And they all go through periods where they want to show themselves, they can function in this world independently. Make their own choices, even if that means failing from time to time. But they want those choices to be theirs, even if that means living with regrets."

Margaret Flannery glances at me, "I see why she likes you. I'm glad she chose to move next door to you and your husband. Not everyone would listen and try to offer sage advice. So many don't even listen these days."

"You and your husband are clearly loving parents; Sarah couldn't ask for a better environment to grow up in. And having the opportunities you can afford her with your firm; she is very fortunate."

"And next you're going to tell me it's all up to her now?" Margaret guesses.

"No, because you already knew that and don't need to hear it from me. But I'm glad your husband is continuing to mentor her. She will look back and realize just how much you have shaped who she will be."

"And then there's Demetrius..." Margaret Flannery touches my arm with a smile at a thought she's not likely to share. "She is going to have an interesting life; that's about all I can say about that."

"I've found him to be thoughtful and a bit introspective. He should be a good husband for her." I'm not looking for an explanation of her evaluation of Demetrius White. But I do want to reassure her if it's a negative evaluation I've not had it.

"They'll make a life for themselves," Margaret continues. "I just hope she's ready to carry a football team to term. He wants lots of kids. I don't know how she will handle that being an only child. She likes having all our attention and not having to share it. Demetrius is one of six kids. He loves having brothers and sisters around all the time. Before they married Sarah came to us and asked if she was making a mistake since their expectations were very different. She intends to be a professional woman. Having a whole brood of kids will be difficult."

"But you clearly have the resources to give her help raising kids. She'll have to find her own level and they'll just need to communicate every step of the way. Being in communications I would expect she'll figure that out."

Margaret Flannery nods agreement, touches my arm before turning to go, "I hope so."

CHAPTER THIRTY:

Rory James, Senior Vice President and Partner, Continuum Media

When I called gBeto, told who was calling and there was a nearly minute long silence before she said anything, I wasn't sure she would come. She had to be surprised to hear from me, after more than twenty years. After we decided to go our separate ways, even though we have been in the same city most of that time. But here she is, walking into the wood heavy dining room of McGlynn's Pub and Restaurant. She looks around, spots me and approaches. I was hoping for a smile, but she does not. If anything, she seems to be approaching this lunch with dread. All the same, she looks great.

"I should have expected you to eat here," she begins as she sits across from me.

"Actually, I don't very often, even though it's Irish food. Never liked what my mother made. It's not like home, thank goodness. Anyway, it's a long walk. I tend to eat closer to my condo."

"You live around here somewhere?"

I smile, "Practically across the street from my office. It's just me. Having a big house somewhere doesn't make much sense. Putting up with the traffic just to get in and out of the city. Just to stare at green grass? That's never been me."

We stare at each other for a moment as all the memories flood past me in a blur of emotion. I'm ecstatic to see her. I'm likely to cry. But at the same time, I'm retreating to the reasons we went our separate ways, which pulls me back. "I loved you when you were bone thin, but

I have to say you're much more attractive now."

gBeto shows a weak smile, probably remembering what she looked like in high school. "I got my act together."

"I never had any doubt," I smile at her.

"You changed your name, why?" I didn't realize she knew that.

"I had to cut my ties to East Hill in my business. Too many people judge you by where you came from. I had it legally changed right after graduation. Probably among the best things I've done given recent events." I let hang there for a long moment. "You married."

She nods although I can't be sure if it's to my point of changing my name or her getting married. "Nathaniel's been good for me. Balances me out. Keeps me focused," she reflects for a long moment then continues, "But you said you're all by yourself. Did you ever marry?"

I shake my head not sure I can answer her question without revealing feelings I don't want her to see. After a too long moment I clear my throat and respond, "I'm married to my job. Always have been. Only now, I'm the boss, and I never knew how much difference that would make."

She seems to reflect on my answer, looks down and nods, once. "What did you do after school? College?" she asks trying to fill in gaps.

Deep breath, got to sell it. "I started selling anything anyone would hire me for. I figured out quickly I was never going to be a rocket scientist. The only thing I was good at was convincing people to buy stuff. It never occurred to me there was more money on the sales side than anything else I could do, but it worked out that way. Funny thing though. Because I never went to college? No one would hire me today. Without a degree I'd never even get in the front door. The kids I'm hiring today? I'll hire them without the degree because I don't have one, but they have to get one within five years, or I terminate them."

"Have you… terminated anyone for that reason?"

LOVE

"I have," I reflect for a moment, "Sent a loud message to the rest of the team I was serious. After she completed her degree, I rehired her and she's now one of my best people. You just never know."

"You keep in touch with anyone from high school?" she asks, still curious about what I've been doing with my life.

"I see Mick like once a month, he's all the family I have left. Mom and Dad passed away a couple years ago."

"Wow, they died young. We're they even sixty yet?"

"Dad would have been fifty-eight and mom fifty-five."

"Did something happen to them?" gBeto seems genuinely interested. I'm a little surprised.

"Natural gas leak. They were still living in the old house. They never moved, even though I offered to get them a better place. Stubborn. Gas line came apart at a rusted coupling and filled the house with gas while they were asleep. They just never woke up." I still can't believe they're gone. "What about your folks?"

"Mom passed away last year. Dad's still in the same house, dirt floor and all. But he retired and my sister moved in with him. She divorced after just a couple years of marriage and vowed she'd never do that again. She's been working as a teacher's aide all these years. Paid her bills, but not much more. Saw taking care of Dad as an opportunity to save a few dollars. It seems to be working out."

"It's funny how some family will take whatever you'll give them and others, if they didn't make it themselves, they don't want your charity even though you can easily afford it."

"We've both come a long way from the old neighborhood," gBeto observes introspectively.

"We have and I couldn't be happier for you. Attorney General. That was just inconceivable back then."

"Being a partner in a media company? Equally so."

"Do you think the decisions we made back then drove us to what we've become?" I ask to see what she's thinking about this conversation.

"It had a lot to do with it. I never want to be poor again."

"Same with me, but it's strange. The more money I've made the less important it's become. I could live on a lot less. Move to a cheaper place that would still be comfortable. Not buy luxury goods, or eat in the better restaurants. Since it's just me, and I'm pretty well set with the business, I just don't know why it's important to make a lot of money."

"But you haven't gone off to Tibet to become a monk and contemplate the meaning of life," she points out.

"Hadn't thought of it, but maybe I should consider..." I look away to visualize Tibet.

"I wasn't serious," she leans forward to make sure I know. "The good Catholic you are, I just wouldn't see you in Tibet studying Buddhism."

"I'm not such a good Catholic anymore," I admit. "I go when I have a guilty conscience, or just need to be with other people for a while. But it doesn't have the same meaning to me as when I was growing up. Probably needed it then to make sense of the world. But as I got older, I don't know as it explained anything to me anymore."

"That's a big change for an altar boy."

"Yeah, well, Mick was an altar boy too," I need to move this along as nostalgia really isn't my thing either.

"You know I'm prosecuting him," gBeto instantly sees this isn't just an opportunity to catch up.

I nod, "I see he brought up your year away," I hang out there for her to get it out of the way.

242

LOVE

"He did," she is apparently wondering why.

"I asked him about that," I want her to know the source of my insight.

"And?"

"He thought you'd never prosecute him because of our relationship and what he knew about it. When you did, he was just pissed off he misjudged you. He thought if he raised the issue the media would go looking for an explanation and you'd have to back off to keep him from saying more."

gBeto looks away clearly absorbing the information. After a moment of silence, she turns to me almost angry, at least hostile, "Is that why you called me? To get me to back off your brother?"

I hold up my hands, "Whoa. Do you really think that little of me?"

"Then why am I here?" she demands to know. "Why did you even tell me that?"

"You mean why now? After all this time? Just when you're prosecuting my brother? Why didn't I just stay in my quiet life and leave you alone? Is that what you're asking me?"

"Yes. That's exactly what I'm asking you," gBeto leaves no doubt.

"How much do you remember about my family from high school?"

"Your family?" she softens realizing she's misjudged. "I don't know what you're asking me."

"Do you remember anything about my relationship with Mick?"

"You never seemed that close is all I remember," gBeto reflects.

"Do you remember all the bruises?"

243

I see gBeto stopping to think, "I thought that was your father because you never talked about him, not even at the holiday time."

I shake my head, "Mick beat me like nearly every day. I was his punching bag for every slight he suffered, every mocking comment another kid would make about him being a stupid Irish nobody. His nickname was Potato-boy. The problem was Mick wasn't very strong or very coordinated. Anytime he got into a fight at school he always took the worst of it. I was an easy target because I'd never fight back."

"Why didn't you?" gBeto asks apparently never putting any of this together.

"Because he was my brother." I shrug.

"You would take a beating from him nearly every day because he was family? Where was your father, your mother? Didn't they ever step in?"

"They barely knew we were there. We were just mouths to feed. Besides, Mick was expert at leaving marks in places you normally wouldn't see."

"Why did you think I'd see them then?"

"When we made love, you pointed them out. You may not remember, but I clearly do. I was ashamed that you saw them. Embarrassed that maybe you'd think less of me. Afraid you wouldn't want to do it again, thinking I couldn't stand up for myself."

"I don't think I ever thought that about you," gBeto responds softly and seems to have dropped her hostility.

"I've known Mick was out of control for a long time. The childhood anger and hostility he developed has never gone away. I really think that's why he decided to become a cop. He was never there to help anyone. He was there to get even. He's never confirmed this, but I think he was abused by Father Mulcahy when he was an altar boy. They spent a lot of time together. Father tried to get me to come to his apartment too, but I always found an excuse not to."

"Why are you telling me this?" she reaches out and puts her hand over mine.

"I know you can't discuss the case and I'd never ask you to. Mick doesn't know I'm talking with you and I'll never tell him. But he said something the last time we talked that made me start thinking. I didn't know it but he had run into Bo Madison before."

"What?" gBeto clearly didn't know.

"There's a club called Just Enuff Cabaret."

gBeto stares at me but waits for me to say more.

"Mick knows the owner and worked there occasionally as a bouncer for three or four years. If you investigate what happened, you'll likely have a motive that I don't think has come out yet. It was like a year ago or more."

"How do you know about this? Did Mick tell you?"

"Indirectly. Bits and pieces, you know? When he first started, he'd said something to me that I should stop by because the girls were really something. He knew I wasn't into that, but he was just busting me because he thinks I'm a monk or gay or something."

"Are you? Gay?" gBeto asks catching me off guard.

"I guess you could say I'm neither since..." I can't finish this sentence as I'm overwhelmed. I change the subject. "Anyway, he mentioned to me another time that a number of athletes came by the club and he'd be happy to introduce me. It didn't occur to me until I was listening to him rant about the charges against him and everything that one of the athletes he mentioned that night was Bo Madison. I remember him talking about how big he was for a running back."

"He knew who he was," gBeto confirms, "May have talked with him at the club. But how does this link him to wanting to kill him?"

"I think you will find that answer if you find people who were in the club the last night Mick worked there."

"Payroll records would give me the date," gBeto notes.

"I would talk with the owner if I were you. See what he remembers."

"Is he covering up for Mick?" gBeto wants to go down a path I hoped she wouldn't.

"If you owned a gentlemen's club, would you want to have anything to do with a police shooting trial?"

"That's why you pointed me to the payroll records," gBeto realizes. "Proof he worked there. Did the internal affairs people know about this?"

"Your husband would likely have a better idea than I would." I see gBeto pull back at my mention of her husband, but then she must see what I'm suggesting.

"I'll ask Nathaniel," she acknowledges I may be correct in my assumption. "Why are you doing this? You know it will help me convict him."

"As I said, Mick has been out of control since he was a kid. He won't seek help to deal with whatever's driving him. This may be the only way he'll get it under control."

"And you're afraid he will kill someone else."

I can't say more, as I've probably already said too much. I let her assume what she will. She apparently understands it has been hard for me to do this at all, and particularly now.

"You did the right thing. And I'm glad you reached out to me. I think of you often. Hoped you had found what you want from life."

I can't answer her, pulled back into the time when we were together. I turn to a different topic. "Have you ever wondered...?"

"What would have happened if we chose differently?" she completes my question. "Every day."

"Really? I thought it was just me." I look at her again the way I always did.

"We were just kids… way in over our heads. We really didn't have any choice where we lived, how we lived then. The future was waiting, but it could have been very different…"

"No food, barely making ends meet was the only life we knew," I reflect. "And even though I love you more than anything, the life we would have had staying there…"

She looks at me as if appraising what I've just admitted, then looks down before continuing. "We agreed. That's all you have to remember. It wasn't you wanting to try to make a go of it and not me, or the other way around. We made a choice. We live with the consequences of our choices."

"I found her," I have to tell her.

"Who?"

CHAPTER THIRTY-ONE:

gBeto Dahomey Brown, Attorney General, State of Texas

"All rise, this court is now in session, Judge Sondra Flack presiding," the bailiff calls.

This is the first case I've prosecuted since being elected attorney general. I wouldn't be here if LaMance hadn't tried to take advantage of the situation. I don't blame her. It's not likely she would have been elected on her own. She saw her chance, hoping if she were appointed to succeed me, she might have had the support to continue on. *But that's all over.*

Judge Flack looks down at me, "Attorney General, it is a rare privilege to have you in my court prosecuting a case before me."

"Your honor, it is my privilege to argue before such a distinguished Jurist."

The defense attorney, Ralph Simpson, asks for recognition, "Your honor, I hope the stature of the prosecuting attorney will not be a factor in the decision of this court."

Judge Flack shakes her head, "Mr. Simpson. This case will be decided by the skill you and the Attorney General display before this jury and no other factors. The governor or the president could come argue before me and it wouldn't make any difference."

"Thank you, your honor, I just wanted to be on record."

After opening statements where I asserted we would show premeditation and the defense asserted supposition and innuendo was the best we would be able to produce, we replayed the videos and recounted the facts of the case for the jury. I am surprised Mr. Simpson does not object to some of the evidence provided, but I've been very careful to characterize evidence clearly. What someone saw versus what someone heard versus what someone was told by a third party. I purposely worked to ensure Mr. Simpson had to accept the evidence as presented.

We broke for lunch and Aamaal, who is at the table with me, spends the whole time on her phone talking with the investigators who have been acting on Rory's tip.

When she finishes her call I ask, "Well?"

"The owner provided the payroll records, but if we want him to testify, we will have to subpoena him."

"He wasn't willing to provide any insight as to what happened that night?"

Aamaal shakes her head, "Might get answers under oath," she suggests.

"Issue the subpoena and tell Scotty we need to know what we have today," I respond unhappy, but Rory told me it wasn't likely the owner would want to be helpful. "This trial is not going to last long at the rate we are moving."

The first witness I bring to the stand is Lieutenant Childers who was the lead investigator for the internal affairs investigation and report.

"Lieutenant Childers, your team of six investigators, including an officer from the Houston department, examined all of the evidence and interviewed witnesses."

"Yes."

"Did you find evidence of premeditation on the part of former officer Michael St. James in his encounter with Bo Madison on the evening in question?"

"No."

"Would you say your investigation was exhaustive of both former officer St. James' professional and personal activities?'

"Yes,"

"Did you interview all of his part time employers over the past ten years?"

"Department records do not indicate former officer St. James had any part time employment over the past ten years," Childers sounds confused.

"Is it department policy that officers must disclose any part time employment both in terms of start and ending dates of such employment?"

"Yes. If former officer St. James had been working for any other party during his term of active duty without disclosing it, it would have been a departmental policy violation,"

"On top of the other eight you cited in the report?"

Lieutenant Childers frowns at me but grudgingly responds, "Yes."

"Did you make any effort to try to determine if former officer St. James had worked part time during his term of active duty."

"We don't investigate supposition."

I turn just in time to see Scottie enter carrying the papers I need, I walk over to retrieve them from her, "Your honor I would like to submit these payroll records from the Just Enuff Lounge, where the former officer occasionally worked as a bouncer over a period of nearly four years, a term of employment that ended approximately twelve months ago. Please note that the payroll records state that former officer St. James was and I quote, 'terminated for cause.'" I look over at the defendant who is completely impassive.

"Lieutenant Childers, I have just shown you that your team

missed at least one fact in the investigation you conducted. Would you agree?"

"I have not reviewed the payroll records you have entered, but I would have to acknowledge that we may have not caught something that was likely immaterial."

"Immaterial?" I walk over towards the jury. "Lieutenant Childers, would you say that the fact Bo Madison frequented the Just Enuff Lounge and former officer St. James frequently worked there as a bouncer is immaterial to this case?"

"That would depend on whether there was a nexus." Lieutenant Childers responds coldly.

"Meaning whether there was an incident between the two men at this club. Is that what you're saying?"

"Yes."

"Lieutenant Childers, you will hear from at least three witnesses who were in the club on the night former officer St. James was terminated for cause, that there was an altercation between them."

"An altercation?" Lieutenant Childers looks over at the defendant and frowns.

"These witnesses will state for the record that former officer St. James was sleeping with one of the dancers at this club. That on the evening of the former officer's dismissal, Bo Madison was in the club with three friends who had played football with him at UT."

"Objection your honor, the prosecutor is leading the witness," from Mr. Simpson.

"Your honor, I am providing information to Lieutenant Childers which his team of investigators missed in their examination of events to determine whether their report has any relevance in this case."

"Proceed," from Judge Flack.

"On that evening, Bo Madison struck up a conversation with the dancer who the former officer was sleeping with. Former officer St. James objected to Bo Madison having that conversation and tried to rough him up. According to the witnesses he then forcefully ejected Bo Madison from the club. The next day Bo Madison and his former team mates returned to the club and lodged a formal complaint with the owner who terminated former officer St. James as a result. Now Lieutenant Childers, none of this is in the report your investigation filed with the city. Why is that?"

"Evidently because we did not ask the defendant in our interview if he deliberately violated department policy by working part time elsewhere without reporting it to the department."

"Despite the fact you identified eight violations of policy," I point out.

"Our recommendation was that he be stripped of his licenses and certifications and terminated from the department. We could have continued to pursue any number of possible additional violations but it would not have changed what we thought should be the outcome."

"Termination with no chance of re-employment in the State of Texas."

"Correct," the lieutenant apparently wants to end the discussion here.

"But if you had uncovered the prior encounter with Bo Madison, would that have changed your recommendation?"

"Meaning would we have advocated for prosecution?" Lieutenant Childers seeks to confirm.

"Or any other recommendations," I widen his options for response.

"From the nature of the discussions we had I don't believe so. What you uncovered is unrelated to the events of the officer involved shooting. They happened nearly a year before from what you said, and you do not cite any other interaction between them subsequent to that night."

"If I got you fired, Lieutenant, do you think you would remember me a year later?"

"Very likely," he admits grudgingly.

"The record shows former officer St. James has an anger management problem for which he has been enrolled in therapy on two occasions, although he did not complete the course of therapy in either instance. Is that normal department procedure? That once determined to need help with an issue, an officer is enrolled but has no obligation to complete?"

"I wouldn't know," the Lieutenant respond sullenly.

"But you are an expert in department policy and procedure, are you not? I mean as the person in charge of internal affairs investigations, who cited eight violations of department policy and procedure in the report, it would seem you have to be an expert to be able to cite them."

"I can tell you what the policies and procedures are, but I can't tell you how they are administered, or not, as the case may be."

"Really lieutenant? If there were a policy in the department that hasn't been enforced in two decades you would not know?"

"We don't have policies on the books that aren't enforced. We review them every three years and either modify or withdraw them."

"Then the policy regarding attendance at anger management therapy classes is an active policy. It is being enforced. And yet I see nothing in the policy stating it is a voluntary program. If referred to a class you can still decide not to participate."

"That's not how I understand the policy," the lieutenant confirms.

"But that's what happened twice. Is there something written down anywhere that says former officer St. James was exempt from the policy?"

"No."

"And yet this violation of policy wasn't cited in the report either. Why didn't your investigation find this violation? Does that take it up to ten?"

"I'm not counting because these aren't findings," the Lieutenant responds clearly uncertain now.

"Actually, it was two separate violations. I think we're up to eleven. Is there anything the former officer did right?"

"The former officer did many things right," the lieutenant snaps at me. "Too many things to count as a matter of fact."

"Would you reinstate him to active duty?"

"Yes ma'am, I would. He was a fine officer, who was often an exemplary example for our younger officers.

"Like his ability to hit center mass with three consecutive shots when only one would have ended the life of Bo Madison?"

Lieutenant Childers apparently realizes he's headed down a slippery slope and has already said too much.

"Lieutenant, coming back to my earlier question. Knowing there are multiple holes in the report of the internal affairs investigation, would you agree that it should not be the definitive report on what occurred that night between Bo Madison and former officer Michael St. James?"

"It is substantially correct. There may be one or two facts we missed, since parties to the events chose not to come forward with information."

"If you were a Black man in this town, your best friend was killed by a White cop would you stand up and say boo? Particularly about an event that happened a year earlier? If you say yes, it's because you're not a Black man and haven't grown up in fear of the police as these young men have."

"Objection," Mr. Simpson voices. "Foundation. The prosecutor is speculating about a generalization that has no direct bearing on the case at hand."

"Objection is sustained. Mrs. Brown please confine your speculations to the campaign trail and focus on facts and evidence in my court room."

"Your honor, it is a fact that Black men grow up in fear of the police in this city. If you would like me to bring in witnesses to verify that fact, I will be happy to do so."

"Mrs. Brown, I hear what you're saying, but let's confine the facts and evidence to this case, specifically."

"Yes, your honor. No more questions for Lieutenant Childers."

"No questions your honor," Mr. Simpson gives him a pass.

"My next witness is Ronald Wojowicz, owner of the Just Enuff Lounge who my associate is bringing into the courtroom just now."

Once Ronald Wojowicz is sworn in, I go for the jugular, "Mr. Wojowicz, you are the owner of the Just Enuff Lounge, you employed Michael St. James as a bouncer and fired him for cause. What happened?"

"The pervert tried to shake me down. Wanted a job as a bouncer so he could watch the girls for free. He was banging one of my dancers. Kept getting into fights with customers over her. I had to fire the bum. He was costing me business."

"On the night you terminated Mr. St. James was one of the customers he roughed up Bo Madison?"

"I didn't see him in the club that night, but he and his friends paid me a visit next day and made a complaint. I talked to my barkeep and he confirmed what happened."

"Did your barkeep confirm that Mr. St. James yelled at Bo Madison that he would kill him if he caught him with his girl?"

Mr. Wojowicz looks at the defendant and shakes his head. "That's not what I was told."

I stop, feeling my racing heart, turn and look at the overweight club owner. "What were you told?"

Mr. Wojowicz looks at me, "I'm still under oath and if I don't tell you I can be prosecuted?"

I nod.

The club owner looks at former officer St. James and responds, "My barkeep told me… now I didn't hear this but my barkeep's never told me anything that didn't prove out… anyway, he told me he heard him…" he points to the defendant, "Scream at Bo Madison that he'd kill him or any nigger who tried to sleep with the girl he was banging."

"Is that why you terminated the defendant?"

"Hey, I have a lot of Black customers, mostly on Wednesday, you know? I can't have a guy at the door driving them away. That would cost me."

CHAPTER THIRTY-TWO:

Thomas Flannery, CEO and Partner Continuum Media

Rory and I have lunch at the Capital Club once a month to review how the business is doing, out of the office, in a neutral setting where we can hopefully be objective. This has been instrumental in some of the best decisions we have made over the past decade working together. Besides, the food is generally excellent.

Today we are discussing what audience and advertisers we might find for a blog site on urban mobility, an emerging topic Rory likes, because he doesn't own a car anymore, taking Uber or Lyft wherever he needs to go. "But does anyone care about that anymore?" I'm asking him. "Other than autonomous vehicles there's nothing new to talk about. And they're a ways off as they have been for the last decade."

"Because of our reputation of balance, I think we can attract a number of advertisers," Rory begins. "The vehicle manufacturers who are trying to get people to buy their electrics, and the charging companies who want people to put chargers in their garages, and all the shared ride folks, and the engineering companies that want to redesign cities to accommodate the self-drives. I really think the advertising revenue is there and will grow over time."

"I'm not so sure about the readers…" I point out. "And if the readers don't appear, the advertisers will disappear. We don't want to start something that doesn't deliver the audience. We've never had that happen in our whole ten years."

I look up and see Margaret and gBeto Brown coming towards us. I didn't know Margaret was coming into town and why the attorney general? *Must be something to do with one of the foundations Margaret is supporting. At least I hope that's what it is.* But to my surprise they come to our table. Rory rises and I follow, "To what do we owe this pleasant surprise?"

"We're having lunch with you," Margaret informs us.

"Do you know my partner, Rory James?" I ask gBeto.

"We actually grew up together," Rory responds.

"In that case, please sit down," I turn to Rory and say, "We can finish this discussion back at the office with some statistics on similar product in the market."

"I have that," Rory responds.

"Was this just a spur of the moment…" I begin, not even sure what to call it.

"gBeto gave me a call and asked if we could have a conversation," Margaret informs us. "I remembered you and Rory were meeting today. It seemed the perfect opportunity."

"We should have thought of this before," I suggest. "Now that Sarah and Demetrius have moved in next door to you and your husband, we really should get to know you better. Let you better understand the type of neighbors the kids are likely to be."

"Actually, gBeto and I had a nice conversation on that very topic at the Komen luncheon. But seeing us both should give her a little more depth to her understanding, a little more insight into the balanced perspectives we hope have been instilled in our little girl."

"I'm pleased you were able to chat and yes, we are an open book. Just regular people who have done well and want to give back for our good fortune. But I'm sure you can see, we do tend to enjoy the fruits of our labors, have a tendency toward the finer things in life now that we can afford them. But that wasn't always the case. When Sarah was about ten, Rory and I started our business with nothing more than an idea, a few dollars we'd saved and expertise we'd honed over the previous decade in that particular business arena. There were many a sleepless night wondering if we had enough cash to be able to make payroll. Nights when we were trying to identify things we could sell if we needed to, wondering how to improve cash flow. And Rory was the one who made it all possible, out there every day selling advertising for our products, building a loyal following of ever more important advertisers. For the first three years I don't think I had a sound night's sleep. And then it all turned around. We had extra cash in the bank. We suddenly had enough to be able to make payroll for a month. Suddenly I wasn't singularly focused on that one thing. And Rory, just kept at it, adding accounts, adding more sales people to increase our reach and range. That's the story of how we became able to enjoy our life a little more than we used to. The experience Sarah had, watching us build something that has become important in our niche of the industry."

"As you can tell," Margaret interjects. "Thomas is very proud of what he and Rory have created, built from nothing, what is now in our blood and Sarah's."

"Do you work in the business too?" gBeto asks Margaret.

"I was the CFO, the head of procurement, the chief personnel officer, facilities manager, and I can't even think of what other titles Tom gave me at one time or another. So yes. I still manage the HR team and I sit on the audit committee of the board reviewing the books. Places where my prior experiences can help. An independent eye on who we're hiring and our trends in spending."

"Very important roles," gBeto acknowledges. "But what do you do as a family? Things that are fun, relaxing, things that balance you out from the pressures of managing a business that employs many others?"

"In the early years there just wasn't money or time to do much..." I begin.

"What about the years before you set up the business, when you worked for someone else? Sarah would have been young." gBeto asks. "What did you do to expose her to the world?"

"We took her to museums in New York, to off-Broadway plays we could afford," I begin again.

"We took her to Disney World several times. Starting at age two as I remember," Margaret picks up in answering. "She loved it there. I don't know if it broadened her interests, but she asked a lot of questions and when she got home, even at a young age, she would write stories about what we saw and what we did."

"I think that's the first time I knew she would eventually follow in our footsteps. Then I knew I needed to start making bigger strides. I needed to create something that would someday be hers," I reflect. "Well, what else would you like to discuss?" I ask to keep things moving knowing Margaret tends to have no sense of time and I don't want to spend the whole afternoon here.

"Actually, Tom, there's something gBeto and I would like to talk about with both of you."

Now I'm really confused. First, I didn't know they even knew each other, and now they want to talk with both Margaret and me. I look at Margaret, "Did you know anything about this?"

"She didn't," gBeto responds. We thought it important to talk with you together."

"Sure. What's on your mind?" I decide it's time for me to listen.

"A little history is needed here," Rory starts out to my surprise. Seems like he was in on this hijacking of our meeting.

"gBeto and I were high school classmates. We got to be good friends in chemistry class and ended up as lab partners. That's when I got to know what an extraordinary woman she is and I have to say I fell in love with her."

"I didn't know any of this," I admit.

"I never talked about it. In fact, until last week, we hadn't been in touch since we graduated from high school."

LOVE

"Last week?" Holy shit! As Attorney General is she opening an investigation into the firm? "Is that why you want to talk with us?" Give us advance warning?

"Yes and no," Rory responds. "What we wanted to talk to you about is Sarah.''

"Sarah?" Margaret is now confused. "What about Sarah?"

Rory starts out, "We both grew up extremely poor. We were young and had no idea what we were doing, but we loved each other and the result is we had a child. But we had just turned sixteen. Our parents couldn't help us as they had no room for us in their tiny homes and no money to help us get started. Even before the child was born, we decided we had to give it up at birth. gBeto never saw the child and until this week didn't even know the sex of the child."

"You're saying Sarah was your child?" Margaret gets there a whole lot quicker than I do.

"She is," Rory responds. "I was at the hospital when she was born and stayed in the background when they took her down to the nursery. I watched you come in, be introduced to her and watched you take her away. I wanted to make sure someone would have her who could take care of her in the way we couldn't, emotionally, financially or even basic understanding of how to care for a child. I followed you outside and watched you get into your car. I memorized your license number and when my brother joined the police force, I asked him to look it up for me, not telling him why. I had your names and an address. I drove past your house with my brother once and I was sure everything was good. I didn't say anything to gBeto."

"Sarah doesn't know she was adopted," Margaret warns us. "You're not going to tell her?"

"Margaret, I've worked with Tom for what? Fifteen years now? I haven't said a word to her in all that time, even though I knew. I admit when she came to work for the firm, I was happy just to see what she was becoming, had become, and what a wonderful person she is."

261

"Why are you telling us this?" I'm getting angry that I didn't know he's been stalking my daughter all this time.

"I didn't become your partner just because of her," Rory tries to explain but I'm not really listening. "We were just such a good team at McIntyre. When I applied for a job, I didn't know you were there. But I took the job because you were. I thought I might get to see her once in a while, but it never occurred to me, even when we formed the partnership that she might come work for us. She was less than ten back then. I wasn't sure we'd even survive a year. But I rolled the dice with you and it worked out, better than I could have imagined. I like being part of this firm, working with you and everyone. I can't imagine doing anything else. But I thought you had a right to know, particularly since she's living next door to her biological mother now."

"And you suggested she buy there," I suddenly remember angrily. "Were you trying to set something up?"

"No, I didn't know gBeto's address. Never occurred to me to check that out. I recommended the neighborhood because of the schools and the others who live there. Influential people like Anne Rutherford who's like the godmother of Texas politics. And she's right across the street." Rory looks at gBeto. "I wanted to be helpful since who you know is a lot more important than what you know."

I turn to gBeto. "You didn't know?"

She shakes her head, "I hadn't put anything together. A couple flashes when she'd say something Rory used to say. But I just thought that phrase must be coming back. Couple of her mannerisms caught my attention but I hadn't figured out they were Rory's. I didn't know where Rory was. Didn't know he was your partner, or that Sarah has had a chance to get to know him as a person. I didn't make any connections."

"It was a shock to you too?" Margaret responds, still trying to absorb this news.

"With all that's been going on in my life recently I wasn't looking to add any more complications. But you need to know I told her about my pregnancy."

"Why did you do that?" She must be wanting her daughter back.

"She confronted me that Rory's brother told her I dropped out of school for a year. If she figured out why, she'd know why I'd never try to convict him."

"Your brother?" I don't know what they're talking about.

"Mick St. James… the cop who killed Bo Madison? He's my brother."

I shake my head never having put that together but then it occurs to me, "Is that when you decided to call her?" I ask Rory.

"I didn't know she'd told Sarah, but Mick told me he was trying to use the pregnancy to get gBeto to back off."

Margaret has been listening but looking down the whole time. Now she looks up, "I take it you're afraid it's going to come out?"

"We will abide by your wishes, she's your daughter and always will be," gBeto wants to raise a point. "We gave up any right to be a part of her life when she was born. Neither one of us has tried to interfere in over twenty years. It's not fair to upend her whole world at this point. However, what if she ever does one of those Ancestry DNA tests? What if she gets sick and has an immune deficiency or gets cancer or has to answer a simple family medical history? She won't be able to provide factual information. She might get the wrong treatment because the doctors don't have the right information about her. I think you should have the option of telling her if you decide to. I would rather she hear it from you than deduce it from a test result that comes in the mail. I don't know."

Margaret looks at me now, waiting for me to say something.

"We're not looking for you to decide anything today," Rory responds before I can. "This is too big a decision. But we wanted to tell you together and have both of us here when we did. I only told gBeto about Sarah because one thing I know about her is she would eventually figure it out. I didn't want her not knowing what she should do with the information."

"What would you have us do?" Margaret is still absorbing this much quicker than I am.

"Only you can decide that," gBeto responds. "Now that you have all the information."

"And you will…" I start my next question but Rory cuts me off.

"Take our cues from you. Neither of us will treat her any differently, say anything to her that could cause her to question her parentage or diminish in any way her love for the both of you. We will remain, as we are today, background people who will try to be helpful when asked."

"And if we tell her?" Margaret asks. I would not because I don't want to make them think we would even consider it, but it sounds like Margaret may want to.

"The same," gBeto responds this time. "We take our cues from you. I've already told Sarah a little about my childhood. She already knows how hard my early life was, because she interviewed me for her first blog about knowing Mick and why it wasn't a conflict of interest. Funny how Rory's brother precipitated this whole thing. If he hadn't killed Bo Madison we wouldn't be sitting here. I wouldn't even know the child I bore was a girl let alone living next door. I never would have met you both, or reconnected with Rory. Just as you, my life was on a trajectory. Just as you, I'd risen from humble roots to become what I am… like you, comfortable with my place in the world, contributing to the things I believe in. Hopefully making the lives of others better. What I've come to realize, sitting here, listening to you talk about what you built together, and by that, I mean all of you here, is that we all have much more in common than Sarah."

"Which brings us back to the key question: What do we do now?"

I ask. I look at Rory and wonder if I really do know the man who has been my partner all these years. *He's kept a huge secret from me, and that makes me wonder what other secrets is he keeping?* "And all this time I just thought you were gay since there never seemed to be any women in your life."

I notice gBeto look differently at Rory, apparently triggered by my comment. I wonder what she's really thinking about this whole thing. *Rory could have kept it from her even now, but he chose not to. Was that because Sarah was living next door or was it something else?*

CHAPTER THIRTY-THREE:

Anne Rutherford, Political Dowager Almost

When I arrive at gBeto and Nathaniel's, he is at the door and greets me the same way he always does, with a glass of his favorite wine of the moment, which just happens to be a Chilean rose. I smell the bouquet and nod my approval as I always do, whether I like it or not. "They're in the backyard," he points me through to the back door off the kitchen.

As I come out back, I find I'm the last to arrive for Aamaal, Cindy, Estella, and Sarah are already sampling the same rose and chatting with gBeto. I note LaMance apparently was not invited. Never did learn what happened there, but I'm pleased to see that gBeto has no problem taking swift action against even a close confidant when she perceives the need. A strength that will be important if she is to continue her current political career. "Good afternoon, ladies. I am happy to see you all today. The brain trust that will mount the campaign to return our attorney general to office in the fall."

I take my seat between her and Estella. They must have done that on purpose since it was the only seat open, although Nathaniel is carrying out another chair. I wonder who that is for? But then he joins us. "How nice of you offer your insights, Nathaniel."

"I looked and found I just happened to have some unexpected free time today, and since this is the best party in town, where else would I be?" he raises his glass to me and then the other ladies before we all take a sip.

"It would be better if it was the only party in town," Estella remarks. "Then we wouldn't have to worry about campaigns and elections."

"That would take all the fun out of it," I protest. "The American way is to offer ideas and solutions to make life easier for all of us. To employ the power of government judiciously, but effectively. To respect the pocketbook of everyone asked to contribute to the common causes. And to lead. We may be the only party able to do all of those things, but don't tell the others. It's just amusing to back them into corners and show our constituents that we have superior ideas."

"Is that why you love politics?" Cindy asks.

"Of course," I respond with a smile. "I could join another book club and discuss ideas. I could join another garden club and drive my gardener absolutely crazy with suggestions of how he could do a better job. I could travel the world, preferably without my husband since he's just not interested in culture and food, and history. But that would get old quicker than I am. This is the best thing I can think of to apply my mind and resources to."

"And all of Texas is the better for your choice," Nathaniel raises his glass again, as do all of the others.

gBeto changes the subject rather abruptly. "We ought to get the elephant in the room off the table. Just to make it simple for all of you, if we lose the case against the former police officer I will not be standing for re-election."

"You're making this a digital decision," Aamaal responds. "Even before you know what the decision could entail. What does losing mean to you? If he is not convicted of first-degree murder, but of a lesser offense, say second degree manslaughter, is that still a loss in your mind?"

"If the verdict establishes guilt through prior intent that is a win and I'll run. Anything less and I will consider my efforts to fulfill my obligations to the people of Texas insufficient."

"Well then, "I begin in response, "Now that we have that elephant right where we want it, we better figure out how to get this young woman re-elected."

Estella isn't ready to move on yet. "What do you think is the probability of a win, as you've defined it?"

gBeto looks at Aamaal, "You're probably more objective than I am on that question."

"gBeto wasn't present during the jury selection, which is why she thinks I probably have a better read on them than she does," Aamaal responds. "I've counseled her on our jury strategy. I think we did a good job of eliminating the candidates that were most likely to have a preconceived notion one way or the other. No one with a relative working in the department was seated. No one with a relative in a different department was seated. No one with an anti-cop attitude was seated. And no one who admitted to having made a judgment based on seeing the videos was seated. With an equal number of Black and White jurors sprinkled in amongst the Hispanics and Asians, one more woman than men, and mostly registered voters, but none who have actively worked for candidates, I think we have a jury that is likely to be open minded to the evidence provided."

"That's the jury, but how do you think they will vote," Cindy asks. "The deliberation has already gone on longer than anyone thought. What's it been? Twenty hours now?"

"Coming up on twenty-two," gBeto looks at her cell phone.

"Isn't the common wisdom that the longer it goes the less likely a conviction?" Cindy continues.

"There are notable exceptions," gBeto responds although the tone of her voice makes me think she's thinking the same thought, and that's fueling her putting the elephant on the table first.

"You have staked out the course of action in that event," I point out. "I prefer to believe the jury will find him guilty as charged and life will move on for him, for the Madison family and for us. We need to have a plan for your re-election. I know Estella has done her usual fine job of staking out the constituencies we need to address, a first cut at the issues most pertinent to each, talking points for early in the campaign and a roadmap how we can evolve those talking points as the campaign progresses. But it really is simple in my mind. We get more of our people to the polls than they do. We do that and we win. See this really isn't hard when you strip away all of the extra stuff everyone seems to want to focus on."

Sarah speaks up for the first time, "This is all a bit overwhelming for me as a newbie. I don't know what I can say to help the cause, although I will help however I can. When I approached gBeto I suggested I might be most helpful in guiding media placements and talking points since I'm reading everything for Continuum. And I'm happy to do that, but it sounds like I might be most helpful offering to take people without transportation to the polls. Does that make sense?"

"Actually, we all take people to the polls," Estella informs her. "We'll likely ask your husband too. But I think you're absolutely right about the real value you bring to our little group. You have particular insights we will never have and that's a huge asset, although we will need to be respectful of your need to be neutral in the posts you make and select. We can't get upset when she publishes something critical of gBeto as long as it's balanced. We can't get upset when the other side buys ads that appear in blogs that are favorable to us. That wouldn't be fair. I'm just warning you all, since Sarah volunteered to help, we can't be critical of her doing her day job. Besides, she's already done a lot to dispel the image of gBeto the other side has been trying to build recently. We should all thank her for that."

"I want to help any way I can," Sarah adds.

"If you could convince your father to change his registration that would be one more vote," I poke at her since her father contributes to the other party every year in growing amounts as his business has grown.

Sarah nods apologetically, "My father believes in balance. His partner is a generous contributor to your party even though he is not. I'll talk to his partner and see if I can convince him to match what my father contributes. Is that a reasonable strategy?"

I see gBeto nod, "We can't expect a religious conversion on his part just because his daughter moved into the wrong neighborhood."

"Give me time," Sarah nods. "Dad is reasonable. I'll invite him out more often and invite gBeto over. Maybe he can get to know her better. If he gets to know her, I'll bet I can convince him to make a contribution to her campaign, particularly if he knows I'm working on it."

"Sounds like you might have a future in politics," I suggest. "You're coming up with short term and long-term strategies. That's perfect. Politics is all about changing one mind at a time and then going on to the next. Eventually you get to a majority and then you win."

"This is going to be fun," Sarah concludes. "I've never had a chance to work on something like this where you have the ability to make a real impact on people's lives."

gBeto shakes her head, "You make an impact with what you do. You help people be informed and that's the most important thing someone can be."

"We're glad to have you as part of our little brain trust," I take back control. "We need good brains and you are demonstrating you have one. So welcome."

"You're doing well today, Anne," Nathaniel remarks. "You got the elephant off the table and a plan to even the donations playing field. What other miracles are you going to work?"

"I'm going to ask you to do something that may be the most important thing you do today, Nathaniel. Would you refill my glass?" Everyone laughs as Nathaniel smiles and retrieves the bottle.

Estella shakes her head, "There's a smaller elephant I'd like to discuss."

We all look at her and wait for her to continue, she doesn't until Nathaniel returns with the rose. "We need to discuss Nathaniel's administrative leave." He looks up at her with a surprised expression that turns dark almost immediately.

"I get it," Nathaniel responds. "I'm the millstone around her neck even if she wins the case. She's married to the cop who enabled Michael St. James to kill Bo Madison." He then pours more wine into my glass and everyone is silent as he does. "Anyone else want some rose?"

Several point to their glasses and he begins filling them.

"Do you want to tell us what the mayor is saying to you?" gBeto asks Nathaniel.

"What she has implied is the police union has been blackmailing her. Saying if she can't find a reason to fire me, they won't support her re-election. She has sought out a middle ground, a stall, if you will. She asked them to submit a list of improprieties I committed as commissioner and she would investigate each one to determine if any would result in cause. She has the city's internal auditor reviewing each claim. While they're not all financial, the mayor has explained to the union that an auditor would be more credible than someone else since they are trained to look for evidence of wrong doing."

Silence all around. I ask, "What do you think will be the outcome?"

"None of the claims has been substantiated. The latest set recently submitted has been focused on my intent, something that is much harder to conclude was an impropriety since intent did not result in my abuse of my office or a liability to the city."

"What do you mean intent?" Cindy asks.

"They claim it was my intent to reduce department headcount without bargaining since I was actively seeking to remove officers like Michael St. James."

"There are more like him?" Sarah asks, apparently surprised.

"I call them the dirty dozen and Michael St. James was by no means the worst of them," Nathaniel responds to her.

"Is that in the form of a public document?" Sarah continues her line of thought.

"There is an internal memo I sent to the mayor detailing names and a summary of disciplinary actions that have been taken against them over the years," Nathaniel shares with us. "That may be the problem with releasing it, the fact it contains personnel information about employees."

"I could ask the mayor to redact the personnel information, even the names if she wishes," Sarah muses. "The fact such a document exists proves the point that you have been trying to address the very issue brought to light by the killing of Bo Madison. Although I would have to point out since the mayor took no action on your memo, she must carry some of the blame for Bo Madison's death."

"Bringing that to light could cause her to reinstate Nathaniel," Aamaal suggests. "That would also take the lesser elephant off the table for your re-election."

"Could you provide the date you sent the memo to the mayor?" Sarah asks Nathaniel.

He nods clearly thinking through how a blog on Continuum Media would play in the politics of the city. "Since you're on gBeto's campaign team is this crossing the line for you?"

"More rogue cops in the Fort Christian Police Department?" Sarah responds, "Do you think there's anyone in the whole State of Texas that wouldn't want to know they're at risk of a similar potentially deadly encounter with a cop? Regardless of race or religion."

"But you wouldn't have come into possession of the knowledge such a situation exists or a memo detailing it was written if you weren't part of this campaign discussion," Nathaniel pushes.

"Maybe not today," Sarah responds. "But eventually someone

LOVE

would have started asking questions of the mayor. At some point I
would have come asking for a glass of wine and answers the mayor
wasn't sharing. As I see it, I may get the story out earlier than
otherwise by being here, but that's all."

"If you end this administrative leave issue, Anne, you'll have two
elephants and new donor in your bag today," Cindy observes. "We
should do this more often."

I observe Sarah thinking through the discussion we've had. I can
see where this has probably been an eye-opening experience for her,
but her journalistic instincts are very good for someone so young. She
could be a huge asset to not just gBeto's campaign but in the
governor's as well.

Estella shakes her head, "I hate to keep coming back to elephants,
but I have a 'what if', I don't think we considered before."

Everyone looks at Estella waiting, "What if... the trial ends in a
hung jury?"

Everyone looks at gBeto who doesn't respond.

"If it's a hung jury, doesn't that mean they have to retry him?
New jury, new judge. Presenting the evidence and arguing the case all
over again, now that you know the defense and they know the
prosecution. It could easily go past the fall election. What then? Do you
run?" Estella pushes gBeto.

"I hope that's not the outcome," gBeto shakes her head. "I just
want this over one way or the other. I want us all to get on with our
lives."

I watch her look up at Nathaniel who is looking at her. There
seems to be some non-verbal communication between them and then
she answers: "If it's a hung jury I owe it to the people of the state to
retry the case. Can I do that effectively while campaigning?" gBeto
doesn't answer.

"I for one think you should, and if it means we have to do more to give you the time you need, so be it." Cindy responds for all of us.

"It's not the digital solution you are expecting," Aamaal notes. "But you will not have lost the case, just not have won it yet."

"If I were the defense, if I knew you weren't running for reelection, I'd do everything I could to postpone the retrial, hoping to get a new prosecuting attorney who would be less familiar with the case," Sarah suggests, again reinforcing what a good thinker she is. "In that case your decision might actually increase the probability the officer will get off with no time served."

gBeto looks at Sarah curiously and then at Nathaniel. He nods to her just slightly, just once.

"I think you have your answer," gBeto responds as if a load had been lifted from her shoulders.

CHAPTER THIRTY-FOUR:

gBeto Dahomey Brown, Attorney General, State of Texas

Forty-four hours after the jury went off to deliberate, we are called back to the court room. Forty-four hours is a very long time to review the evidence and discuss the merits of the case against him. Murder is always the hardest to gain a conviction at the highest levels. The only thing I can gather from the length of time it took for them arrive at a verdict is they were having difficulty with a single juror who would not agree. There has to be hope they can get to a unanimous decision for them to keep going. If it was going to be a hung jury, I think they would have decided that after the first full day, and pulled the plug. But they didn't do that. The question now is whether the rest of the jury was able to convince the hold out, or did they acquit not able to get beyond a reasonable doubt as to whether he had intent that night.

Aamaal is at the table when I come in. She looks up at me and whispers, "You look awful. Have you had any sleep?"

"What's that?" I respond knowing many questions are about to be answered. I look around and the officers bring in Mick St. James, who is wearing a grey suit with a blue tie and is handcuffed. He is followed by Ralph Simpson, his attorney who looks like he's come to the same conclusion I have about the probable outcome. He nods at me with a slight smile, the one I've seen him show when he's won cases in the past. *Cocky son-of-a-bitch. I'm sure the police union is paying him an exorbitant fee for this case. They certainly don't want any of their other members showing up here. They expect if there is no hope of a conviction, I'll not press charges against others in the future. Obviously, they don't know me very well.*

"All rise. This court is now in session, Judge Sondra Flack, presiding."

Judge Flack enters, takes her seat and nods to us, "Please be seated." She then turns to the jury, "Madam foreman, does the jury have a verdict?"

"We do your honor," the Bailiff takes the decision from the foreman and delivers it to the judge.

The judge reads the decision to herself and I think I see a slight smile form in the crook of her mouth she is evidently trying to suppress, but I'm suddenly filled with hope.

"The jury finds Michael St. James, guilty of premeditated murder in the first degree and sentences him to life in prison," Judge Flack slightly nods to me and turns to the defendant, "Michael St. James you will be remanded to the Texas Correctional Institution in Huntsville, immediately, to begin serving your sentence. I will recommend that you not be granted parole prior to serving twenty-five years of this sentence. You have committed the worst kind of crime in my view, premeditated murder of an innocent civilian. You are a disgrace to the profession of police officers and I am hopeful this sentence will cause all other police officers in Texas, to consider the consequences of their actions when armed and in a confrontation with a civilian."

I close my eyes and breathe deeply for the first time in weeks. I feel the tension drain from my shoulders. If I didn't know better, I'd say even the air in the court room smells fresher. Aamaal grabs my hand and squeezes, displaying a happy smile. "You did a great job pulling everything together and making this verdict possible," I tell her.

I walk over to the defense table as the officers handcuff Michael St. James. "Hello Mick."

"You're still a slut," he nearly spits at me.

"You did me a favor in a way you'll never understand. You made a ghost that has haunted me for decades vanish. I hope we can both become better people as a result of these events, because at least you'll never place another in jeopardy as you have throughout your career."

"Get me out of here, I don't want to hear another word from this bitch," the hatred just pours out of his mouth, but runs over me like a cleansing lotion, healing the cuts this whole proceeding has inflicted on me. I nod to him, although he isn't paying attention now on his way to the waiting vehicle.

Nathaniel hands me his phone. It's Sarah's blog.

A Needless Loss of Life

Today we will likely learn the fate of former Fort Christian City Police Officer Michael St. James. As trials go, this one has not been exceptionally long, although the deliberation has been longer than most. Either way it goes, Bo Madison lies cold and dead in a coffin in Lakeside cemetery. Regardless of your thoughts about the on-going trial, or the guilt or innocence of the officer involved, Bo Madison did not have to die. This death could have been prevented, and other deaths or injuries to innocent citizens and visitors to Fort Christian can be prevented starting today.

Continuum Media has obtained confirmation from Mayor Jennie Richards that over a year ago Commissioner Nathaniel Brown sent her a memo with the heading, 'Action Needed'. The action Commissioner Brown was referring to was the need to either move twelve officers to non-patrol/public contact status, dismiss them for cause or force early retirement. In this memo he referred to these twelve officers as 'The Dirty Dozen'. They are officers who have a history of disciplinary actions against them for flagrant and frequent violation of department policy and procedure. Commissioner Brown labeled them a threat to public safety.

The mayor confirmed a copy of the memo was provided to the police union which has the right to represent all members in actions initiated against them by the city. The mayor attempted to gain concurrence from the union to dismiss the Dirty Dozen as recommended by the commissioner. Discussions continued right up until the shooting of Bo Madison with no resolution. It would seem appropriate to label the police union as a threat to the public safety given their inaction has resulted in an innocent death, when the likelihood of such an event was brought to their attention a year prior.

The mayor was asked why the commissioner remains on administrative leave after the internal affairs report was issued as called for by the ordinance. Her reply was the police union has submitted a list of purported inappropriate actions by the commissioner that should require his dismissal. The city has investigated each and every accusation and not found evidence to support any single, let alone multiple, offenses.

Now is the time for the legislature to look into appropriate changes in the powers and authorities of police unions in this state. Changes that will eliminate the need for citizens to seek protection from those employed to protect them. Now is the time for the mayor to reinstate the commissioner and administratively dismiss the Dirty Dozen immediately. Only then will we all rest easier.

I approach the bench and nod to Judge Flack, "You honor, as always it is a privilege to argue before you. Thank you for all that you do for the people of the State of Texas."

"Attorney General Brown, you did good today. Keep up the good fight." I nod again and rejoin Nathaniel.

He takes my arm and we walk out of the courthouse, into the daylight that is like a new dawn for Fort Christian and us. Just outside Daniel Porter and the Four Horsemen are walking up the sidewalk. I'm not intending to talk to them after they attempted to remove me from office.

"Attorney General Brown," he calls out as he approaches. "A word?"

I turn to Nathaniel since I never told him of their meeting or why I asked LaMance to hand in her resignation. Nathaniel knows I'll tell him when I'm ready. He will never ask. "Why don't you go on home, I'm going in to the office to finish the meeting I was in when they called me to come over."

"I'm going to see Mayor Richards first. She may have something to say to me," Nathaniel releases my arm, eyeing Daniel and the four ministers apparently realizing there is something here I don't want him in the middle of.

"Daniel, Reverends…"

"We just heard… we can't express how relieved we are and how much the joint congregations are thankful for justice for Bo Madison and his family."

"And all the other people who live in our state…" I remind him. "This isn't just about a Black man who died needlessly. This is about justice for all, about taking a bad cop off the streets, about making the homes of every woman, man and child safer. I'll never give up the good fight regardless of what you think, regardless of the concerns of various congregations, regardless of a police union who wants to cover the misdeeds of its members."

Daniel Porter looks at me strangely as Reverend Clyburn steps forward, "gBeto, we've known each other a long time."

"We have as I've known all of you a long time."

"You have to understand our concern was not personal. It wasn't that we don't respect you and have faith in you…"

"No, I don't."

"Don't what?" Rev Clyburn seems confused.

"I don't have to understand your concern was not personal, because whatever you said or say, it was personal. You said loud and clear that you wanted me to step aside because you didn't think I could win this case. For whatever reason. You made an excuse about Nathaniel, but that wasn't it. You didn't and probably still don't trust me."

"With this resounding decision…" Rev Clyburn tries to make amends.

"I should have earned your trust, but I know I haven't. That's my fault. Maybe you just can't trust someone who grew up poor and is self-made and not obligated to any one of you for singular spiritual guidance. Or maybe it's you cut a deal with LaMance that she was going to put in a White man as the prosecuting attorney because you didn't think any woman could put a White male cop in prison. Obviously, you underestimated this Black woman. Or maybe it's you never took the time to figure out what my name means. The Dahomey tribe had women soldiers back from the sixteen hundreds to the nineteen hundreds. A gBeto was a warrior in their language. Every time I hear my name, I know what my parents expected me to be. They were extremely poor and they couldn't give me anything except the courage, strength and intelligence to be a warrior. Regularly kicking the butt of the male soldiers sent against me. And that's what I am."

Daniel looks at me as if he's dumbstruck. The other ministers step back as I say, "Good day, gentlemen," and walk past them on my way back to my office.

As I enter, I am intercepted by my administrative assistant who hands me a note from Walter asking me to come up to his Fort Christian office. The distance is not that far. Rather than wait for a car to come around, I walk it. The sun is warm in the clear blue sky. A slight breeze helps me clear my lungs and dry the perspiration from my neck. I feared this day would end my ambitions, end my career in public service and end my ability to be a warrior for the people. But now I'm likely back in Walter's good graces. He's probably wanting me to crank up his economic development task force, which will take me out of the office a lot. I need to get him to push through Aamaal's appointment. I need someone in charge when I'm not there. I also need him to consider legislation limiting the police union powers. I don't know how I get that one through given my relationship with Nathaniel. I'll likely need a proxy to bring it forward although Sarah's blog may be one way to start with.

As I enter Walter's office, I find Anne and Estella with him talking around his desk. "Good afternoon, Governor Rutherford," I greet them wondering why Anne and Estella would be here. A thought pops into my head but I push it away not wanting to anticipate something that may not materialize.

"Attorney General Dahomey-Brown, thank you for coming on such short notice."

I join them at Walter's desk, "You obviously are aware of the verdict," I begin.

"We were here when I got the call," Walter informs me. "We were discussing your future and since these ladies are the enablers of that future, well, I thought they are where we should start."

"The verdict is positive proof that we've made progress on our primary goals. For that reason, I am prepared to continue as a public servant," I inform them that elephant is retired.

"And I am prepared to ask you to consider a different role starting now. Lieutenant Governor Robertson has informed me that his continuing health condition has turned for the worse and requires him to step aside immediately. As you know he had already decided to not seek re-election, but now he does not feel he can execute his constitutionally defined responsibilities. I intend to submit your name as his replacement this afternoon. Once you are confirmed by the Senate you will become its presiding officer.

"There is one other thing," Walter is going quickly. I'm still stuck on the immediacy of the appointment. "You were appointed to be co-chair with Ronald Amundsen of my economic development task force. You will keep that position in your new role and I expect you to make it your top priority, as I want a report before the election which I can endorse."

I nod as I finally catch up to him, "The staff has been doing the research for the task force, and I believe the first session is scheduled next month. Do you want me to advance that schedule?"

"Yes. The sooner you have a releasable report the better. We need the media to really focus on it for at least a couple weeks before the election. I want every eligible voter to know what we intend to do to create economic security for them before they go into the voting booth. Knowledge is power, particularly when voters are knowledgeable of what the future holds for them under the second term of a Rutherford administration."

"This is all rather quick," is all I can say.

"This has been in the works since before the Madison shooting. If that hadn't happened you likely would have been appointed several months ago. Robertson was ready to step aside, but I convinced him you were worth waiting for. Anyway, the trial was important, not just in establishing in the mind of the public what kind of person you are, but to serve as the foundation of our social fabric. A precedent so loud and clear there will be no mistaking what we believe in. What the people of Texas can expect going forward."

Anne Rutherford steps forward and takes my hand, squeezing it, "Congratulations. You have accomplished exactly what you said you would. Now it's time for you to do more than you ever thought possible."

Estella comes closer, "I'm going to help out on the governor's campaign, but I'm going to also manage the attorney general race as we are going to have to introduce a new face there and we all know that increases the risk of losing it. Don't worry, I'm still on speed dial and will take your calls and texts, but you'll have the A team running your campaign now, so…"

I give her a hug, "I never thought we wouldn't be campaigning together this fall. This is sad. Just let me know what I can do to help your candidate, joint appearances, guest editorials, tell me what you need."

"Sarah," she instantly responds. "I need Sarah working the attorney general campaign. Don't you keep her all to yourself."

Anne interrupts, "There's enough of Sarah to go around. Walter's going to need some of her brain power."

"Who's Sarah?" Walter asks.

"Thomas Flannery's daughter," Anne responds.

"Flannery? He'll be funding the other side's campaign," Walter clearly isn't liking what he's hearing.

"His daughter is on our side, but works for his company," Anne pushes back," Bright, articulate, energetic… exactly what we need to reinvigorate your messaging. She's also going to work on her father's donations. That means you can't say anything bad about him where someone might hear you."

"Don't think I've ever said anything bad about Flannery," Walter backs down from Anne. *Never seen the two of them together before, this is really interesting.* "He's always treated me fairly in his publications. It's just his money decisions I've not agreed with."

"You'll be happy with his help and tell him you are at some point, but let me work that with his daughter."

Walter nods, "Okay ladies, what else do you need from your governor today?"

"What else do you need from us?" I ask immediately.

"I need you to get out of my office. I must get back to the people's work. But you can use the conference room if you want to keep talking."

I follow Anne who has clearly been here before. Estella closes the door behind us and can only say, "Lieutenant governor. This is amazing."

"Thank you, Anne, for never losing faith in me. Seems I didn't do as well with others in the community, but it's turning out all right."

Anne looks puzzled but then apparently takes a guess, "Are you referring to Porter and his Posse?"

"Haven't heard that one before, but yes," I admit.

"I heard something about them," Anne confides. "Having midnight meetings and not inviting any of their congregations in for them. I get the sense there may be a new editor at the Morning News coming in as the corporate brass thinks Porter has been trying to shape the news rather than report it, and it's cost him some circulation."

"Tic Rogers," I suddenly know what she's talking about. "Sarah said a blogger by the name of Tic Rogers sold Porter that piece that started the whole controversy about whether I knew Michael St. James…"

"Oh?" Anne seems completely caught off guard. "Porter almost torpedoed the whole trial?"

"That's what Sarah said when she interviewed me the first time."

"Sounds like Porter knew he was in trouble and was working it from both sides, trying to stir up controversy to sell papers while undermining the likelihood of your success," Anne spins a theory. "I wonder what we would find if we looked into his relationship with the police union."

Estella holds up both hands, "I'm just along for the ride here. Conspiracy theories, they're all yours."

CHAPTER THIRTY-FIVE:

Rory James, Senior Vice President and Partner
Continuum Media

gBeto agreed to meet me at McGlynn's Pub and Restaurant as it seems a neutral place neither of us goes to often. The people there seem to ignore us for the most part. Well, they ignore me because no one knows who I am. Some people stare at gBeto and whisper, probably wondering if she's the attorney general. If so, who is the dude she's with? Probably some lawyer she has to deal with in her official capacity. That's okay, I'm willing to be whoever they'd like me to be.

Except now that's all changed. She's the lieutenant governor, at least for the next several months. Then maybe she'll have a full term in office. She is a never-ending surprise. I never should have let her go.

When she comes in, she looks amazing. Dressed casually, hair is up, different. She almost looks radiant. These clothes are tighter fitting and I can see she's lost weight. Not near anorexic like when I knew her, but thinner than I'd seen her from a distance. I rise to greet her, nod as she reaches the table and we sit. "What happened? You look amazing…"

"Sleep happened," she informs me. "Amazing what eight hours of solid uninterrupted sleep will do for you. Particularly if you can get it for more than one night in a row." She smiles at me now in a relaxed way I've not seen in a very long time. "How are you, now that you have a felon in the family?"

I wasn't anticipating that bluntness but it's deserved. "It's different, although I'd been expecting something bad to happen to him for a long time. I think the Mick-fate, as I used to call it, I most

285

expected was that he'd get into a gun fight with a drug dealer and not be the quickest draw in the west. Then there was the fantasy that he'd stop someone for a routine ticket, give some guy lip and get blasted right there along the side of the road. In all reality my favorite was that he'd be found in bed with some dancer and the boyfriend would come in on them and that would be the end of Mick. I knew he was a danger to anyone he came in contact with, but just killing someone? I never envisioned that."

"You said you saw him like once a month?" gBeto asks as if she's trying to understand my feelings about him.

"Just in the last few years. We were right here in town together, but he went through like three divorces all in rapid fire and then it was hookers and dancers for him. He wasn't going to give away any more of his pension which he never could have lived on anyway. At least he'll have free room and board for the next twenty-five years and maybe more if he doesn't mellow out. Not everyone has that kind of economic security."

"You're being pretty glib about your brother," she challenges what she's hearing.

"I'm in sales. Got to be glib or I'll starve. Been there, done that."

"I remember," she seems to be looking right through me like she used to when we were together. Sees the scars I carried from being helpless to make my life better until I was old enough to get odd jobs. All the money I made went to my parents. They needed it to put food on the table.

"Mick has to deal with what he's become," I give her my thoughts on the subject. "I just have to accept that he's on a journey to self-discovery. I'm not sure what he will think of himself when he discovers who he really is."

"What do you think of him?" not going to let me off the hook. *Same old gBeto.*

"I think I should have been there for him through all those years I didn't see him. But honestly, I don't know what I could have said or done to change where he was going. It all started in the neighborhood. He wasn't strong enough to stand up for himself, he wasn't athletic enough to be accepted as a team player, he wasn't smart enough to invent the next Instagram. He just never figured out where he fit in life. And I couldn't help him with that. I was just lucky enough I met you when I was most in chaos about who I was…"

"I don't remember that," she puzzles.

"You suggested I should get the job at the movie theater. Sell popcorn and candy. I was bone thin then. You said people would buy more just because they'd think they needed to eat something more looking at me."

"I remember you working at the theater, but don't remember suggesting it."

"You helped me discover I could sell things people didn't know they needed, but a suggestion could catch their interest," I remind her. "I worked my way up to a manager at the theater and learned I could teach others how to sell. That just opened up possibilities for me. Showed me I could do more than I ever imagined."

"That was after we made the decision," she reflects.

I nod, "If you'd gotten pregnant a year later, when I was finding out I was capable, I never would have let you go. Let her go."

"You have a lot of regrets," gBeto sounds like she does as well and recognizes them when she hears them.

"I do."

"And that's why you never married, never even tried to get married?"

"I had my moment of happiness. The moment when I felt unconditional love from you. And I screwed it up, literally and figuratively. I couldn't trust myself not to screw it up with anyone else.

Besides, I knew I'd never feel that unconditional love like we had, ever again."

"You just decided you didn't want to go look for it," she's not buying my explanation even though it's what I've been telling myself all these years.

"You're right, I didn't want to go look for it. For a long time, I was hoping after I was doing well that I'd find you again. Erase the mistake I'd made. Start over with you because I knew we'd be happy even though there'd always be a hole in our relationship."

"But I met Nathaniel. You were gone and I wasn't even looking for you."

"I have to admit it hurt when I learned you'd married. But I did what I always did. I threw myself into my work and made even more money, became legendary at McIntyre, and that's why Thomas Flannery took me on as his partner. I owe my success to your marriage."

"Two cosmic forces, bumping off each other with no ability to change their destination," she reflects. "I often reflect my life could have been very different. Just a few decisions, a few people who noticed me, someone making a different choice we were totally unaware of. All those things are shaken, not stirred, to produce the perfect life for either of us."

"Depending on your perspective," I agree. "My life has been a good one on many levels when you look at it from the outside. But I wouldn't relive it exactly the same way. I couldn't, knowing what I know now."

I watch her looking at me, wondering if she dares ask the question or whether she should leave things alone, assume I still love her just as much if not more, even though she has chosen a different life, different husband and different fate. I decide to change the subject, "Have you heard anything from Tom and Margaret?"

gBeto shakes her head.

LOVE

"Then we know what we need to know. You won't hear from me again. We both have our lives to live."

"You have to know when you love something enough to let it go, let it grow and become what it will apart from you," gBeto reflects.

"Are you talking about Sarah or me?"

gBeto looks at me sorrowfully for a long moment, tears form in the corners of her eyes, and she clears her throat before answering, "We all have our separate lives to live, a singular decision changed everything. Now that our lives have taken different roads we must follow them, even though for a brief moment we saw the possibility of what could have been. But our lives took a different turn, two people who were very different then."

"I will always love you," I can't help but say.

"And I will never forget the love that sustained me for many years," she responds.

I reach out and am about to take her hand when I notice Sarah and her husband Demetrius enter the restaurant. I pull back and gBeto looks around, sees Sarah and waves to her.

In only a moment she approaches our table with Demetrius in tow. "gBeto, Rory. I didn't know you knew each other," she smiles at gBeto, "Have you signed him up to contribute to your campaign?"

"How much?" I ask reaching for a check book.

Sarah doesn't miss a beat, "Just want you to match Dad's contribution."

"Do you know the number or do I need to ask him?" I'm now sure her parents haven't had a chat with her about us.

"Lots of zeros," is her answer.

I stop reaching for the check book, "I'll ask and get back to you."

Sarah looks around, "You haven't eaten yet, you mind if we join you?"

"Not at all," gBeto responds and slides in allowing Sarah to join her. I do the same for Demetrius.

"How are you finding living in the 'burbs?" I ask since I live downtown.

"It's quiet," Demetrius responds. "Almost like everyone's dead."

"He's just missing his frat parties," Sarah shakes her head. "Wild times but we need to get past that stage of our lives."

Demetrius glances at her and asks, "Why?"

"Law school is too much like undergrad," she shakes her head. "Wait until he goes to work for a law firm. Then he'll know what it's like to work amongst the living dead," Sarah laughs.

"He can always go to work for one of the state agencies," gBeto suggests. "Then he'll know what it's like to strangle innovation."

"Why are you all suggesting life after school's not much fun?" I ask. "I never went to college and it worked out just fine for me."

"You have a rare talent," Sarah observes. Not many could do what you do," she looks at gBeto and continues, "Or you for that matter. What was it about East Hills that the two of you could overcome the odds to be what you are?"

"We all make choices," gBeto begins.

"And we spend the rest of our lives trying to overcome them," I conclude.

Sarah looks at Demetrius, "Do you have any idea what they're talking about?"

Her husband grins at us and responds, "Not a clue."

The End.

About the Author

dhtreichler is a futurist, technologist and strategist who toured the global garden spots as a defense contractor executive for fifteen years. His assignments covered intelligence, training and battlefield systems integrating state of the art technology to keep Americans safe. His novels grew out of a need to deeply understand how our world is changing, developing scenarios and then populating them with people who must confront how social change and increasingly sophisticated technology is transforming our lives and how men and women establish relationships in a mediated world.

Keep up with all of dhtreichler's latest work and essays at www.davidtreichler.com www.fortchristiansagas.com and www.GlobalVinoSnob.com.

Also by dhtreichler

HAPPINESS

Courage

TRUTH

A Cat's Redemption

CHOICES

HOPE

Emergence

Barely Human

The Ghost in the Machine: a novel

World Without Work

The Great American Cat Novel

My Life as a Frog

Life After

Lucifer

The Tragic Flaw

Succession

The End Game

I Believe in You

Rik's

The Illustrated Bearmas Reader – Ralph's Ordeals

The First Bearmas

www.ingramcontent.com/pod-product-compliance
Lightning Source LLC
Chambersburg PA
CBHW060407260626
47160CB00006B/2468